JUST A TEST

"Are you sure?" Jirah whispered. She ducked behind her sister, staring into the black, shadowy grove. Tree limbs stirred in the icy wind. "It's just a . . . test for wizards?"

Nearra took another tiny step forward, standing firmly on the soil just inside the gate. "It has to be a test. I can do this." She braced her shoulders against the wind.

"Nearra, I think the ground is moving." Jirah's shaking hand pointed past her sister, toward the roots of the cypress trees.

"Are you ready?" Nearra's golden hands balled into fists, and she gulped.

"If you are," Jirah whispered, "then I am."

Together, they began to step into the grove.

"NO!"

THE NEW ADVENTURES

ELEMENTS

BY REE SOESBEE

Volume One
PILLAR OF FLAME

Volume Two
QUEEN OF THE SEA
(July 2007)

Volume Three
TEMPEST'S VOW
(January 2008)

THE NEW ADVENTURES

ELEMENTS
◆
VOLUME ONE

PILLAR OF FLAME

REE SOESBEE

COVER & INTERIOR ART
Vinod Rams

MIRRORSTONE™

PILLAR OF FLAME

©2007 Wizards of the Coast, Inc.

Cover art by Vinod Rams
Cartography by Dennis Kauth
First Printing: January 2007

9 8 7 6 5 4 3 2 1

ISBN: 978-0-7869-4248-0
620-95914740-001-EN

U.S., CANADA,
ASIA, PACIFIC, & LATIN AMERICA
Wizards of the Coast, Inc.
P.O. Box 707
Renton, WA 98057-0707
+1-800-324-6496

EUROPEAN HEADQUARTERS
Hasbro UK Ltd
Caswell Way
Newport, Gwent NP9 0YH
GREAT BRITAIN
Save this address for your records.

Visit our web site at www.mirrorstonebooks.com

On purple clouds
When will I set sail?
Western sea.

ISSA

For my home, which like Nearra's,
is very close and yet very far away.

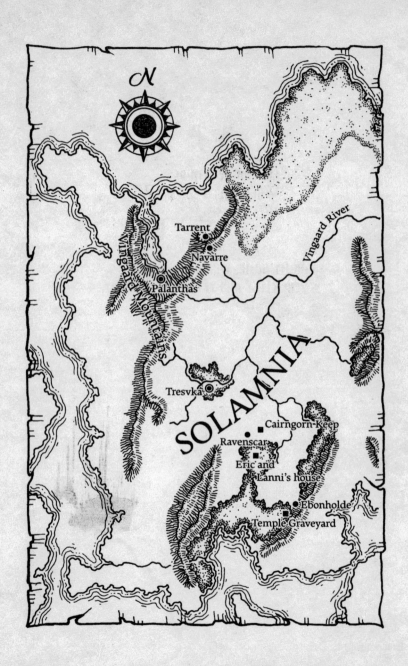

TABLE OF CONTENTS

CHAPTER

1 OF WIZARDRY

"**P**alanthas!" Jirah stared wide eyed at the city around them. The spires of tall buildings rose in silhouette against the distant ocean. Near the center, still a long walk away, a tall tower gleamed above the rest, bright flashes like rainbows glistening at its top. Though the base of the tower was obscured by a thick, dark grove, the tower itself rose in a tall spire from the darkness, catching the rays of the morning sun. "The Tower of High Sorcery," breathed Jirah. "We're really going to see it up close."

The two girls, one light, one dark, huddled together as if afraid the city might jump out and bite them as they walked down the main street of Palanthas. Jirah, her hair black against her pale skin, toed the cobblestones of the road. Her sister, golden hair shifting around her shoulders, chuckled and pushed her forward.

"Aren't you nervous at all, Nearra?" Jirah asked, shielding her eyes from the sun. She stood on tiptoe, trying to look over the buildings before them. "You're too calm! I'd be shaking in my shoes by now!"

"I don't see any reason to be afraid," Nearra said, her voice holding a note of forced confidence. "It's just wizards, and wizards are people. They aren't going to bite us. Besides, remember the dream I kept having on Icefire's ship on our way here?"

Jirah nodded. The only reason they'd come to Palanthas instead of going home was because Nearra had a recurring dream telling her to come to Palanthas. To change the subject from the unexplainable topic, Jirah asked, "Do you remember the stories Grandfather used to tell us about it? The high arches and magic fountains?" Jirah tossed her hair and took a skipping step forward. "He said the Tower of High Sorcery had flowers that grew even in the winter, and flying birds with feathers made of fire."

Nearra snorted. "No. What did he know about it? Grandfather wasn't a wizard. Nobody in our family has been a wizard for generations. He was just retelling stories he'd heard as a boy. The Tower is probably nothing at all like a fairy tale. I heard it's cursed and that terrible things happened there."

"Those are just legends," Jirah retorted. "There are wizards in the city, and wizards always live in the Tower of High Sorcery. The Tower can't be cursed if people are living there!"

Nearra nodded. "I'm just nervous, I guess." She sighed and followed her sister around the corner toward the heart of the city.

Passersby rushed the other way through the streets. Jirah's eyes followed them, and she noted the symbol of Mishakal hanging around the neck of one of the young women who swept by. An odd lightheartedness came over her as they walked. "Nearra?" she said, breaking the silence. "I'm glad we came to Palanthas." She slowed her step and lowered her voice. "I didn't want to go home and see Da until I had something to tell him . . . you know. About my future."

Nearra's smile came a shade too quickly. "Don't worry about that, Jirah. You've got plenty of time to find a career. Anyway, I needed to come here too. Now that I have magic, I need to apply to the Conclave of Wizards and take the Test of High Sorcery. I can do that while you look around in Palanthas, and we'll still be home in just a couple of weeks." She put her hand over her sister's, and they both paused. Nearra's hand, the skin golden and metallic, lay against Jirah's pale, flesh-colored wrist.

Jirah shuddered involuntarily. Hoping Nearra didn't notice, she swept her hand out from beneath her sister's and put her arm around Nearra's waist instead. Nearra's hand fell, and Jirah tried not to look down at it. Those metal-covered hands were creepy. The metal moved like real skin, and Nearra claimed she could feel through them just like real hands—but they looked unnatural.

Cutting her sister off with a too-bright smile before Nearra could apologize, Jirah changed the subject. "Do you think they'll remember us—our family—now?"

"The wizards?" Nearra frowned. "Even if they do remember Anselm, they can't turn us away. I have magic. I have a right to take the test, no matter who my ancestor was." But the question still hung between them.

They rounded a corner in the road, coming into the main hub of Palanthas, and Nearra's steps slowed. Her eyes followed the street forward, and her face paled. Quickly, Jirah turned to see what had captured her sister's attention.

On one side of the road was a dark, forested yard around a twisted, thin tower. Cypress limbs knotted together above a twisted path, cutting off any hope of sunlight breaking between the trees. Dark, turned soil marked the path itself, with faint white flecks here and there like chips of bone on an ancient battlefield. A cold wind swept through the trees, as if winter still huddled in the thick forest even though the spring sun shone down on the street outside. Twisted, black iron bars, forged together as one unit, curled up from the ground, fencing the grove from the street. Jirah thought she saw faint stains of blood on the iron.

Jirah could see the Tower of High Sorcery rising up from the center of the grove, somewhere down the dark and bitter path. Nearra stared up at the black tower rising from the misty trees, clutching her dragon-claw staff to her chest. Jirah gulped as goosebumps rose on her arm. Something evil lived in that grove.

"We can't go in there," Jirah said. Beside her, Nearra stepped closer to her sister.

They stared past the gate, through the thick cypress grove, every nerve in Jirah's body screaming at her to run away. "That's the Tower of High Sorcery?" She shivered, trying not to look too hard at the shadows that darted between the trees. Her voice shook as she said, "It's not anything like Grandfather's stories."

Nearra furrowed her brow and clenched her fists. She took a step toward the gate. "I'm not scared." The street behind them was all but empty, only a few straggling travelers rushing past. No one even came to this side of the road, preferring to stay on the far edge. Nearra took another step and grabbed the bars of the wide, black gate with both hands, but jerked her hands back immediately. "These bars are ice cold."

Taking a deep breath, Nearra seized the gate again. "I'm a wizard. I'm supposed to be here." Her gold fingers wrapped around the black bars as Nearra got a firm handhold. Ignoring the sharp chill, she pushed the iron gate forward and winced as the hinges shrieked.

"Are you kidding?" Jirah grabbed her sister's sleeve and dragged her back. "This place is not exactly inviting us in!"

Nearra let go, but the gate continued to drift inward. The cold wind that shook the cypress trees picked up speed and swelled out toward them. Jirah took a half step back, shocked by the bitter chill.

"Nearra!" Jirah pulled her sister close. Wispy tendrils of greenish mist rose from the roots of the trees on the path, nudging forward like serpents freed of their cages. "What are those?"

"I don't know." Nearra took a step forward, standing in the open gateway just on the edge of the grove. She gulped, shivering against her sister. When she spoke, her voice squeaked. "We have to go in there. Grandfather always said the Conclave meets in the Tower of Sorcery." She took a tiny step forward onto the dark soil. "The test has to be done in the Tower. It's the only place they can do it! That's what all the stories say." She hardened her resolve, squaring her shoulders. "This has to be just a test."

"Are you sure?" Jirah whispered. She ducked behind her sister, staring into the black, shadowy grove. Tree limbs stirred in the icy wind. Even the warm spring sun on their backs didn't steal any chill from the air. "It's just a . . . test for wizards?"

Nearra took another tiny step forward, standing firmly on the soil just inside the gate. "It has to be a test. I can do this." She braced her shoulders against the wind.

"Nearra, I think the ground is moving." Jirah's shaking hand pointed past her sister, toward the roots of the cypress trees.

"Are you ready?" Nearra's golden hands balled into fists, and she gulped.

"If you are," Jirah whispered, "then I am."

Together, they began to step into the grove.

"NO!" The shriek, followed by a clatter of packages against cobblestone, jerked the two girls around before they completed the movement. A frantic elf stood in the middle of the street, juggling books and brown-wrapped parcels as he gestured wildly. Carrot-colored hair stood up in a dandelion puff behind two long braids over his shoulders, and slender elf ears jutted up behind high cheekbones and panicked copper eyes. "Don't go in there!"

He leaped forward, grabbing them by the shoulders and pulling them backward. Packages flew everywhere, tumbling all around them. Jirah tripped, staggering to the ground over fluttering pages and parcels. Nearra let out a little scream as she fell on the cobblestone road, her golden hands splayed against the stone. Jirah tripped over her and fell, pinning Nearra and the elf against the ground.

"Get off me!" His red robes fluttered around what Jirah could now tell was a very delicate frame. Whatever strength he'd used to pull them over was given by sheer terror, not martial practice.

Jirah rolled over with a moan, trying to free herself from the pile. Then she jumped in surprise as the iron gate chomped shut forcefully, like the jaws of a snapping dragon. Inside the forest, Jirah heard a terrible wail, as if the angry grove longed for prey. The cypress trees lashed for a moment—was that wind, or something worse? Her heart jumped into her throat.

"You can't!" wailed the red-robed elf, struggling to free himself from the tangle of Nearra's sleeves and Jirah's legs. "That's Shoikan Grove! Are you mad?" Lying on his back, the red-robed wizard flailed beneath a confused Nearra. "You'll be destroyed!"

Nearra tried to disentangle herself, pushing aside a book. "But we have to go to the Tower of High Sorcery. I have to take my Test of Wizardry." Jirah saw a shudder pass through her sister at the thought of going back in there, and Nearra's voice fell. "How am I going to get in there?"

"Get in there?!" The elf sat up and stared her in the eye. Now that he'd stopped kicking and grabbing at them, Jirah could tell he wasn't much older than they were—well, in elf years, anyway. His features were pleasant if overly delicate, and his body was as thin as a rail. The red robe he wore was far too large for him, as if it'd been made for someone burly and broad. "Nobody goes in there. Well, almost nobody. You mean . . . you don't know?" His coppery eyes darted back and forth between the sisters with an almost comical attitude of stunned surprise.

"Know what?" Jirah asked swiftly, eager for the answer. She pulled herself to her knees and stared at him. "We know about the Tower of High Sorcery. Our ancestor was a wizard. His stories have been passed down for generations in our family."

"Generations. Human generations—still, a very long time. Then you don't know, do you?" The elf sat with his legs wide, reaching out with shaking hands to gather his books and packages around him. His thin body and tentative movements reminded Jirah of a bird building a nest. "The Tower is cursed. Has been for centuries. If you don't know that, you are really behind the times. You said your ancestor was a wizard? Haven't any of you been wizards since then?" He stopped to search their faces. "No, I see not. The-the Tower of High Sorcery in Palanthas is cursed. No one goes in there. Well, almost no one." He stared around the empty street for a moment, then muttered, "Except the Master of Past and Present!"

"Who?" Jirah asked in a loud voice. Nearra winced.

The wizard silenced her with a hiss. "Sssh!" He clamped his hand over Jirah's mouth. "Don't say it again. He might hear us." Letting go of her, the bony wizard stood up on shaking legs. "Come with me. I'll explain everything."

Jirah handed the elf his packages, loading down his arms with books and other sundries. Nearra eyed the wizard's tottering burden with faint amusement. "I'll just carry these for you. You look like you could use a hand. I'm Nearra, and this is my sister, Jirah."

"Aspiring wizards, no doubt?" The elf managed a worried smile. "Nagato. I'm Nagato."

"My sister's a wizard. Not me." Bitterness seeped into Jirah's voice. She fought it with a vaguely fake smile. "You're Kagonesti, aren't you?" Jirah blurted. Nearra tried to shush her, but it was too late. "That's a little weird for a wizard." Most Kagonesti lived apart from the rest of the world, protecting the forest and having little to do with magic.

Blushing faintly, Nagato clutched his packages tightly and headed down the street. "Yes, well, that's true. It's a long story. Erm, I . . . um." He raised an eyebrow, warming slightly now that the Tower of High Sorcery was farther behind them. "First, let me tell you about the Tower."

Jirah couldn't tell if he was being helpful or just moving past an uncomfortable topic. She'd have to ask Nearra later. Nearra was always better at reading people.

Nagato continued, "The Tower of Palanthas was cursed long ago so that no one could enter until the Master of Past and Present returned."

"Master of Past and Present?" Nearra asked.

"He returned a few years ago, in 353. Took over the Tower, and now it's his. The only people who ever go in there now are his apprentices—and even they are afraid of Shoikan Grove. It's an evil place." He shuddered. "The Master's name is Raistlin. Ah yes," he said, tilting his head at the looks on the girls' faces. "You've heard that name before, I wager."

"Raistlin—one of the Heroes of the Lance!" Nearra squeezed the packages she was holding, and Jirah thought she heard something snap. "But Raistlin is a Black Robe. He controls the Tower?"

"Exactly. And he doesn't care much for visitors—friendly or otherwise."

"Nagato, if the wizards can't get into the Tower," Nearra asked tentatively, "how do they take the Test of Wizardry?"

"They don't. Well, not here, anyway. The test is given in Wayreth, mostly. We're trying to change that, negotiate with Raistlin, but, well, he's not much of one for talking. And it's very difficult to give the test outside of a Tower of Sorcery." Nagato smiled ruefully. "But several members of the Conclave are here, and you'll need to get their permission to take the test at all. So wherever you've come from, your journey isn't in vain."

"So if they're not in the Tower, where are they?" Jirah trotted along beside him, trying to keep up with the elf's long strides.

"Well, these are powerful and important wizards. They don't live in an inn or a barn, to be sure." Nagato sniffed with an air of disdain. "The Wizards' Conclave built a grand hall to use until the Master of the Tower came and opened the tower for them. They meet in that building—have for a few hundred years, or so I'm told. It's called the Hall of Three Moons." Nagato gestured toward a white building on the other side of the road, arms fluttering in his wide sleeves. "And here we are."

CHAPTER

2 HALL OF THREE MOONS

Nagato stopped closer to a building just within the shadow of the Library of Palanthas. It was of modest size, but the ornamentation was elaborate, as if trying to make up for the diminutive stature of the building. Three full moons—one black, one red, and one white—rose in a stained-glass arc, a magnificent window within the high marble doorway. The sunlight shone through the stained glass, mixing red, white, and dark blue lights across the inner floor.

Nearra and Jirah followed Nagato hesitantly, stepping briskly forward only when the Red Robe elf clucked at them like a mother hen. "Come along. Don't just stand there in the street like urchins."

The girls followed Nagato into the main foyer, staring at the magnificent marble columns, veined with light blue, that held up the high ceiling. Men and women of all races walked the floors of the main hall. Red robes caught the light of the stained glass window, side by side with velvet black cowls and silvery white dresses.

"There are wizards everywhere," Nearra whispered, awed. She gripped her dragon-claw fire staff, wishing she'd chosen a more formal dress than the simple blue one she wore. Some of the wizards greeted Nagato with a wave or a smile, but the Red Robe grinned shyly in passing and did not stop to speak with them. Nagato led the girls through the building's main chamber, toward a series of staircases leading to balconies above.

As they followed Nagato up the stairs, Nearra saw that he hurried toward an archway into a larger room. "It looks like they're having a meeting." A cluster of wizards walked out of the room as they entered.

"Then we shouldn't disturb them." Nearra tried to grab Nagato's sleeve and pull the wizard back.

Nagato hushed her gently, rushing on. "No, it's perfect. Look, it's breaking up. They must have just finished. These are exactly the people you should ask about your test. How lucky they're all here!"

They entered a side room, where several tall, leather-bound chairs were arranged around low tables. A soft burgundy rug covered the floor. The room looked more like a lounge than a meeting chamber, relaxed and comfortable. A small fire glowed in a fireplace with a mahogany mantel, keeping the room warm and bright. Wizards of several orders whispered cordially to one another near the fire.

"Hold these for a moment." Shoving his packages into Jirah's arms, Nagato dashed to a straight-backed gentleman, catching his attention with a polite greeting.

"What am I, a pack mule?" Jirah tried to complain, but there were so many eyes on her that it came out as more of a whimper. Nearra smiled in commiseration and took a few of the parcels from Jirah's arms, juggling them with her vallenwood fire staff in the crook of her elbow. The staff's crystal, held by a carved dragon claw at the top of its length, sparkled as it reflected firelight from all angles.

The gentleman speaking to Nagato spared a glance toward the girls, an eyebrow quirking sharply. Nagato smiled and bowed, backing toward them with moderate grace. "He's coming." Nagato scrambled to take the packages back. "Be on your best behavior, ladies. Councilor Justarius is in charge of the Hall of Three Moons, the Wizards' Conclave itself!"

Justarius walked with a gait far slower and more stilted than the young elf's. He took his time crossing the chamber, pausing occasionally to speak to another wizard or shake someone's hand. He had a gentle demeanor, but sharp eyes that took in everything around him. He leaned heavily on a red-stained wooden cane, despite his stiff, straight posture.

"Why does he limp?" Jirah whispered, tugging Nagato's robe.

Nagato answered, "Justarius? It is a scar from his Test of High Sorcery. All wizards who have taken the test have some scar, either outside or in, from their experience." Around them, more wizards began to leave the room. Nagato's voice fell reverently. "Whatever happened to him then gave him that limp."

"Have you taken the Test of High Sorcery, Nagato?" asked Nearra. Nagato gulped, turned white, and said nothing. With a sigh, Nearra assumed that was a yes.

"Ah, here he comes." Nagato beamed.

Justarius was human, a man with kind eyes, a weary smile, and a face lightly lined with laugh wrinkles. In his scarlet robes, he looked like someone's father. Nagato bowed before the elegant wizard, the elf's red robes fluttering in imperfect imitation of the regal demeanor of his peer. Quickly sensing that it was the appropriate thing to do, Jirah and Nearra repeated the motion.

"Justarius." Nagato smiled politely, gesturing to Jirah and Nearra. "I want to introduce you to some acquaintances of mine. This is Nearra and her sister Jirah." Several wizards followed the limping councilor, standing behind him as the sisters were introduced. The wizards eyed the girls warily. A young elf with long, steel-silver hair covering his dark eyes actually sneered. Nearra felt her smile fade.

"You're wizards, are you?" Justarius's eyebrows rose curiously. He shook the girls' hands with a firm, pleasant grip. Nearra was grateful for his agreeable tone, so different from the glares of the others.

"Just me," Nearra answered, trying not to stumble over her words. Jirah shrank beneath Nagato's packages. "I'm here to take my Test of High Sorcery, sir."

The room fell to silence as more of the wizards took an interest in them.

"Well, well! Then you've arrived at the right place." Justarius smiled at them both.

Nagato beamed. "You go ahead and talk. I'm going to put these packages in the library." He took the parcels and books from Nearra and Jirah. "I'll be right back." Over the stack of items, Nagato made an excited gesture to Nearra and grinned. "Good luck!" he whispered. Then he headed toward the door, balancing his packages as he went.

Left suddenly alone with a leader of the wizards in Palanthas, Nearra managed a weak smile. Justarius seemed to understand that the girls felt out of place, and he asked politely, "Do you come from a lineage of wizards?"

Jirah blushed, clearly uncomfortable, but Nearra raised her chin and plunged in. "Our ancestor was a wizard named Anselm. He was a mage here at the Tower of High Sorcery in Palanthas." She heard faint gasps from the room. Obviously, some of the wizards here still knew the name.

"But Anselm was cursed," Justarius said kindly. "Magic was removed from his descendants."

A Black Robe stepped forward, folding his hands into the sleeves of his robes. "He was cursed for betraying his fellow wizards. He didn't deserve to be one of us." The man gave Nearra a look that said he thought much the same of her.

Justarius chuckled. "Now, now, Yomon. Let the young lady talk."

"We broke the curse, my sister and I," Nearra explained. She suddenly felt Jirah's fingers in her own, bolstering Nearra's confidence. "Anselm paid the cost of his betrayal. For generations, our family has been punished for a crime that none of us committed. That time is over now. I'm ready to start a new history for my family—one in which we can erase Anselm's stain on our family name."

"And these?" Justarius reached for her hands, taking them in his and turning them to look at her palms. "Are these part of your unusual story?"

"I was taken by a Black Robe and used in a ritual to bring back one of the most powerful evil sorceresses in Krynn's history. Jirah, my friends, and I were able to fight her off, but the sorceress's magic remained in me.

"I used it to seek out the tomb of my ancestor Anselm. My hands are marked by one of the magical items involved in that curse. An evil wizard named Tylari stole golden gauntlets that controlled the wind, and without those gauntlets, we couldn't break the curse. We had to defeat him to free our family. After he was destroyed, the mark of the golden gauntlets he was wearing somehow transferred to me." She flexed her golden fingers, suddenly ashamed. Justarius released her hands.

"Defeated a wizard—two wizards!—at such a young age, and with no true knowledge of magic?" a pale woman said, shaking her head admiringly. "That is impressive."

It wasn't just two wizards, Nearra knew, but she didn't want to get into a complicated discussion of all that had happened.

"Nearra, allow me to introduce Viridia, leader of the Order of White Robes here in the city," Justarius said. "Now let the girl talk, my dear Viridia. I suspect there is more to this tale." Justarius turned back to Nearra. "Go ahead. You broke the curse?"

"No, sir. Actually, it wasn't me. It was my sister, Jirah." Heads swiveled, and Jirah turned beet red at Nearra's side. "She broke the curse," Nearra continued, "but she had to give up her ability to use magic. Ever. That was the price. There's more, but . . . but . . . that's what happened. I don't think the details are important." Nearra took a deep breath and plunged on. "Now that the curse is broken and I have control of the magic I've been given, I want to take the Test of High Sorcery and become a true wizard."

"That is some story," Viridia sighed. She was five or so years older than Nearra, wearing a white robe as if she had been born into it. She had curly golden hair cut in a short, perky bob. Although Viridia was a grown woman, the sparkle in her eye made her seem young and fun loving. Nearra smiled despite her nervousness. "Hello," the woman said cheerfully. "I'm Viridia." The White Robe shook Nearra's hand energetically and smiled past her at Jirah.

"So you are here to take your Test of High Sorcery?" Justarius tilted his head and considered Nearra. She nodded, suddenly aware again that every person in the room was staring at her. Justarius said nothing for a long, uncomfortable moment. Some of the wizards around the room whispered, others grumbled in disapproval. "How do we know, young lady, that you have any magic at all? Regardless of your family's history, you will have to prove to the Wizards' Conclave that you can perform magical spells before we even consider giving you the Test of High Sorcery."

"Yes, sir. I am aware of that." Nearra held out her hand and concentrated. She could feel heat rising in her face and neck. "Sh . . . sh . . ." Nearra gulped, and the faint light that had begun to twinkle on her palm faded.

A grandfatherly wizard in wrinkled red robes leaned forward to peer into her palm. He whispered, "Go on, girl." She caught his eye, and the wizard winked and grinned behind his thick white beard. "You can do it."

Taking heart from his kindness, Nearra steeled herself and took a deep breath. "*Shirak*."

A soft glow of light blossomed from her fingers, swirling into a ball against Nearra's golden palm. It wasn't very bright, not even as big as the flame of a candle, but it did not waver. Several of the wizards muttered loudly, others openly decrying Nearra's magic with cutting jibes. "I've seen better mage-lights from fireflies!" one cried, laughing. Another retorted, "Are you certain she cast a spell, or is that just the reflection of the torchlight on her freakish hands?" Laughter burbled through the room and mixed with uncomfortable silence.

Justarius held up his hand and the commentary subsided.

The grandfatherly Red Robe at Nearra's side winked again, chuckling to himself, and took a step back. "That's a lovely staff you have, dear. I see that you are well worthy of it." He sat down in one of the leather chairs, smiling to her encouragingly.

"She has proven that she possesses magic. That alone makes her worthy of our test," Justarius said in a commanding tone. Slowly, as if conferring on her a great burden, Justarius placed his hands on Nearra's shoulders and stared deeply into her eyes. "The Test of High Sorcery is a dangerous thing, especially for one so young, so unproven. You have served as no one's apprentice. How did you come by your skills?"

Nearra shrank into herself a little. This was a more difficult story to tell. She saw Nagato slip back into the room near the archway, and his hopeful smile raised her spirits. "I served as a maid in Cairngorn Keep," she began.

"Maddoc's keep?" an elf in white robes asked, raising his voice.

"Yes," she answered truthfully. "He was trying to raise the spirit of the sorceress Asvoria to steal her power. To do that, he placed her soul . . . into me." If Nearra thought there had been muttering before, it was nothing compared to the whispers that flooded the room when she said this. "I overcame the soul of the dark queen with the help of my friends. But her departed spirit left a lasting impression on me—a knowledge of magic that, I must confess, is not entirely my own. I learned wizardry from Asvoria, but I learned to respect its power by fighting to break the curse that Anselm brought down on my family."

"You come before the Conclave of Wizards with a wild story like that?"

Nearra could see the young Black Robe elf who had heckled her before pushing his way through the crowd. She hadn't noticed his thick features before, muscular and tall for an elf. His forearms were tattooed with brightly colored images, and steel-silver hair hung down below his shoulders in long waves. His voice was gravelly and mocking. "You learned magic from a dead sorceress and broke a curse generations old. Oh, pardon us, Miss Wonderful, if we don't bow down and ask you to be a proper wizard. Why should you take the Test of High Sorcery at all, with that kind of power? Just jump right in! I'm certain that if you want to be in charge of the Conclave, Justarius won't mind stepping aside!"

Several wizards laughed, and only a few were polite enough to cover their mouths. Justarius frowned at the bold speech and leveled a withering glance at the black-robed Silvanesti. "Loreddion, your thoughts on this subject are not required." The young elf growled, fire flashing in his eyes, but he stepped back. "Go," Justarius told him.

The dark elf snarled, but did as he was told. As he stalked past Nagato in the doorway, he deliberately slammed his shoulder into the shy Kagonesti without apology.

Justarius turned back to Nearra. "If what you told us is true—and I see no reason to discount it, with the rumors we've all heard from Cairngorn Keep—then you may, in fact, have the ability to take the Test of High Sorcery. But are you certain you don't want to wait, Nearra? Perhaps apprentice under one of the wizards here in Palanthas, learn more—"

"No," Nearra interrupted. Fire rose in her spirit. "I've earned this. I can do it. Please let me try."

Justarius looked at the other wizards of the Conclave, his eyes resting on the leaders of both White and Black, then to the elderly wizard who stood near Nearra's elbow. "Let her try," whispered the old Red Robe, his face crinkling into a white-bearded smile. "She's proven she has the courage—and the magic. Who are we to question whether the gods have guided her here?"

Something about the old wizard's tone drew Nearra's attention. Did he know about her dream? She glanced at him, but the grandfatherly wizard only smiled and patted her hand innocently. "All things come in their time, my dear. Perhaps now is yours?"

Nearra drew her attention back to Justarius. "I'm ready for my test, sir."

"Yes," Justarius agreed, and he patted her firmly on the shoulder. "It would appear that I cannot change your mind on this. Does the Conclave have any argument?" Around them, the other wizards remained quiet, only a few whispering disapproval of Justarius's decision. "It seems that people around here still listen to you, Chyrcan," Justarius nodded to the elderly man. "Then so shall it be."

Justarius sighed. He faced Nearra and pulled himself to his full height. For the first time, Nearra could tell that he was a wizard of great power, a man to be feared and listened to. He was no ordinary wizard with a limp, but one of incredible ability and talent. Yet there was sadness in his eyes when he faced her. "We have no access to the Tower of High Sorcery, but it is possible to take a test without its facilities. Come back to the Hall of Three Moons two hours after sunrise tomorrow, Nearra, and you will face your Test of High Sorcery.

"But remember!" Justarius caught her eye once more. "If you should fail, you will sacrifice all of your magical knowledge and ability—everything you have gained. No one fails the test and remains a wizard."

Nearra gulped and nodded, unable to speak.

"If you fail this test, Nearra, you will die."

CHAPTER

3   By Paladine's Grace

I didn't think it would be so big . . ." Jirah's voice trailed off in awe.

The Temple of Paladine rose above them like a great white sea-bird, the wings of white marble outstretched to either side of a lovely grove of plants and green waving grass. Clerics in white and gold circled inside the building, greeting citizens as they passed between the arched wooden doors. The platinum sigil of a great dragon, shining with obvious care, was worked on the wood. High overhead was the great dome of the church, still covered in scaffolding. From here, Jirah could see workers waving to one another as they built the roof of the church.

"They're still building it. It'll be even grander when they're done," said Nearra. Even so, she paused before she walked toward the high doors. Jirah had to grab her sister's hands to drag her along.

Nearra liked to pretend that nothing impressed her, but there was no way she could keep that bland look on her face here. Not in the Temple of Paladine himself, in the city of Palanthas!

Jirah stopped just inside the doors and looked around—the clerics sweeping past, the parishioners praying in the temple, the priests cleaning the marble statues flanking the altar at the end of the room. "It's so beautiful," she whispered. "I love it.

"Excuse me, I . . ." Jirah tried to catch the attention of a cleric passing by, but the woman did not stop. As the cleric rushed down between the pews, Jirah muttered, "I guess someone really needed her. Oh well, I'm sure that someone else . . . excuse me, sir?"

This time, she tried to step directly in front of one of the acolytes. He gave her a stern look and pushed past.

"Do I have salad on my head?" Jirah put her hands on her hips and glared.

"They're just busy. Palanthas is a big city. I'm sure they—"

Jirah didn't let her sister finish. "Excuse me!" she demanded, planting herself in front of a portly cleric carrying a basket of sandwiches and wine. "I need to speak to a cleric."

"What? What?" The fat man stared down his nose at her as though the black-haired girl were some sort of bug. "Are you injured?"

"No. I need to speak to a cleric. I want to join the church."

At this, the cleric was visibly taken aback. "You want to join the church?" He paused and stared at her. "Well, I can't make that kind of arrangement. You'll have to find Gloria—she's the rector. She'll be the one to decide if you're suited for the task." A condescending note crept into his voice as he hiked up his basket. "I wouldn't hold my breath about being a cleric, little girl. You aren't the kind."

Jirah stared, gaping as the cleric marched away. "How rude!"

"They do that," said a quiet voice from one side. Jirah and Nearra turned to find a young man standing nearby, dusting one of the dragon statues in a nook. "There was a problem with some wizards a while back. Oh, it's all worked out now, but some of them still call it the 'Day of the Purple Wizard' and make faces when they pray." The thin boy wore the robes of an acolyte of Paladine, though his mass of curly, dirty-blond hair and his fatigued smile separated him from the other clerics. The most polished thing about him was the whisk of his dust rag.

"Purple wizard?" Nearra frowned. "That sounds familiar . . . Tell me, was this purple wizard a kender?"

The acolyte perked up. "You know Sindri?"

"Oh wow," Nearra chuckled.

Jirah rolled her eyes. "He traveled with us for a while, traveled with her, really"—Jirah pointed at her sister—"and then with me when we were looking for her. That's a long story." She stuck out her hand toward the boy. "I'm Jirah. This is my sister Nearra."

"I'm Adyn. Adyn Thinreed, cleric of Paladine." The girls shook his hand one by one. "I met Sindri—and his friend Catriona—when I first came to Palanthas. They helped me find my way."

"They're our friends too," Nearra said, smiling into his eyes. For a moment, Jirah felt like neither of them remembered that she was standing there. She cleared her throat loudly, and Nearra blushed and looked away.

"You're a cleric of Paladine?" Nearra asked.

"Yes. Though"—he gestured floppily with the dust rag—"you wouldn't know it to look at me." Jirah heard bitterness behind the boy's smile. "I'm here to help people and serve Paladine in the greatest city on Krynn." His smile faded, and he took another swat at the dragon statue. "Apparently by cleaning the pews so their bottoms don't get dirty."

"Can you help me, Adyn?" Jirah asked. "I need to speak to a cleric of Paladine about joining the priesthood." Suddenly shy, her voice faded away. "I need to speak to Gloria."

"The rector? Sure, she's my boss. Come on. I'll take you to her office." Adyn tucked the polishing rag away and smiled at her. They followed him to the side of the main hall, through a small, dark

REE SOESBEE

door into a corridor of soft wood and warm tones. A brownish red rug on the floor softened their footsteps.

"What's a rector?" Jirah asked, keeping her voice low.

"She's the priestess in charge of running the temple—"

Perking up, Jirah ran on over his words, "Arranging festivals, organizing the holy-day celebrations?"

"No," Adyn replied with an embarrassed shrug. "Actually running the temple—cleaning the halls, making sure everyone gets paid, counting the supplies . . . stuff like that." His face reddened. "The kind of stuff I do."

The three of them walked down the hall, past closed doors with doorknobs shaped like little dragons. At the third door, Adyn stopped and knocked. A female voice from inside greeted them with a cheery, inquisitive tone, and Adyn opened the door. The small office's walls were lined with shelves containing colored paperweights, bright trinkets, and sheaves of scrolls. A simple wooden desk in the center of the room overflowed with pens and odd items. In a comfortable chair, a human woman sat gazing out the window. "Yes, Adyn? Ah, you've brought visitors." Gloria closed the book in her lap and peered at them over the top of her glasses. "What can I do for you, young ladies?"

"Gloria, this is Jirah and Nearra. They're friends of Sindri," Adyn said.

The woman's eyebrows shot up into her salt-and-pepper hair. "The little wizard? Oh dear, oh dear! Is he back?" She clutched the book to her chest. "The last time, I lost two wine goblets and a small cask of oil. Is he with you?"

"No, Gloria—they're not kender."

"I can see that," she snapped lightly, and smiled. "What can I do for you?"

Jirah stepped forward, twisting her hands in her skirts. She curtseyed awkwardly. "I want to join the priesthood." If a kender had jumped out of Jirah's skirts, Gloria's eyebrows could not have been more firmly rooted upward.

"And why is that?" Although her tone was gentle, Jirah could feel the woman's eyes scanning her.

"I heard Paladine's voice."

Gloria exchanged a concerned look with Adyn. Nearra quickly interjected. "She did. And he told her to come here."

"Well . . ." Jirah squirmed under Gloria's keen observation. "He didn't say that. He just asked me to give up magic. But I thought . . . I mean, since he spoke to me, and all . . ."

"Give up magic?" This time it was Adyn speaking.

"Wizard magic. Our family has a heritage of wizardry. In order to restore the family's ability, I had to give up any magic I had." Why was it that when Nearra told the wizards about breaking the curse, they all acted like it was the most natural thing in the world, but these priests stared at her as if her ears were on fire? Jirah let her voice trail off, then burst out, "It's true! And I want to be a cleric."

A long, strained moment of silence fell on the small office. Finally, Gloria placed her book on the desk and reached for Jirah's hands. "Well, giving up mage craft won't stop you from becoming a cleric if you have the gift for it. Come here, dear, let me look at you."

Jirah stepped forward and shyly placed her hands in the old woman's. Gloria pulled her close to stare at Jirah's palms, then turned the girl's hands over and looked at her small fingers. Every second felt like an eternity while Jirah watched her. Gloria closed her eyes and murmured a prayer, and Jirah felt a faint tingle run through her spine.

Then, with a sigh, Gloria sat back in her chair and let go of Jirah's hands. She took her glasses from her nose and set them in her lap. Jirah stood in the center of the room, the entire world

REE SOESBEE

pressing down on her shoulders. Her voice came out with a squeak. "Well?"

Gloria sighed, drumming her hands on her glasses. "I'm sorry, dear. Paladine doesn't speak through you."

"But that's to be expected, right?" Nearra said. "She hasn't been trained as a cleric yet. There's a lot to learn."

"No, dear." Gloria dismissed Nearra's comment with a wave. "Being a cleric isn't like being a wizard, young lady. It is a gift that one is born with—or is chosen to carry. If Paladine wanted you as a cleric, Jirah, you would have a mark. Now, that doesn't mean you can't serve Paladine if you feel truly called—as a worker, perhaps, or in some other way. But you will never be a cleric of this church."

Jirah felt her heart sink into her shoes. Tears crowded her eyes, and she brushed them away with an angry hand.

"You can't be sure," Nearra argued. "You could be wrong."

Gloria rapped her knuckles on the desk sharply. "Little girl, you may know something about wizards, I can see that. But you don't know anything about the ways of the gods. You cannot force them, or wheedle them. You either are"—she spread her hands—"or you are not." She turned to Jirah. "I'm sorry, dear," Gloria said gently. "Paladine may have spoken to you, but he doesn't speak through you."

Jirah threw open the door with a loud bang that made Adyn jump. She could hear Nearra calling her name behind her, but it didn't stop Jirah. She didn't look back. Hot tears stung her eyes. Why was it always like this? Nearra got the wizards to give her the Test of High Sorcery right off the street. Why was everything so easy for Nearra and so difficult for her?

Jirah chided herself. This wasn't Nearra's fault. The soft carpet blurred before her eyes, hazing in a mist of red and brown. Nearra was a good sister and a loyal friend. Yet it had seemed, for a bright moment, that everything would work out, that there would be a place for her in Paladine's service, something to do with her life. Jirah slammed her hand against the door at the end of the hall, throwing it open with all of her anger. There was a shout on the other side, and the door jarred against something hard.

"Hey!" It was the fat priest who had scolded Jirah earlier. He grabbed the offending door in one hand, dark eyes blazing. "Watch where you're going, you little guttersnipe!"

People in the temple turned from their prayers as the man's voice spiraled higher. Jirah could feel their eyes on her, and her heart shrank three sizes. The big man yelled again. "What were you doing in the offices? Are you a thief? Were you stealing from Paladine's temple?" The pitch of his screams echoed, and Jirah froze.

"No, no, I wasn't." She held out her hands to stop him from yelling again. It didn't work.

"I'll have the city guard in here in three minutes! They'll haul you away, do you hear me! Turn out your pockets—I want to see what you stole! You, there," he gestured wildly to one of the other priests who stood gaping nearby. "Get the guard!" He grabbed at Jirah's shoulder. She screamed and darted past him, wanting nothing more than to be far away from the church, the priests, and her failure. A street urchin? Is that what she looked like?

Is that all she was?

The priest yelled, storming after her. Parishioners darted to either side to get out of Jirah's way. A priest near the front gates managed to get his arms around her and pull her back, holding Jirah helpless in front of the small crowd. The priest marched toward her, eyes flashing with righteous anger. "Turn out her pockets!"

"What are you doing, Macus? Unhand her!" Adyn appeared

behind the other priest, Nearra hard on his heels. "Let her go! She hasn't done anything wrong."

The fat priest's face grew blotchy. "She's a thief!"

"She is not!" Nearra stepped in front of her sister, staff in her hand.

The priest holding Jirah quickly let go and stepped away when faced with an angry wizard. Jirah's knees buckled and she fell to the floor, gulping for air. She could taste the salt of her tears, feel the scratches on her shoulder where Macus had grabbed her.

Nearra's voice carried clearly in the temple. "How dare you! We are strangers in this city, and you treat us like this? Is this how the church of Paladine welcomes visitors?"

"But . . ." Macus's voice was weak now, but he pointed in Jirah's direction, rings flashing on every finger.

"She's no more a thief than I am," Nearra said. "We were invited to meet with Gloria in the rector's office. Or don't you remember your own directions?" Nearra stomped her vallenwood staff on the floor for emphasis, and the red crystal at its tip flashed warningly.

Macus paused, beady eyes darting back and forth from Nearra to Adyn to Jirah. Suddenly aware that he had made a scene for no reason, the fat priest recoiled. "She was in the offices . . . I couldn't have known . . . I was just protecting the church—"

"Jirah, are you all right?" Adyn knelt down beside her. He held out a handkerchief and she took it, wiping her face unabashedly.

"I'm fine," she gulped, pulling herself to her feet. "I just want to leave."

"She *should* leave!" Macus cried. Nearra glared at him again. "Right now," he muttered more quietly, straightening his white robes and twisting the rings around his thick fingers.

"We're leaving." Jirah flashed him a glance as sharp as her

sister's. The pitying look on Adyn's face summed up Jirah's whole afternoon. She couldn't meet his eyes.

"Jirah, are you all right?" Nearra's hand was on her shoulder.

Macus sneered after them as they stepped back into the sunshine. "I'll be watching for you."

"Trust me," Jirah whispered, "we won't be coming back."

CHAPTER

4   FEARBREAKER

It's over. I'm going to have to sell fish at the market. Or learn how to shine shoes. Or worse, be a woodcutter," Jirah muttered, slumping in her chair and pushing away her sandwich.

"Hey. Da's a woodcutter."

"I know," Jirah replied. "That's why I said it. Do you think he's happy?"

Nearra grimaced. "No. He's been trying to be a wizard all his life. Of course he's not happy." She refilled their cups for the fourth time that evening.

The inn around them bustled. The dinner hour was raucous, with patrons lifting their glasses over their heads and shouting for more wine, calling to greet their companions as the door swung open to allow the tavern's usual crowd. The girls had a small table near the fireplace, where the flame's warm crackle drove out the chilly spring evening.

Feet trampled across the floor, tavern maids pushed back and forth with full platters, and a pair of bards sang bawdy tunes by the bar. Still, even amid the hubbub, Jirah felt very alone. She looked up at Nearra. "I'm glad you're here."

"Of course I'm here." Nearra smiled gently, blue eyes compassionate. "I'm your sister. Where else would I be?"

They shared a smile.

Nearra emptied her glass and reached for the pitcher on the table. She filled her tankard, then poured another inch of the liquid into her sister's cup as well. "You think your life is over? Tomorrow, I'm going to become the first untrained wizard in more than four hundred years to take the Test of High Sorcery. Nagato"—she hiccupped, smothering it with her hand—"Nagato told me so. If I die—"

"You aren't going to die!" Jirah said, but Nearra kept talking.

" . . . then I'll still go down in history. How about that?"

Jirah took another long drink from her cup. "We are both so completely doomed."

A small voice piped up out of nowhere at the other side of their table. "Yup. All three of us."

Jirah and Nearra spun in their seats to face a kender sitting in what had just a moment ago been an empty chair. "Where did you come from?" Nearra burst out. She lifted her cup and stared at the liquid. "I haven't been drinking wine, so I shouldn't be seeing things."

Jirah reached out and poked the kender with an experimental finger. "She feels real."

"Ow! Hey! I'm buying the drink. The least you could do is drink as much as I do." The kender plunked a second pitcher before them and sank into her chair. She was a rough-looking sort, not the usual kender at all. She wasn't smiling, chattering, or stealing anything that Jirah could see. The only stealthy thing she'd done was to sit down at their table unnoticed.

The kender poured all of their glasses full, a dour frown covering her features. She was small, like most kender, but her arms were extremely muscular, and she had no hoopak staff on her back. She wore leather armor with metal shoulders and plates sewn on, and at her side a small metal baton swung from a leather loop on her belt. Beside the pitcher sat a helmet with a faceplate like a cat's head, with black horsehair pouring from a topknot set into the metal. The kender's hair was a rich brown shot through with light streaks, and her eyes were as piercing and green as an old tomcat's. She had no topknot tying her hair back, but instead, long braids hung several inches past her shoulders. A variety of small trinkets and carvings were knotted into the dark caramel-colored braids. Some adornments even sprouted out from behind her ears, covering her shoulders in feathers and ivory.

"All three of us, dead as doornails. Or worse. Left by thieves and murderers to rot in a desert." Jirah and Nearra stared as the kender slumped over the table. "Might as well dig our own graves. We've been abandoned by fate, betrayed by providence . . ."

Jirah waved her hands about in front of her, closing her eyes and shaking her head. "Wait, wait, wait. Who are you?"

"I'm dead."

"No, before that part."

"Oh." The kender set down her cup and reached to shake hands with Jirah. "I'm Koi," she said, gripping firmly. "Koi Fearbreaker."

"I'm Jirah, and this is my sister, Nearra. We're dead too."

Nearra laughed, taking another sip of her drink. "Will you two stop that? Nobody's dead. Why are you so glum, Koi?"

The kender girl sighed and kicked her feet under the table. "I'm in Palanthas on behalf of my village. We have a problem—a magical problem. But I can't find anyone to help me with it." She shrugged.

"I'm a wizard," Nearra said between sips. "Maybe I can help you."

For a moment, the kender perked up. "I knew I sat down at this table for a reason! My village has lost its fire. I need to get it back."

"Lost its fire?" Jirah asked.

Koi nodded. "They all went out one night. Poof. Just like that. All the fires in Haymore—that's my village. We can't relight them. Even wizard fire, all kinds of flame. Gone." She wiggled her fingers through the air like falling stars. "My village is cold. I've heard others too, all the wonderful places near the village, like a plague, spreading through Kenderhome. But because it started in our village, we are the ones to handle it, so I volunteered. But none of the wizards in Palanthas will even listen to me. They all just stuff their hands in the pockets of their robes and run away as quickly as they can."

"You came here all alone? That's brave of you." Nearra smiled, clearly enchanted with the kender.

"Brave?" Koi snorted. "I don't think any kender knows the meaning of the word. I know I don't. Do you know what my last adventure was?" When the girls shrugged and shook their heads, Koi continued. "There was a dragon in the northwest pass, a young one who'd just moved into one of the caves there. One day a couple years ago, we saw it flying overhead, over the mountains near Haymore. And I thought to myself, 'Self,' thought I, 'Now's your big chance.' "

"Big chance?" Jirah repeated. The glasses seemed to have magically emptied themselves, so she grabbed the second pitcher and refilled them.

"I've done just about everything, you see? Sailed the ocean. Fought a pack of wolves with my bare hands. Insulted the Pajwah of the Bullywugs and played checkers with the Grand Executioner of Blöde. I've traveled from Kenderhome to the Great Moors, from Khur to Caergoth. What's left? Nothing. Except, thought I, a dragon. 'A dragon'll do it, Koi!' says I. 'Finally,' says I. And so I creep up to his cave."

"Alone?" Nearra whispered. The two girls leaned forward. Jirah watched the firelight dance on Koi's features as she spun her tale.

"Of course alone! It wouldn't have been a real test if there'd been anyone else along!" Koi snorted. She spread her hands above her shoulders, sneaking through the cave even as she described it. "There was the cave, deep and dark, and freshly dug when the dragon awoke. There I was, sneaking through it, nothing but my hoopak and my armor. And then suddenly, at the end of the tunnel—BLAM! A gigantic red dragon. He had teeth as long as my arm, eyes the size of cart wheels, and claws that could slice through a door made of steel! But he was sound asleep! Well, that wouldn't do at all, so I decided to wake him up."

Jirah couldn't help herself. She squeaked in fear at the description. "Why?"

"Well, dragons don't give off dragonfear when they're asleep! Not really. Well, all right, I couldn't tell, to be honest. So when I got close enough, I threw my hoopak at his nose."

"Did he wake up?" Nearra asked, breathless.

"Yup." Koi slumped back down into her seat and took a long swig of her wine. She looked up at the two of them, and to her surprise, Jirah saw tears in the corners of the little kender's eyes. The kender paused for a moment to roughly wipe them away, and then rasped, "I didn't feel a thing."

"What?" the two sisters chorused.

"Not a thing!" Koi slammed her cup down on the table. "Dragonfear is supposed to be the scariest thing in the world, the absolute worst. Don't you see? That was my only chance to feel real, true, honest *fear*. And nothing happened, so I stole from him—I stole this." She pulled out a bronze feather trinket from her hair and waved it at them. "And I lost my hoopak—the dragon stepped on it and snapped it into little splinters. But even that didn't scare me. My hair didn't stand up on my head, there was no sick feeling in my stomach—my heart didn't even pound once. Not once! Nothing," Koi wailed. "I'm hopeless."

"You're a kender!" Jirah cried out. "Of course you can't feel fear!"

"That's just it! Everyone else can." She looked woeful, big round eyes brimming with tears. "I want to feel it. Just once. I've chased fear across Krynn and back and never found even a hint of it." Koi put her head on the table with a sob. "I'm doomed. I'll never find it."

"Oh, poor Koi!" Jirah patted the kender softly. "I'm so sorry. I know what it's like to have a dream and not be able to reach it." She haltingly told Koi about what happened at the Temple of Palanthas, not skimping on her description of Macus and his blustering. Koi was listening intently, though her eyes still had tears in them.

"That's so sad," Koi sniffled, wiping her nose on a table napkin. "You should come home with me. Kender don't care who calls themselves a cleric, as long as you throw a good party on the holy days. We have 743 of them in my village, you know."

Nearra whispered, "There aren't even that many days in a year!"

Apparently Koi heard her, because the kender countered, "Sometimes we have three or four on the same day, all at once. It's easier to schedule them . . . oh. But you can't come home with me. I can't even go home." Her face screwed up again and she reached for the napkin. "They can't cook anything—can't keep warm at night. They're all leaving the village, but it's the same for miles around. If I don't find a way, and soon, Haymore will be completely empty."

"Listen, Koi." Nearra reached across the table and handed the kender another napkin. "Tomorrow I go before the conclave to take my Test of High Sorcery. I want you to come with me. We'll tell them all about Haymore and your story. I'm sure they'll listen to you then."

Koi perked up, green eyes shining. "Really?"

"Really."

"You're the best! I just knew this was the right place to sit down." Still wiping the tears from her eyes, Koi smiled broadly.

"Why us?" Jirah asked. "Why did you come to our table?"

Koi cocked her head and glanced down at Nearra's golden hands. "Well, to be honest, you seemed like the weirdest people in the room. You might have been murderers, or cultists, or assassins. You might even have been sea elves in disguise or dragons in human form!" Planting her elbow on the table and leaning against her fist, Koi sighed dreamily. "I guess I just thought I'd give fear another shot."

"Nothing?" Nearra raised an eyebrow.

"Nope." Koi sighed and emptied her glass. "Ah, well. There's always tomorrow."

CHAPTER

5   A Cold Dawn

It took Nearra a moment to place the high-pitched noise that had awakened her. She was lying on her back, staring up at the dark ceiling. She heard the noise again, something outside her window, but her sleep-addled mind couldn't place it. A high, shrill . . . then there was banging on her door.

It was a scream.

Nearra sat up. Was it her terrible dream again? She tried to shake off the malaise of sleep, blinking her eyes wildly. Then, in the haze of the morning, she heard the scream once more. Nearra threw off the covers and dashed to the window as Jirah threw open the door. Koi was on her heels, wearing an odd linen night-shirt and long green and white striped socks. Nearra hurled open the shutters and leaned out over the street.

Dawn touched the horizon, illuminating figures running pell-mell through the street. People stepped out of their houses, yelling back and forth, and a woman in pale yellow skirts raced—screaming—toward the temples.

Jirah's voice rang out clear as a bell in the faint morning. "What's going on?" Her dark head popped out beside Nearra's pale one. Koi bounced to their side, prancing up and down behind them.

One of the citizens in the street looked up at them. "A curse has afflicted the city!" he yelled. "All the fires have gone out!"

On hearing this, Koi shrieked, "I knew it! The plague! It's spreading from Kenderhome all the way here!"

Jirah bounded to the small fireplace in the room, kneeling to pull out tinder and a piece of flint. Striking them together, she waited for a spark, but none came. She blew on the tinder, staring at the soft wood shavings for any sign of light.

"Let me try." Koi snatched the flint from Jirah. She pounded them together, faster and faster, but the tinder sat empty on the hearth, no flicker or spark illuminating the curls of cedar.

Nearra stood over the fire and extended her finger. "*Api.*" Something started to flicker at her fingernail, a brief tuft of orange light swelling and trying to grow—and then it fizzled out, smoke rising from her skin. She frowned. "*Api!*" Again, nothing happened.

"Even fire spells don't work." Jirah sat back on her heels and ran a hand through her hair. "This is amazing."

Koi wailed, "It's just like at home! Everyone's going to die. We have to talk to the wizards, Nearra." The kender flapped her hands, scattering the shavings. "We have to talk to them now! I've got to get my armor on!" She raced from the room, dropping the flint stones in her haste.

"Good idea." Nearra grabbed her dress and jerked it over her head, tying her golden hair in a loose knot at the back of her neck. She reached for her staff. "Let's go."

Dark hearths in the blacksmith's shop echoed the empty ovens of bakers. Nearra couldn't stop herself from looking in every house, where black fireplaces and ash-covered hearths stood under cold, black cooking pots. "No warm food today," Nearra murmured. "No hot oatmeal or stew, no cooked meat."

"The kids aren't playing." Jirah peered at a family slamming shut their windows and doors. "Everyone's afraid."

"They probably think the Cataclysm is happening again," Koi said morosely. "Wasn't that one of the first signs of the Cataclysm? The fires going out in ancient Istar?"

"Do you think that's what's happening?" Jirah jumped forward, trying to catch up with her sister's long strides. She pointed. A gang of rough-looking men carrying clubs and other weapons were gathering in the bazaar. Nearra could hear shouts coming from the gang. "Why are they so angry?"

"I think Koi put her finger on it. The legends of the Cataclysm are still very strong, especially in Palanthas. They're afraid."

Jirah tugged on Nearra's sleeve and caught Koi by a long braid of the kender's hair. "Look, they're headed toward the temple of Paladine. If we're going to get to the Hall of Three Moons, we'd better hurry," Jirah said.

Nearra couldn't have agreed more. The three of them rushed through the streets, almost running in their anxiety to get to their destination. In their haste, Nearra almost missed a shrill yell down an alley. A young woman with three small children huddled against a corner of one of the buildings in the alley. Two men from the riot gang were approaching on the other side, carrying heavy vallenwood bats.

"She's a priest!" one of them yelled, and Nearra could see that it was true. The woman wore soft blue robes embroidered with the twisted figure eight of Mishakal. "They caused this! They're starting the Cataclysm again!"

The woman, hardly older than a girl herself, crouched to protect the children. Nearra yelled out before she could stop herself. "You leave her alone!" In that instant, when the two armed men turned to face her, Nearra was glad to feel her sister step up on one side of her and the kender on the other.

Nearra marched forward, her staff in her hands. "You're going to hurt an innocent woman and three small children? If you're trying to pacify the gods, you're making a terrible start." She placed herself between the woman and the advancing threat.

Koi drew a small baton of steel from her belt. It was about as long as her forearm, thick as the hilt of a sword, but completely smooth. She held it out in her fist like a short staff. "One more step, buddy, and you're going to get more than you bargained for."

The men jumped forward, bats swinging. "What are you going to do, wizard girl? Shoot fire out of your eyes? In case you hadn't noticed, there's no fire in the whole city. But we're going to bring it back, if it means we have to burn down every temple in Palanthas."

"Then I guess I'll just have to stand between the city and the flame." As Nearra raised her staff in the air, the thought flitted through her head that they weren't her words. The crystal twinkled, calling on its magic to aid her. "There may be no fire, but I bet I can still summon ice. *Es dingin dalam!*" She spoke the words of magic without hesitation, and her golden hands glowed. The staff's crystal flickered, and a frosty wind swept through the alley, sweeping trash aside in its wake.

A thin sheet of pale white crusted the men's skin. The frost turned to snow, and the snow to ice. A bat fell to the ground, clattering wood against stone, as both attackers were imprisoned in blocks of ice, mouths still open and feet poised to rush forward.

"Wow," Koi breathed, hanging the steel baton back on her belt by its leather loop. "You really are a wizard."

Jirah chuckled. "Nice trick. Looks familiar."

Laughing lightly, Nearra smiled. "I always liked that bow. Too bad you gave it to Rina. It might have been useful," Nearra teased, referencing one of the magical items the sisters used to break Anselm's curse.

The color drained out of Jirah's face. "I couldn't use it anyway. It worked on magic, remember?"

Smile fading, Nearra looked away. "Oh. Right." Her eye fell on Koi as the kender helped the young priestess with her children. "You'd better get them to the temple quickly. I'm afraid that feeling is going to become common in this city until fires return."

"Thank you. I will." The woman smiled at them all and raised her hand in blessing. "May Mishakal be with you." Jirah flinched and looked away as the priestess hurried the children out of the alley.

"We'd better hurry to the Hall of Three Moons. The streets aren't going to be safe to travel for very long," Jirah said. The curved streets of the city led around the great wheel, past Shoikan Grove and right up to the steps of the Hall.

"Nearra! Jirah!" Nagato's voice called from just inside the hall. "You're early! Have you heard? All the fire—"

"All the fire in Palanthas has gone out," Koi sighed, wrapping her arms around herself and weaving back and forth.

Nagato deflated, opening and closing his mouth. "Well, yes, actually." He paused, and Nearra introduced Koi. Nagato continued, "The wizards are meeting inside to discover what it could mean. Three priests came by this morning at the crack of dawn—right when the fires went out. They only left a few minutes ago, and all the leaders of the orders are in the meeting chamber, arguing over what's happened."

"We know what's going on," Nearra said.

"What?" Nagato's eyebrows shot up when Nearra volunteered this. "How could you?"

"Koi's here all the way from Kenderhome. The same thing happened to her village."

Nagato crowded closer, keeping tight to Nearra's side as they pushed through the wizard's hall. White, Black, and Red Robes milled about like geese in a pen. Some argued, others ran frantically about, and three men in black robes stood guard over the front door of the hall.

"Nagato." A gravelly voice caught their attention. Steel-silver hair glinted in the light over a face as young as Nearra's but far more severe—the dark elf Loreddion. "Justarius is looking for you." His black robes twisted about his ankles as he came to an abrupt stop before them. He eyed Nearra and Jirah, then looked down at Koi with a sneer. "You brought a kender? He's not another purple wizard or something, is he?"

"She." Koi squared her shoulders and strode within inches of Loreddion's robes, jabbing her finger into his belly. "And *she* isn't a wizard. But *she's* very good with a dagger. Are you sure you want to annoy someone who's three feet tall and holding a sharp knife, bub?" She reached down for the hilt of her weapon, holding it in one hand while she jabbed him again. Her smile was fierce and sharp, little teeth pointed like a feral cat.

Loreddion stared down at her for a moment, lips parted in surprise. He grunted as she poked him a third time. Amazingly, Loreddion didn't set Koi on fire, strike her with lightning, or even put a curse on her—he just started to laugh. The laugh was dark and deep and rich, his voice low and pleasant. "You're all right, kid." Loreddion cuffed Koi behind her ear playfully.

He looked up at Nagato, and the smile faded back into his usual scowl. "Justarius wants you. Follow me."

They followed the Black Robe into a chamber on the first floor. Like the one before, several tall, leather-bound chairs were arranged in a half circle at one end of the rectangular room, but this time there was no table. There were more than twenty chairs, each one with a wizard seated in it. Others, neophytes and trainees, skittered around the edges. In the center of the circle was a single chair unlike the others. Instead of dark wood, it was light, the cushions a soft cream edged in gold. Justarius sat in this chair, his head bowed over steepled fingers. While the others chattered, he said nothing.

Nagato bowed as he entered the room, and Nearra and Jirah followed his lead. Koi, much like Loreddion, simply strode in, but where the Black Robe stalked to the rear of the room, the kender stood in the doorway with her hands on her hips, staring at everything around her in amazement. Justarius looked up as they entered, and Nearra could see concern deep in his eyes.

"Sir?" Nagato ventured quietly, and the conversation in the room faded to silence.

"Ah, Nagato." Justarius took in the small group at the doorway. "Oh, dear. Nearra. Yes, your test was scheduled for this morning, wasn't it?"

She replied softly, "Yes, sir."

"I can't see how it's possible," one of the Black Robes started, but Justarius raised his hand and the man fell silent.

"No. No, of course not. Your test will have to be rescheduled. Nagato, I need your skill in the library. Chyrcan remembers something about a book he read once that described similar occurrences, but none of the other librarians have your skill." Justarius sighed.

"Excuse me," Nearra said tentatively. Several of the wizards looked up from their papers.

Justarius turned to her with a quizzical expression. "Was there something else?"

She nodded to him in answer. "I'd like to introduce you to Koi Fearbreaker . . . of Haymore Village."

Nearra recognized Yomon as the old man grumped, "Very nice. A thieving kender. Possibly at the very bottom of the list of necessary items."

Viridia slapped at the arm of her chair sharply. "Yomon! Stop it." She adjusted her white robes around her knees and crossed her legs in the leather chair. "Go on, Nearra."

Nearra turned to Koi, and the kender began to tell her story. Although it was the same one Koi told them in the inn, this time she elaborated and spun the yarn of weeping kender children in cold homes. "They sent me here to see if you could help me, but now I think that maybe we can help each other. This could be happening all over Krynn. It's some kind of magical plague, I think," Koi finished, waving her arms expansively.

"It's no plague." Chyrcan came shuffling in the door behind them, sparing a smile for Nagato on his way past. "I remember part of the passage. It referred to a magical artifact known as the Pillar of Flame. The Pillar controls fire in a vast radius—possibly even across all of Krynn. If such an artifact exists, it could be the source of our problems."

Koi bit her lip thoughtfully. "Something like that could reach all the way to Kenderhome?"

"It could reach everywhere." The bearded Red Robe walked toward Justarius. "But my memory is old and faulty. If we could find that book, perhaps it could tell us more."

Chyrcan looked expectantly at Nagato. The young wizard straightened, his voice breaking with nervousness at addressing the entire assembly of wizards. "If it exists in the library that I tend, I shall certainly find it."

"Chyrcan, do you think that this book you remember might reveal the location of the Pillar of Flame?" Viridia asked. "I think we should send someone to seek it out. If it exists, then we must find it and discover what's affecting it."

Yomon grumped, "It's nothing but a legend, Viridia. There are so many wild tales of magic items, artifacts, powerful sorcery from before the Cataclysm—and they're all bunk. I doubt this book Chyrcan remembers exists, much less some 'Pillar of Flame' or all-powerful artifact that controls fire. It's foolishness! We need to gather a militant squad of wizards and lock down the city." The elderly human stomped to a window of the room, throwing open heavy black drapes and flinging the shutters open. The sound of angry citizens echoed into the room.

"There! Do you hear them? That is the sound of Palanthas dying!" Yomon stood before the window, fist raised. The morning sunlight vanished into the darkness of his black robes. He leveled an icy stare at Justarius. "The city is in panic. By nightfall, every temple in the city is going to be surrounded by rioters, looters. Listen to them."

Nearra could hear voices outside the Hall of Three Moons shouting. Someone cried out to Paladine for mercy, and another condemned Takhisis's wrath. Yomon stood in the window like a great dark angel, the wide arms of his robe cutting off the sun. "This city will live or die based on our strength. We have to hold it up, Justarius. We are the keepers of power, the ones with the duty to keep this city safe. Only we have the strength to keep the peace. We must prevent them from hurting themselves.

"Because if we do not, then mark my words," Yomon scowled darkly. The panicked voices in the street became a backdrop of rising terror. "Palanthas will tear itself apart."

CHAPTER

6   SEEKING A SPARK

"How long are they going to argue?" Koi asked, lugging another crate of apples from the cart. She carried it through the short passage to the Hall of Three Moon's kitchen. Apprentices wearing short, gray robes took the crate and started unpacking the apples into small picnic baskets.

"I don't know." Nearra folded a towel over one small basket, feeling the heft of the cold meats and cheeses in the little basket. "Possibly all day."

Sighing, Jirah handed out another basket. A line of women seeking food that didn't need a fire snaked down the street. "I'm glad I'm not there." Looking down at the road, she fumbled for another basket of fruit. "At the temple, I mean. The wizards seem to be much more involved. I think they really have a good lead here with this Pillar of Flame thing. At least they're doing something." She kicked a rock over, watching the ants flee in panic. "The clerics don't seem to be doing anything at all." Night would be on the city in just a few hours. Jirah shuddered to think about what would happen when evening came.

Viridia popped out of the kitchen behind them, munching on a pear. "Is Nagato still in the library?"

"I think so." Nearra smiled down at a small boy and fished a bit of day-old bread from her pocket. He grabbed it gratefully and dashed off into the crowd. Jirah watched him get lost in the sea of strangers, wondering if he would be warm when he slept that night.

"I wanted to talk to you for a moment, Nearra. No, Jirah, please stay," Viridia quickly added when she saw Jirah flush. The White Robe sat on the stair and patted the seat beside her.

Jirah sat on the stair with Nearra, keeping her eyes glued to the floor. Nearra smiled and gracefully positioned herself by Viridia's side. The White Robe bit into her pear again and watched the commotion at the temple with an appraising eye. "They're afraid," she began. "Fire is what made man out of an animal. Take it away, and we become beasts again." The sunlight played on Viridia's blonde hair and made it hard to look directly at her pure white robes.

"I want to tell you something, Viridia. I wasn't sure if it was important before, but I want you to hear it." Hesitantly, Nearra told Viridia the tale, stepping through the words hesitantly. "It begins on a ship, out in the sea . . ."

It was a dream. It had to be a dream.

People were dying.

Nearra stood on the deck of a ship at night, feeling the prow rise and fall beneath her feet. This wasn't Icefire's ship. It wasn't any ship she knew or had ever been on. Nearra looked over the edge again and saw faces in the water. Red blood tinged the white waves. Asvoria killed them, hadn't she? The sorceress who had once taken over Nearra's mind still haunted her thoughts, sifting unknown memories through those that truly belonged to Nearra. As she had done in so many dreams before, Nearra tightened her hands into fists and tried to drive the images

away. She closed her eyes. "You're dead, Asvoria," she said through clenched teeth. "You can't haunt me anymore."

She stared about, seeing red-stained ocean in every direction. Was land anywhere at all? She looked up at the stars, and they were all wrong. Where was the shining dragon? The red moon? She couldn't make out any constellations, nothing she understood. Where was she?

"What are you looking for?" The voice made her jump. It carried easily over the whipping of wind and the loud, tense shudder of sail. Nearra spun back toward the front of the ship. There was a sailor sitting near the prow. She could have sworn she was alone. Nevertheless, he sat there, whittling and humming. The sharp knife flashed in his hand, carving a lump of ivory. Light danced on the blade as it chipped away at the bone.

"I . . . don't know." Her voice sounded too soft, drowned out by the wind and the waves.

The sailor shrugged idly. "Then you'll never find it." The sailor raised the ivory piece and showed her his craftsmanship. The carving was of buildings, high spires and tall temples lifting their heads over the small houses of a city. "There is a great change coming, and you will have to play your part. You are born to be a leader, Nearra. Now is your time."

"A leader?" Nearra shook her head, golden hair flying in the wind. "You're wrong. Davyn is a leader. Icefire on his ship, he's in charge. Not me. I just take care of people." The sailor seemed so strange, friendly and yet distant. But his smile was encouraging, and Nearra returned it hesitantly.

The sailor quirked an eyebrow. With a smile, he asked, "Is that so very different?"

"No," Nearra shook her head. "I had to do those things. If I had my choice, I would have stayed in my father's cottage and lived a quiet life."

"So you choose peaceful ignorance over making a change in the world around you?"

"It's better than being a queen," Nearra said, "like Asvoria."

"Do you really think so?" The sailor lifted his scrimshaw again and peered into the tiny windows. "Asvoria taught you lessons, Nearra."

"She taught me lessons, all right. She showed me how to be cruel."

"More than that. She released the magic in your soul." The sailor's eyes held a twinkle, and Nearra was forced to agree. "You remember being a queen, but you do not think you can be a leader." The sailor chuckled. He turned the scrimshaw in his hand, and Nearra thought she saw little lights twinkling in the windows of the buildings. "You have magic, but you are afraid to be a wizard."

"I'm not afraid."

"No? Have you taken the Test of High Sorcery?"

Nearra flushed. She remembered how many times she had avoided the city, stayed too long in this inn or that one, stopped when she could to handle small tasks. She looked down at the prow and it seemed that the angel figurehead was crying bloody tears.

"You are needed to lead, Nearra." The sailor smiled at her, blue eyes twinkling gently. "I need you to go to Palanthas. You will understand when you get there." He lifted her chin. "I believe in you."

She paused, taken aback by the complete honesty in his voice, the sadness and the earnestness fighting within the words. Something here was important.

"This is a big responsibility, Nearra. For as long as you can remember, you've been protected by others. Now you must take care of yourself—and those who will choose to follow you. You must see my city restored. Go to Palanthas. Then you will go home."

Nearra furrowed her brow. "Restored? What's wrong with Palanthas?"

He lifted her hand to his knee and placed the ivory carving against her palm. The old sailor smiled and winked at her. "It's about to become very cold, Nearra. And you must stand between Palanthas and the flame." The sailor's strong, calloused hand closed around hers, and she felt the rough edges of the carving biting into her palm. The coldness swelled into dread, making her limbs heavy. The sound of the sea roared in her *ears, the dampness of the spray fell on her face. The boat pitched above the waves and landed jarringly back into the ocean. Nearra was tossed forward. She grasped for the rail and clutched the ivory scrimshaw to her chest. When she looked back up, the sailor was gone.*

In the sky, among the strange and unfamiliar stars, the gleaming figure of a silver dragon shone once more.

Viridia didn't frown or even look surprised, but listened carefully through Nearra's full rendition. When Nearra was done, Viridia paused a long moment to think, then asked to hear it again. Nearra repeated the tale, leaving nothing out. When Nearra reached the part about standing between Palanthas and the flame, Viridia stopped her. "Do you know what that means, Nearra?" she asked.

Nearra said shyly, "I thought it meant to come to Palanthas."

"It probably did. This dream sounds more like a foretelling than your mind playing tricks on you by night. You've been sent here, Nearra, for a reason. I think Paladine spoke to you. And I think he spoke to your sister too." At this, Jirah sat up straight, the flush returning. Viridia smiled pleasantly, finishing her pear. "The story you told about breaking Anselm's curse? You both did that, despite all the obstacles placed in your path. I think both of you were sent here in the hour of Palanthas's need." Viridia tossed the pear behind a bush and stared into the sky. "You were born south of here, weren't you, girls? Near Ravenscar?"

"Yes. Our parents still live in the woods not far from the town," Jirah quickly replied.

Viridia smiled, unusually pleased by this simple bit of information. "You can't take your test, Nearra, not until the fire is returned to the city. So I'd say you have a pretty significant investment in the outcome of this problem." She noted Nearra's golden hands and paused. She lifted one and looked at it. "What color will your robes be if you pass the test?"

Nearra blushed. "White. I hope."

Viridia smiled as if a great burden were suddenly lifted from her shoulders. "I'm going to ask you to do something for me, Nearra. And I want you to promise me that you will." Viridia shook her head. "I've learned that power doesn't make someone right for a task. You have to find the right person for the job. Or, in this case, the right person for the job has to find you." She patted Nearra's golden hand. "Promise me?"

"I promise."

"And Jirah?" She leveled her gaze into Jirah's eyes. A weight descended on Jirah's shoulders.

She shook her head. "I can't . . ."

"Please?" Viridia said quietly. "I can tell that you're afraid of something, Jirah. I'm not going to ask what it is, but I've always trusted my feelings. Whatever it is that brought Nearra here also sent you." Viridia fluttered her fingers in the sunlight. "There's a greater power moving us, and we should believe that the gods have a plan."

Behind Viridia, Jirah could see Nearra making a tense, pleading gesture. Jirah rolled her eyes and looked down at the hem of Viridia's robe. "All right."

"Thank you, girls." The White Robe stood up suddenly, her cheerful demeanor becoming determined and intent. Jirah quickly understood what made this woman the leader of the White Order in Palanthas. "You'd better come inside soon. The conclave's going to be announcing its decision in a moment." Viridia swept into the kitchen with a bright smile for Koi, ruffling the kender's hair in passing. In a snap, the White Robe was gone.

Jirah and Nearra watched her go with dumbfounded expressions. "Huh." Jirah exhaled.

"What are you guys doing?" Koi asked, wiping her hands on a dishtowel. "All the wizards are getting together in the main foyer. I think there's going to be an announcement. We're probably going to be told this is a hopeless cause, and we should abandon the city at once. Won't that be something?" She sighed. "The great exodus of Palanthas."

"Cut that out, Koi," Jirah snapped lightly. "Maybe it's not as bad as you think."

Dozens of wizards filled the foyer of the Hall of Three Moons. They stood on balconies and along the walls, some leaning against pillars, others standing stiff by the front door. Nearra and Jirah pushed their way through the throng until they could see the main stairway. On the wide stairs, Justarius and Yomon soothed the crowd, gathering their attention. Nagato stood at the foot of the stair, clutching a careworn text in his arms. Viridia stepped up onto the stairs beside the other two wizards, nodding formally to them. Justarius raised his arms, and the assembly fell silent.

"Wizards of Palanthas," Justarius began, his voice echoing through the hall. In the respectful silence that followed, Jirah could hear the crowds in the street outside. The wizards at the door kept their backs slightly turned, protecting the main entrance of the building. "We, your ruling council, have made a decision regarding the fate of this city.

"All wizards of Palanthas will turn their efforts to guarding the city. We must, as Yomon has said, protect the citizens even from themselves in this time of crisis." Justarius lowered his arms. "We studied the information found in our libraries"—he gestured toward Nagato, whose face quickly flushed as red as his robes—"and determined that this magical defect is occurring because of an artifact known as the Pillar of Flame."

A soft *oooh* passed through the crowd. People started whispering.

Justarius pounded his staff on the ground lightly, and the murmur fell to a hush. "The three orders of wizards have determined that a small group shall be sent out to find more information about this artifact. We know very little about it, and if it is the source of the city's problems, then we must learn more."

Koi whispered to Jirah, "This city's problems . . . that's smart. He's trying to make it look like it's a smaller problem. He isn't mentioning that the plague's all over Kenderhome, and probably across most of Krynn." Several of the wizards around them stared down at Koi in surprise, and Jirah jabbed her in the ribs.

"Shhh!" she hissed. "Justarius is talking."

"Each of the three orders of magic will send one individual to seek out the Pillar of Flame and return with the information we seek. We have not chosen the most powerful or the most experienced. Those wizards will be needed to maintain order in the city. Instead, we need those with insight and talent to investigate this issue." Justarius scanned the crowd sternly.

"The Order of Red Robes chooses Nagato as our representative on this journey," said Chyrcan. If Nagato was bright pink before, he was the color of a cherry now. He stumbled toward the stairs, clutching his book. Several times, Nagato opened his mouth as though to say something, but words never came. His eyes flickered among the sea of faces. When he reached Jirah, his mouth moved again, and she could have sworn he said, "*Help.*"

"Oh no," Nearra whispered. "Viridia can't have meant . . ." She raised one golden hand to her mouth.

Yomon stepped forward, pulling his black robes tight about his body. He glowered down at the crowd. "This is foolishness. There are a hundred things that might be responsible for this strange plague, a hundred enemies who may have leveled this curse against our city." Many of the black-robed wizards in the crowd grumbled in agreement, crossing their arms and muttering darkly to one another. "I will waste none of our strength on this fool's errand. Loreddion!" he snapped. "You're going."

The dark elf opened his mouth to protest, but quickly snapped it shut. Looking at Yomon's fierce stare, Jirah thought Loreddion made the right decision. Loreddion glared at his superior, stalking over to where Nagato stood. When he got there, he growled at the little Red Robe. The smaller elf scurried a few steps away.

Finally, Viridia stepped to the front of the stairs, standing very stiffly. Despite her diminutive height, the pale wizard looked like a glowing sunflower in the light from the stained windows high above. "The White Order of Palanthas recognizes this mission as imperative. However, we do not choose to send one of our own wizards on this journey. Instead, we choose Candidate Nearra, who will be taking her Test of High Sorcery once this crisis is resolved."

"A mere candidate?" Yomon roared. "You can't do that! Why, she's not a wizard at all!"

Justarius frowned as well. "Viridia, really. It mocks the importance of this task to choose someone ill prepared for the mission. Choose again."

The wizards around Nearra shrank back, leaving her to stand alone in the crowd. Viridia put her hands on her hips and faced the leaders of the other orders. "I have made my decision, and I will not alter it. If you refuse to accept Nearra, then the White Robes will not support this task." Justarius and Yomon seemed taken aback by her vehemence.

Jirah crept closer to her sister's side, Koi right behind her. Nearra wrung her hands together, trying to look stalwart but managing only a weak sort of stuck-to-the-floor expression. Jirah felt sorry for her, but also felt a tinge of envy still, deep down.

Jirah smiled up at Nearra encouragingly. Nearra's smile in return was strained. She looked back up at the three wizards on the stairs, and Jirah could see her sister's hands twist in her robes again.

"Is Nearra going to be all right?" Koi whispered. Jirah shrugged silently and shook her head. She had no idea. Nearra looked nervous, biting her lower lip like that. All the wizards in the hall were staring at her.

"This is my decision, Justarius. If you wish my order's assistance, then you will accept it." Viridia was a pillar of strength on the stairway, glaring at the two other leaders. At last, Justarius sighed and nodded.

"Very well, Viridia. If your order supports this, then so it shall be."

All the wizards around Nearra scooted away, leaving her standing alone in the crowd with Jirah and Koi standing on either side.

"These three young wizards . . . er," Justarius corrected himself. "These three young individuals are now charged with this mission: to seek out the Pillar of Flame and discover if it is involved with Palanthas's current difficulty." He leaned on his staff and looked down at them. "I wish you luck. Of course, the resources of the Hall of Three Moons are open to you. As to the rest of you, go out into the city. Ensure the public safety. Do what you can for Palanthas until our young adventurers return."

Justarius leveled his gaze upon Nearra. "Our hopes now rest entirely on you."

CHAPTER

7 LESSONS

"Why me?" Nearra asked. She shivered. Windows opened to let in the day's warm sun had not yet been closed, allowing a brisk breeze to blow through the library. Late afternoon light filtered in, red with the setting sun and quickly fading. Nagato hunched over a stack of books in the center of a wide table, rustling over some bit of information or particular phrase.

"Why did Viridia pick me?" Nearra asked again. She sat on a wooden bench in the library, watching Nagato scurry among the piles. Bookshelves all around them were piled high with scrolls, scraps of bound paper, priceless books older than elves. Maybe one of them would have the answer to the Pillar of Flame—or at least, a place where they could start looking.

"Come on, Nearra. You're the obvious choice." Loreddion leaned against the wall in a shadowy corner of the library, tossing a coin and catching it again in soft rhythm. "Oh, no! Ooo! I had a dream. The gods sent me. I'm special, like a unique little snowflake in the middle of a winter storm," he imitated her mockingly. The scorn in his voice could have set Nagato's books on fire. "Isn't that wonderful?" Loreddion laughed.

"Leave her alone." Koi glared at him. "You're just mad because she's your equal on this mission, and she's not even a wizard yet." The kender climbed up onto a chair so she could stare eye to eye with the dark elf. "Can't you just go cast some spells or something, like Nagato did? Some kind of divination spells that will keep you quiet for a while, so the rest of us can work?"

"Divination isn't my kind of magic. It's for weaklings," Loreddion sneered. He snapped the steel piece so hard that it spun across the room and embedded itself in the wooden frame of Koi's chair. "I'm mad because this is a stupid mission. I should be out there, fighting whatever's trying to hurt my city."

"Your city?" Jirah snorted. "You think you're already head of the Black Robes?"

"I will be." Loreddion brooded behind the sheet of his steel-colored hair. "You just watch and see." He stalked to the windows of the room, closing the shutters with loud bangs.

Koi sighed and started working the coin out of the wood of the chair. "He'll get over it once we're on our way."

A sound at the library door caught Nearra's attention, and she looked up to see the oak panel sliding back to allow another wizard to enter. "Chyrcan?" Nearra called, surprised that she recognized him.

The elderly gentleman smiled, hobbling along on a wooden cane carved like serpents twisted together. He fluttered his hand, forbidding Nearra from getting up. "No, no, dear. I'm just here to check in on you." That statement was met by a snort from Loreddion, who moved beyond the bookshelves to close the windows in the rear of the library. Chyrcan ignored him. "Any luck?"

"No." Nagato moved aside some of the books and pulled more from the shelves of the library. "I can't find this document you remember. It's just not here. Maybe someone removed it." Nagato bustled from shelf to shelf, muttering softly to himself. "We've got to find something before nightfall. We're lucky Solinari is full tonight. This city's about to become the darkest place on Krynn."

Chyrcan sat on the wooden bench beside Nearra. "Must have been quite a shock to you, being chosen like that. Over so many qualified wizards from the city," the Red Robe said to Nearra.

"That's just it. Why me?" she asked, exasperated. She spread her golden hands above her knees and sighed. "I've never even been to Palanthas before."

"Have you ever thought that might be the very reason?" Chyrcan lowered his head, smiling at her. He reached into a sleeve of his robe and pulled out a pair of reading glasses, spinning them lightly between his fingers as he talked. "Viridia is a very clever woman. She's older than she looks, and an exceptional leader. Perhaps your neutrality to the city was critical to your selection." Chyrcan reached to take a book from the table, turning the pages lightly.

Jirah came over, carrying an armload of scrolls for Nagato. She set them on the table with a grunt. "Are you saying that Viridia didn't trust the wizards in Palanthas?"

"Oho!" chuckled Chyrcan. "My dear, you're very clever." He shook a finger at Jirah. "But don't be too clever. If you let anyone catch you saying that sort of thing aloud, you could find yourself in great trouble." Chyrcan pushed the reading glasses onto his nose and leaned forward to skim a scroll Nagato left lying on the table.

"How do you know this library so well, Nagato?" Nearra asked.

"My master was the head librarian for the Hall of Three Moons. When I was abandoned in Palanthas as a child, he took me in. The libraries were really the only place I felt comfortable. Most people assumed I was a Kagonesti warrior, an archer, or a barbarian of some sort. Something fierce." He hung his head, immersing himself in a book. "Human children can be cruel to outsiders."

"Nagato hid in the library," Loreddion mocked as he pulled down a black-wrapped scroll from one of the higher shelves. "If he'd had any kind of backbone, he'd be a White Robe instead of red. I've never seen him stand up for anything, even himself." He tossed the scroll with a flip of his hand, making Nagato scramble frantically to catch it before it hit the ground. The Red Robe shrank back into himself, closing his mouth and scurrying behind the table as Loreddion stalked closer.

Loreddion glared at Jirah, Nearra, and Koi in turn. "I grew up in Silvanesti, right on the border of the lands marked by the high tower there, the tower that housed the dragon Cyan Bloodbane. I was there the day that great green wyrm took over the tower and seized Silvanesti for his own. You think the tower here is cursed?" Loreddion snorted. "Bloodbane spread the darkness of nightmares for a hundred miles and more—a personalized torture for anyone who came too close. And besides that, goblins and draconians were everywhere."

"That sounds horrible." Nearra couldn't help but feel a little sorry for the bitter young elf.

He turned a baleful glare on her. "Most of the Silvanesti left. Driven out. It was 'too much' for them. Simpering weaklings, White Robes and flower pickers, they all ran away when it got too tough." Scorn dripped from every word Loreddion spoke. "But not me, and not my mother. We stayed. We did what we had to to survive. When the War of the Lance was over and my mother died, I came to Palanthas to learn magic."

Nearra asked cautiously, "Is that why you chose the black robes?"

Loreddion reddened and spun away from her. "I'm done here.

This research is stupid. This mission is stupid. I don't know why I'm even going on it with you idiots!" He thumped his fist against the wall. With a roar, he yelled, "This is so dumb!"

"And what would you suggest we do instead, Loreddion?" Chyrcan asked.

"Summon spirits of darkness, evil beings loyal to Takhisis. We could arrange a summoning circle in the rear courtyard and offer them as sacrifice in exchange for knowledge. No one can hide from the dead. They carry their secrets with them, and whatever cursed Palanthas and Kenderhome must have made bargains with the powers of evil, sacrificed a few animals, gotten the attention of dark gods. They can tell us a lot more than some dumb scrolls." He growled, his voice dropping an octave in a menacing rumble. "We're wasting our time here."

A morbidly curious little squeak came from the kender. "Spirits of darkness?" While Nearra and Jirah blanched, Koi perked up and climbed on her chair again. "That sounds like something I'd want to see. Are there spirits of fear too? Maybe I could make a deal with them. I'd like them to loan me fear for a while. Do you think they would?" For the first time since Nearra met her, Koi looked almost cheerful.

"What does a kender want with fear?" Loreddion looked interested. "All the kender I know are all high and mighty about not knowing fear. I thought the kender battle cry was 'Oh, how interesting.' Are you sure you're a kender?"

Koi bristled. "Watch it, Mr. Dark-and-Spooky. I can still stick you with a dagger."

"Yeah? And I can turn you into a toad," he snapped back. The two glared at each other for a moment, then broke into perfectly matched smiles.

"You have to sleep sometime," Koi said. The smile faded and the kender switched back to being grumpy. Nearra saw the smile still playing around the corners of the kender's eyes.

"I found something!" Nagato stood up from behind the tall stacks of books, waving a sheaf of parchment. He pushed aside the books on the table, toppling some of them haphazardly to the floor. "This is a text about the Cataclysm. That's why I didn't look at it to begin with."

"What does it say?" Nearra asked. Stepping around the table, she huddled over the green leather-bound book with Nagato.

Nagato translated, and a hush fell over the room. " 'When magic began to seep away from Krynn and the gods left the world, the people of all the cities panicked. The wizards of the great orders gathered together. Some felt that wizard magic was cursed by the Kingpriest's demands, exactly as the clerics had been. Others believed that wizards were the sole holders of magic until the gods returned. Still more felt that the magic of the wizards would fade and die in quiet succession over the next few years, and the moons would slowly vanish from the heavens.

" 'A small group of wizards decided to take steps to protect the knowledge of sorcery. They gathered together books, scrolls, and magic items, and hoarded them against the day that wizard magic left the world. Thus, they thought, when the gods returned and wizards retrieved their magic again, nothing would be lost.' " The elf paused. "That sounds rather clever, but I can't see how it . . . ah. Here we are.

" 'This group gained power among the wizard orders and used its talents to store the magic of these items for future generations. Among these storage containers were the Great Pillars of Magic, ancient receptacles of sorcerous power. The group seized control of these receptacles and stored with them many other items of magic.' "

"They were magpies?" Koi asked, stacking the books that had fallen to the floor.

"Sort of," Nagato agreed. "Here's more . . . 'When other wizards refused to help them, these wizards of the Crescent Cabal . . .' Crescent Cabal? I've never heard of them before. How odd." He tilted his head and chewed on the pad of his thumb for a moment.

Prodding him gently, Nearra asked, "That's what they were called?"

"Yes. It goes on to say that there was a war within the wizard orders, and that the Crescent Cabal tried to take over the five Towers of High Sorcery, stealing all the items and magic and texts for themselves—in order to 'protect it,' of course. They continued stealing and creating magic items, hoarding knowledge in case wizards lost their magic. They insisted that magic was going to leave the world. Then the rest of the wizards joined together, afraid that the Crescent Cabal was gaining too much power. The cabal was destroyed. Its leaders were kicked out of the orders. Their names were stricken from the records." Nagato turned the paper over, scanning faint spidery text on the other side.

Jirah sighed, head in her hands. "Like Anselm," she said quietly.

"What happened to them?" asked Koi.

"Well, there's a note here." Nagato ran his fingers over it, trying to pick out the words. "The first part was written just after the Cataclysm, when the Crescent Cabal was 'destroyed' by the other wizards. But according to this, they weren't destroyed at all. Not surprising, I suppose. By then the Crescent Cabal would have had quite a storehouse of magic items. The wizards wouldn't have wanted to destroy those."

"Too much power to be lost if they did?" Jirah asked.

"Well, that too, but the main thing is that it's very dangerous to destroy a magic item if proper precautions aren't taken. Breaking a wand or melting down a magic sword can lead to disastrous results. The magic inside breaks free and does whatever it was designed to do—but completely out of control. Spells go crazy as the magical energy is expended until it burns itself out, and that can be explosive."

"Huh." Jirah considered this.

"How old is that note?" Nearra peered over Nagato's arm. "It looks less faded than the writing on the other side."

"At a guess, I'd say it was added in more than a hundred years later. Look here. It says that the cabal continued its activities. There are notations of items stolen that are attributed to them years after the orders said the cabal was gone. And these artifacts—the Great Pillars of Magic—were never located by the rest of the wizards. They searched and searched but never could find them." Nagato thumbed through a different book, looking for a separate passage. "When the orders were hunting down the cabal and destroying them, this book mentions a time in Palanthas when fire spells were acting very strangely. The fire didn't go out as they have now, so I didn't notice the similarity, but with this other codicil . . . Yes, perhaps the cabal was using this Pillar of Flame to affect fire spells, to try and fight back against the orders in Palanthas. That could be what is happening now as well."

Nearra frowned. "But the Crescent Cabal—if they exist now—must have tons and tons of magic items. They've been stealing things from other wizards for centuries."

"I doubt they're the same organization they once were. They were founded on surviving the Cataclysm and the loss of wizard magic, which never happened. Yet they kept stealing things, hoarding texts and spells. There are items listed as stolen hundreds of years afterward, and nobody knows how—items from inside the Towers, from inside the Hall of Three Moons." Nagato shuffled frantically about, piling certain texts together. "Here. Here. This one. And this one. Little things, not big things. Enough that wouldn't be noticed, but look at this. All the items that went missing were related to elemental magic. Fire. Water. Wind. Anything."

"They're still taking things?" Jirah breathed.

"Those items could have been taken by anyone. There's no proof this 'cabal' is still active," Loreddion sneered. "Or that this 'Pillar of Flame' even exists."

Nagato looked up from his books. "But it does."

Silence fell across the room for a moment, broken only by a shutter banging against the window. Even the crowds outside were quiet, letting the wind speak bitterly in their place. When Nagato spoke again, it was with more surety than before. "It exists. There's too much information for me to believe that it doesn't."

"So what now?" Jirah asked. "If we believe that the Crescent Cabal is behind this, or at least, that someone has control of the Pillar of Flame, then we have to do something about it."

Loreddion grumbled, "We have to find the Pillar. And nothing in all this mess has given us any idea how to do that."

"I think you've done enough research, Nagato," Chyrcan said quietly from his seat on the bench. He slipped his reading glasses back into his sleeve, closing the book in his lap. "I believe the conclave will want to know what you've found."

Loreddion stepped forward jerkily, as if his limbs refused to move even when he commanded them. His eyes sharpened. "Wait, you want to tell everyone?" He pushed past Chyrcan and slammed his fists onto the table. "First of all, if this isn't true, you're just going to embarrass us all in front of all the other wizards in Palanthas. They'll laugh us out of the city."

"And what if it is true?" Nearra stood up and stared Loreddion in the eye.

He swung his head to face her, silver hair straggling down over his face. "Then it's likely that the Crescent Cabal still has members among the wizards here." His voice held a dark threat as his hands gripped the table. Nearra felt a cold ball forming in her stomach and took a quick step back. "If it is true," he continued darkly, "then all we're doing is warning them that we're on their trail. Do you think that's such a good idea?"

"I'm going to tell them." Nagato scrabbled together several of the scrolls and papers he had been studying into a stack, as if afraid that any more discussion would make him change his mind. "The wizards of Palanthas expect to find something, and I'm going to show them we're worth their trust. With this scrap of parchment and this book"—he bundled the two together tightly—"I think we have enough proof." Nagato patted the greenish leather cover of the old text, fingers gently stroking the burnished patterns on the spine.

"One book? You're crazy." Loreddion started forward, but Koi pushed to the side of the table and stood between the elves. Loreddion stopped, snarling down at the kender, who didn't move. "It's your funeral," he said grudgingly, folding his arms.

Nagato lifted the pile of books. "I'm going." He scurried toward the door of the library, balancing the weight of the material against his thin chest. "Are you coming, Nearra?"

"Of course I am." Nearra reached across the wooden bench for her dragon-claw staff. "You don't have to come if you don't want to, Loreddion, but I think Nagato's doing the right thing. Maybe, with the information we've found, one of the wizards can give us a direction to go to find the Pillar. We'll never know if we don't ask." Nearra gestured for Jirah to go out ahead of her, and paused to give Chyrcan her hand. The old wizard stood wearily and thanked her.

"Are you coming?" Koi challenged the dark elf. Loreddion looked for a moment as if he were going to swat the kender. "Are you scared?" she taunted him, cocking her head like a wren.

"No," he replied mulishly.

"Me neither." The kender stared up at the elf with a challenging look. "So let's go together." Before he could complain, she grabbed Loreddion's sleeve and dragged the dark elf from the room. His protests faded down the hallway along with her stomping steps.

Chyrcan squeezed Nearra's hand as he said, "Don't worry, my dear. I'm sure everything will work out all right in the end."

CHAPTER

8   IN THE DARKNESS

"That was horrible." Nagato sank into the chair, head falling into his hands. "I want to die."

Koi swatted him with a towel. "You did fine!" She paused, then corrected herself. "Well, at least nobody attacked you with knives or spells or corkscrews or anything."

"They laughed at me. They actually laughed." Nagato spread his hands over the arms of the overstuffed chair. "I almost gave Yomon a heart attack. He turned red. Did you see him? I thought his eyes were going to fall out." Nagato let his head fall back against the red armchair. "I thought Justarius was going to kill me."

Nearra pulled her feet up on the couch across from him as Jirah rocked back and forth, sitting on the empty hearth. The house was small but cheery, with handwoven tapestries covering slightly shabby walls. Koi, Nearra, and Nagato sat in the den, cold mugs of chocolate on a table shaped like a cart wheel. In the dim light of the room, Nearra could see the outlines of Nagato's sparse furniture. The last rays of the setting sun gave her light enough to tell who was whom, but not a lot more.

There were a few books on the shelves, showing more care

taken in their placement than Nearra could see in any other part of the room. Everything else in the room was haphazardly placed, having been flung about with abandon.

Jirah put a piece of wood into the empty fireplace. "I like your house," she said to change the subject.

"It was my master's. When he died, he left it to me." Nagato looked around at the overstuffed furniture. "It's all I have. I hope they'll let me stay here when they laugh me out of the city."

"Oh, stop thinking like that," Nearra chided him. "You did fine. It isn't your fault they didn't listen to you."

"There's no proof—only old texts." Nagato got up from his chair sadly, leaving his cup on the table. "I'm going upstairs to bed. You three are welcome to stay here tonight. There are extra blankets, and the couch is comfortable. So is this chair." He patted the back of the old armchair as he headed for a ramshackle set of stairs in the back hallway. "I just want to go to sleep and pretend I'm going to wake up in a world without me in it." Halfway across the room, he tripped over Koi's outstretched legs and windmilled his arms in the gloom.

The kender didn't even bother to giggle. "See you in the morning, Nagato."

Jerking his robe straight with an ill-tempered tug of his hands, Nagato harrumphed softly. "Good night, Koi. Sleep well."

Nearra sighed as she watched Nagato shuffle up the stairs. "Poor guy," she said softly after he was gone. "It really wasn't that bad."

"Did you see Loreddion?" Koi shook her head. "I thought he was going to sink through the floor. He looked like he wanted to be anywhere except in front of all those wizards when Nagato was talking." She sighed emptily. " 'Is that all you brought us, Naaaaa-gato?' " she said in a rough approximation of Viridia, tossing her hair back and forth over her shoulders in an imitation of the White Robe wizard's curly bob. " 'A few books and some scrawled passages about some ancient artifact?' "

Koi hunched forward, pulling one of the blankets from the couch over her head like a hood. "And then there's Yomon. He's even worse." Her voice dropped to the croak of a toad, echoing the old mage's withering tone. " 'A waste of tiiiiii-me, Justarius!' " She growled, " 'These children are uuuuu-seless! Better we turn this mission over to a bunch of . . . of . . . of hamsters!' "

Nearra sighed. Koi's imitations were too close to the truth. The wizards had been cutting, angry that they hadn't turned up anything concrete. They'd turned their frustration and anger on poor Nagato most of all. "Well, there's nothing to be done. We can get a fresh start tomorrow."

Koi and Jirah agreed, and after finishing their cups of cold chocolate, the three girls lay down to sleep, Nearra on Nagato's plump chair, Jirah on the couch, and Koi curled up by the cold fireplace. A hush fell over the household, broken only by the soft sounds of the kender's snoring. Outside, in Palanthas, the city lay in complete darkness.

Nearra awoke sometime in the night to the feeling of a small hand clamped over her mouth. She started up but was pulled back with a jerk and a quiet hiss. "Sssssh! Listen." It was Koi's voice. The kender's green eyes shone like a cat's in the glow of the silver moon. Solinari was bright in the high window, illuminating Nagato's kitchen and casting shadows through the front room. "There it is again. I think Death is scratching at our window."

This time Nearra heard it too—a scratch at the front door of the little cottage, and then a squeak of hinges. Koi lifted her hand from Nearra's lips and grabbed the small metal baton that usually hung at her waist. Nearra gently awakened Jirah.

The hinges squeaked again, and Nearra could see two shadowy figures in the front hall. She didn't think they could see her or the others behind the couch, but she didn't want to take chances. She leaned out, keeping her body low, and reached for her crystal-tipped staff.

The intruders must have seen the movement because there was a sudden curse in the doorway. Nearra heard steps coming toward them and could make out twin silhouettes breaking into a run at her. She rolled off the couch, holding her staff up like a shield, and felt the wood shiver with impact. She looked at the staff and saw three small darts sticking out of the vallenwood. "Ew!" she cried, jerking them out as she ducked back behind the couch.

"Thieves!" Koi leaped forward, jumping from the hearth onto the table, then high into the air, clearing Nearra and the couch in a single bound. She landed with a thud on both feet, the metal cylinder outstretched in her calloused hand. "Get out, or I'll kick your—Hey! Where are you going?"

Ignoring Koi, the thieves rushed by, one darting up the stairway and the other dodging around to the side of the couch to face Nearra and Jirah. It was human- or elf-sized, lithe, and definitely male. Whoever he was, he was dressed in tight black leathers, a black bandanna tied closely around his face. His belt was laced with thin silver threads, perhaps reinforced with metal or silver of some kind—Nearra couldn't quite tell. But she could tell—instantly and immediately—that he was interested in her.

"*Labala perak!*" he said unexpectedly, extending his fingers. Thick silver webbing spun out of his hand and soared toward the sisters. Jirah squealed and tried to leap away and Nearra scrabbled to the other side, but both of them were caught in the webbing. Nearra could swear the thief was smiling beneath his mask.

"I said stop!" Koi stood on the couch overhead, spinning the metal baton between her fingers. "And I . . . mean . . . STOP!" She leaped again, landing between the webbing and the thief. Her baton flashed out, connecting with the thief's knees in brutal blows.

The thief yelped and staggered backward. He hit the shelving on the walls, toppling all the books to the floor and shattering a few knickknacks that had been used as bookends. Growling, he pounced at the kender, unleashing another barrage of darts that flew toward Koi. She spun to the left and right, allowing the darts to go past her.

From her vantage point, coiled in hundreds of sticky strands, Nearra could only stare. The kender was faster than anyone she'd ever seen—faster than her elf friends Icefire and Elidor. Koi moved like a small, feral animal, jumping up onto the table again and corkscrewing through the air as she propelled herself toward the intruder.

Koi's baton thumped the man in his stomach with terrible force, bowing the thief forward with a rush of exhaled breath. "All right, Death! Take that!" she snarled, then punched him in the back of the head with a fisted hand. He fell to the ground, knocked flat by the kender's fury. There was a loud crash above them, and Koi spun to stare at the ramshackle stairs. "Are you guys all right?" she yelled to Jirah and Nearra.

"I think I've almost got my hand free," Jirah said, struggling against the confining webbing.

"We're fine! See to Nagato!" Nearra wriggled her fingers and whispered softly, "*Api.*" Nothing happened. "Argh," Nearra made a face. "That's a fire spell. You're supposed to get out of a web spell with a fire spell, but we don't really have that option. " She frowned and tried again. "*Cilin bisau!*" A small blade of light slid out of her finger, like a sharp extension of Nearra's fingernail. She sawed at the strands, and they slowly fell away.

Seeing that Nearra would be free soon, Koi ran toward the stairs and took them two by two. Nearra heard more struggling, followed by a loud crash. "Koi!" she yelled.

"You can't have him, Death!" The kender roared, continuing her half-joking obsession with death. She hurtled out of sight with her weapon in her hand. There was a yell, and another thump, and a form in red robes came flying down the stairs as though hurled by a powerful force. He crashed into the wall at the bottom of the stairs, shattering the weak banister and bouncing along for a moment on the remains of texts and fallen pillows. Nagato looked up, dazed, at Nearra's feet, and she saw blood streaming from a cut on his forehead.

A moment later, the kender and another figure came tumbling down the stairs to land ignobly atop Nagato. Koi clawed at the thief's face, trying to rip away his mask, but the black-garbed figure picked her up and threw her over the couch.

Koi realized that she was outnumbered. She spun on the balls of her feet and backed away, holding out the baton with an angry grin. "Come on, bruisers. You've got no idea what you're up against. When I thought you might be Death himself, I was interested. Now I'm starting to get bored."

The thieves approached her from both sides, readying themselves to strike. Nearra tugged desperately at the silvery strands, trying to get her arms free so that she could cast a spell, do something to help. One of the thieves reached behind his back, drawing a lump of brownish sod from a small pouch on his belt, murmuring to himself.

"Koi! He's casting a spell!" Nearra warned.

The kender looked outraged, stomping her feet. "Hold on to something!" she yelled to Nearra, then she leaped straight into the air, holding the strange silvery baton. It caught the light of the moon outside the window, and a pale glow rose from its smooth surface. "*Pesquedescadora!*" Koi howled, and the cylinder flashed purplish blue. Koi landed hard on her feet, continuing the motion and bringing the baton down as hard as she could to the floor. As the end of the metal rod slammed into the floorboards, there was a sudden, strange rush of air.

It was as if all the air in the room were sucked into the rod in a single sharp intake. The pillows of the couch leaned toward Koi, papers hung in the air, and books flipped their pages in a moment of savage expectation—and then the air rippled. The earth buckled beneath Koi's strike, rippling outward in a wide motion as another purple flash exploded from the baton. The earth heaved and rolled, the cylinder forming the epicenter of its own little earthquake.

The couch was flung outward, and the chair leaped into the air. "What's going on?" Jirah screeched as she was pitched high into the air. The strands of the web snapped and she crashed into the ceiling with a sharp cry, arms spinning. The ground buckled and heaved again, rising up to meet her in another swelling wave.

Nearra, too, was flung by the earthquake. She crashed into the couch, waves reverberating all around her as the whole house shifted. She could see through the front door into the moonlit street, where the ground continued to ripple for several paces. Beyond that, everything seemed stable. As the shaking ground threatened to reunite Nearra with her dinner, that still area beyond the earthquake looked like heaven. The overstuffed chair flew over Nearra's head, forcing her to duck as the earth rippled again. She struggled to find her footing, but it was like trying to ride a bucking horse.

The two thieves fared slightly better, scrabbling across the ground with each wave. One of them grabbed a book that was flying through the air as it bounced down the stairs.

"My book!" Nagato yelled. Indeed, Nearra recognized the green leather, the strange embossing on the spine. It was the book they had been studying in the library. Though they'd already read it,

Nagato thought it might hold more information they could use. They needed that book! Nearra leaped through the air toward the men, shoving off from a hump of earth that shuddered beneath her feet.

Nearra swung her crystal-tipped staff widely. It connected against one thief's face with a shudder that reverberated down the length of the wood. Stumbling, she fell to the ground beside him, the earthquake stealing her balance. "Koi! Whatever you've done, turn it off!"

"I can't!" The kender grabbed what was left of the shelves and tried to pull herself up off the buckling floor. "It doesn't turn off. It just goes for a while and then stops. There's nothing we can do except hold on!"

"Get the book!" Nearra found herself lying beside the other thief as a particularly violent shudder sent them dodging the over-stuffed armchair again. The thief launched a punch that caught Nearra in the jaw, and suddenly, more than the floor was reeling. She felt her staff jerked from her hands, and a sharp blow to the chest sent her spinning toward the fireplace.

Instead of impacting with hard stone, she hit something soft. In a tumble of legs and arms, both she and Jirah fell to the ground before the hearth. Her sister looked furious.

"We have to stop them!" Nearra yelled. All around her, she could see the little house buckling, the walls twisting like paper as the roof swung back and forth. The two thieves crawled along the shaking ground, pulling against the doorway to help themselves. "They're getting away!"

Koi swung like a cat through the air toward the thieves. She landed in the doorway and faced them, swinging the metal baton like a sword. The two men rushed her, one knocking her aside, taking advantage of the staff's much longer length. She stared after them as one ran north and one ran south on the street in front of the house. "Which one do I chase?" She stared back and forth between their attackers.

Nearra had only a moment to decide. Seeing her staff carried off in the hands of a black-masked thief broke her heart, but she cried out, "Get the book! It may be our only hope to save Palanthas!" With that, Koi was away.

The earth around them shook again, but rippling with less vigor. Its tantrum slowly subsided, then fell still at last. A long moment passed, but the earthquake was gone. Nearra heard something made of glass fall in the kitchen, and a few papers slowly fluttered through the air. Jirah groaned beside her. Over the toppled couch, Nearra saw one red-sleeved arm flutter wearily.

"I think I'm going to be ill," Nagato moaned, sitting up under a pile of pillows. He pulled away a knitted comforter and looked at the demolished interior of his home. "Now I know I'm going to be ill."

"I have no idea where Koi got that stick." Jirah stood up, her steps shaking like a newborn lamb's. "But I can tell you this right now—she's not allowed to bring it inside anymore." She righted the overstuffed armchair, brushed aside the broken legs of the cart-wheel table, and sat down.

"I got it from a dragon. I already I told you that story." Koi's small shape in the doorway was outlined by the silver moonlight. She held up a square of blackness and said, "I got the book. But the other guy—he was just too fast, Nearra. I'm sorry." Her shoulders sagged dejectedly. "The least I could have done was die trying, but here I am again. Perfectly fine, thanks for asking."

"At least we got the book back," Jirah sighed.

"Funny thing about that," Koi's head cocked, and Nearra could see moonlight glinting from her bright eyes. "They really wanted it, but they didn't seem to care that it's a book, and a fragile one at that. I mean, the guy I was following all but ripped it apart.

74

Look." Koi held the book into the sliver of white light and showed them a tear in the leather of the spine. "He was ripping it up like crazy." As she tilted the book, something small and bright glinted beneath the spine.

"He was probably trying to destroy it. If that book contains information that we need, then destroying it is the most direct way to ensure we don't have it." Nagato lifted the book from Koi's hands. "I won't be able to get a good look at the damage until morning, but in this light, it appears that only a few sections are missing. We might get lucky. The thief couldn't have known what sections to rip out specifically, nor find them in the dark on the run. He might have missed something." Nagato pulled gently at the book's leather wrapping. "Nearra, Jirah. Look at this."

Behind the leather binding of the book, there was another cover—one made of thin steel.

"That must be worth a lot," Koi whispered.

Nagato continued pulling, gently sliding the leather away from the original cover of the book.

Jirah leaned back against the doorway, crossing her arms with a huff. "I know who sent those thugs. It had to be Loreddion and Yomon. No wonder Loreddion was so mad we were going to tell the wizards everything tonight. He tried to stop us before we went. He yelled at us when we said we were going anyway. I don't trust him."

Nagato looked unconvinced.

"I don't trust Loreddion either, Jirah," Nearra said. "But there's no proof that either he or Yomon was behind this attack. We are obliged by the Conclave's orders to keep working with Loreddion unless we can prove that he did this. Do you think your suspicions are enough proof?"

Grumpily, Jirah shook her head. "No."

"Then all we can be sure about is that we were attacked, and

PILLAR OF FLAME

that whoever arranged for these thugs is connected with the Crescent Cabal." Nearra paced through the rubble and pondered the problem.

Nagato's head snapped up. "Do you really think they were with the cabal?"

Nearra shrugged. "We know the cabal still exists. Loreddion was right—they probably have members even today among the wizards of Palanthas. Whoever attacked us is connected with them, and they don't want us to find the Pillar of Flame."

"Look at this." Nagato slid away the last of the false leather binding, revealing the full steel of the book's actual cover. There was a pattern etched into the metal. Nagato's finger slid along the edges of it—a tangle of three interlocking crescents, all on fire. "This must be the mark of the Crescent Cabal."

Jirah's eyes widened as she took it in. "By Paladine," she said, the words tumbling out. "I know that symbol."

CHAPTER

9 HOME

Morning light trickled through the window, slowly driving out the darkness. Nearra puttered about the room, trying to put everything back in place. The remnants of Koi's earthquake still littered the floor—books and trinkets under toppled furniture, pillows and rugs scattered from wall to wall. A pile of broken crockery, shattered ceramic plates, and a few cracked glass bookends were piled in a big towel to be taken to the trash. Nearra gently added a broken flowerpot to the pile, plant and all.

Jirah watched her sister and tried not to look up at Nagato or the steel book that lay on the table. The silence in the little house was terrible, and Koi hadn't stopped staring at Jirah for an hour.

"Can you stop cleaning?" Jirah croaked, forcing out the words. "It's driving me crazy."

Nearra froze, her hands clenched around a pillow. "Are you sure? About where you saw the sigil?"

"Yeah." Jirah slumped down in the overstuffed chair and played with a new rip in the arm. "It's on our barn. He found a strange carving somewhere in the woods—I didn't ask him where. It was just another weird research project, and he made a rubbing of it.

It was really pretty, with crescents, images of the moons, and some old hieroglyphs. We painted it on the barn that summer when you were at Cairngorn Keep. Before you . . ." Jirah gulped. "Before you went away."

"Does your father have a lot of these 'weird projects'?" Koi asked.

"You have no idea." Jirah spread her hands, sketching in the air. "There was the three-headed puppy he found and brought home. It ate all the cows in a four-mile radius before they finally chased it out of town. Then there was the enchanted parasol, the one that brought rain. And the curse-breaking potion recipe from the alchemist with the glass hand. Remember that, Nearra?"

Her sister chuckled uncomfortably. "Not everything Da does is weird. He's also researched spells for wizards, helped catalog archaeological finds for those Red Robes in Solanthus, and he wrote copies of historical texts to make steel during the summer when wood doesn't sell well." Nearra slid her hands through her hair. "Our father's always been obsessed with magic, and with breaking the spell on our family. He's spent his life surrounded by magic but unable to use it. It's been difficult."

Then, in the silence, Koi started to laugh, low and tragic.

"Stop it. It's not funny." Nagato gulped. "We have to do more research. We need to find out more about the cabal—who they are now, where they meet, what they're doing with all the things they steal."

"Like my staff," Nearra reminded them, but Koi only shook harder in convulsions of laughter. The kender clapped both of her hands over her mouth in an attempt to control herself, and Nagato glared.

"I can't help it," Koi laughed. "Nagato still looks like he swallowed an orange. I'm sorry, I'm sorry." She gasped for breath, making her low laughter sound all the more horrible. "I always

REE SOESBEE

laugh after a good fight. Almost anything sets it off—hoo!—I can't help it!" She rolled off the couch onto the floor, kicking her feet against the table as her dark, wicked laughter continued.

Nearra sat down on the couch beside Nagato. "We can't stay in Palanthas. They know we're here. The agents of the Crescent Cabal attacked us in your house, Nagato."

An image of Loreddion huddled in some dark alley with the two attackers from last night flashed through Jirah's mind. She could see steel exchanging hands, coins clattering softly into a palm. Koi's chuckling slowed to small, fitful bursts, then fell quiet. With a long, loud sigh, the kender reached up to scratch her nose. Looking down at her, Jirah burst out, "I think we should ditch Loreddion."

"Jirah!" Nearra chided, reaching to pile some scattered papers on a table. "The wizards told us to work together, all three orders. We can't leave Loreddion. It wouldn't be right."

"Well, we can't stay here either." Koi slowly lurched to her feet, bumping into the table and knocking the papers over again. "But there's only one thing we can do. We should go to your parent's house. Look at the barn. Find out where your father saw the original." Koi turned to squint at Jirah. "And we're bringing Loreddion." She checked the metal baton at her belt, and Jirah winced.

"I don't think that's such a good idea," Nearra said, paling. She reached for the pile of papers again, shuffling them together.

Jirah reached to grab her sister's elbow, stopping Nearra's frantic act. "Why not?" Nearra didn't answer, her face turning red. "Stop cleaning. I'm serious. Nearra, are you afraid to go home?"

"No!" Perhaps realizing she'd spoken with far too much vehemence, Nearra tried again. "No. I'm just not sure that's the right way to go." She tapped the papers on the table and lay them down in a pile again.

"You're kidding! We have to go! That barn, along with this book, is our best lead." Koi tossed her head, braids flying about with excitement. She knocked the papers aside again, and they scattered to the floor. Nearra cried out and reached for them, but Jirah stopped her.

"She's right." Jirah shoved the papers across the ground. She stood up to be closer to Nearra. "You're freaking out. You have been since I brought up the barn. What's wrong, Nearra? I thought you wanted to go home. After Palanthas, we were going to go tell our parents everything. Has that changed?"

Nearra wiggled uncomfortably on the couch. "I thought we'd go home and tell Da wonderful things, Jirah. The curse is broken. I was going to be a wizard and wear my robes home. You were going to become a cleric." Nearra sighed. "What are we going to tell him now?"

Suddenly it hit home for Jirah. She could see her Da's face, telling stories about the wonderful things his daughters would do with their lives. She imagined telling him about breaking the curse, and then about losing her magic forever. How could she explain to her father everything that happened without looking like a failure?

"You're right, Nearra." Heart sinking, Jirah wedged herself onto the couch beside her sister. "We can't possibly go home."

"You're both crazy." Koi rolled her eyes. "This is our best shot. What's the worst that could happen? We die? Is that any different from sitting around here? Nagato, what do you think?"

The Red Robe didn't speak right away, clearly weighing the possibilities. "Koi is right. It's our only real option. If Jirah is correct about the sigil on the barn, then the origin of that rubbing might have more information about the Crescent Cabal."

"I'll get Loreddion!" Koi bounced up from the floor. "We'll meet you outside the southern gates of the city in three hours.

It'll take at least that long to get horses, provisions, and all sorts of traveling supplies. How far is it to your parents' house, Nearra? Well, never mind, I guess we'll find out when we get there!" Koi bounced toward the front door, the trinkets in her hair flashing in the sunlight.

"How are you going to pay for the horses?" Jirah squeaked.

Koi jerked an ivory trinket—a carving of an elephant—from her hair. "I'll sell this. It doesn't mean much to me. I'm not even sure where it came from. And if that isn't enough, well, I'm certain the shopkeepers won't mind loaning us a few things to make sure the trip goes well. After all, we're doing this for Palanthas. If they won't help us, I'll just remind them of the dark, cold death they face when winter comes. It'll be a snap," she finished, straight faced.

Nagato tried to smile, scooping the book up in his arms and clutching it tightly to his chest. "I'll put this somewhere safe, then go to the library and pack up a few of the scrolls with the most relevant information." Still talking softly to himself, the shy elf slipped up the stairs.

"For Palanthas," Nearra repeated, with a distinct lack of excitement.

"For Palanthas," Jirah agreed listlessly.

Both sisters slumped back against the couch with a sigh.

A small cottage was nestled in a forest dell, tall trees arching over the edges of the clearing. Smoke curled gently from a gray stone chimney. The area in front of the cottage was filled with rambling rose bushes, while the rear of the cottage had been built into the hillside. Green grass and flowering plants cascaded down from the roof along the hill. A mossy path led through the forest to the cottage door, and sunlight dappled the horses' flanks as they picked their way down the lane.

Loreddion and Koi shared a horse, the kender's feet flapping lightly on either side of the saddle. Loreddion rode silently with his hood up, so Jirah couldn't see the dark elf's face. The kender, on the other hand, had hardly stopped talking the entire trip. She wanted to see Ravenscar, she wanted to explore a cave, or ride off the road and look at an unusual animal track.

Jirah shared a horse with her sister. She laid her head on Nearra's shoulder with a sigh. Until they'd actually gotten in sight of the house, she had hoped something might get in the way, somehow intervene. Maybe Paladine would send them a sign, something to send them back to Palanthas. Or even Ravenscar. Anywhere but here.

"Can I help you?" a bright voice called from inside the house. Jirah sat up to look over Nearra's shoulder. A woman stood silhouetted in the doorway, holding a towel in her hands. Her blonde hair, pulled back in a ponytail, was shot with silver. Although her face was softly wrinkled, her blue eyes were bright and pleasant—eyes identical to Nearra's and Jirah's.

The towel slowly slid from the woman's hands, fluttering gently to the ground. The woman's eyes grew wide, and her hands flew to her mouth. "Nearra . . ." she whispered. "Jirah." Tears slid down her cheeks as her face broke into a wide smile. "You're home!"

Nearra leaped down from the horse's back and raced toward her mother. Jirah was slower, sliding off the horse reluctantly. But her mother's arms wrapped around them both. Tears rained down from the woman's cheeks as she held her daughters close.

"My mother cries too when I come home from a trip," Koi said and nodded understandingly. "But I don't think it's for the same reasons."

"Mama." Nearra stepped back. "This is Nagato, Koi, and Loreddion. Everyone, this is Lanni, our mother."

"Come inside, come inside. I have some warm chicken on the

spit and a nice tub of buttermilk for you and your friends." Lanni reached to shake their hands as the others slid to the ground. She did not hesitate to welcome Loreddion, nor did she put her fine china on a high shelf when she escorted Koi inside. Jirah tied the three horses to a hitch and followed the rest inside.

"We've been so worried, your father and I. After we lost contact with Nearra in Cairngorn Keep, Eric went to find you. And while he was gone"—Lanni glanced under lowered lashes at her younger daughter—"Jirah vanished."

"I'm sorry, Mama." Jirah felt hot tears welling up in her eyes. "And I'm sorry I stole the Trinistyr. But Mama, I have to tell you something very important—"

"As long as you girls aren't hurt." Lanni hugged them again. "And you brought the Trinistyr back, yes? That will ease your father's mind. He's been frantic for months, worrying about the two of you, and about that awful dragon statue."

"Mama, listen," Nearra tried to edge in.

"I know how important breaking the family curse is to you girls, and to your father, but I wish you would all stop risking your lives! Magic isn't everything in the world. I'm sorry," Lanni said offhandedly to the two wizards seated at the kitchen table, "but it's not." She put her hands on her hips and chided the girls. "You three need to stop acting like Anselm still controls this family's destiny. There's more to life than spells and artifacts—"

"Mama!" Jirah stood, raising her voice over her mother's protests. "I broke the curse."

Every sound in the kitchen suddenly stopped. Birds weren't singing outside, and no one moved at the table. In the silence, Jirah heard the kitchen door creak slowly shut. A tall figure stood in the doorway. "Da?"

The man in the doorway had long, handsome features, his black hair streaked with gray. His eyes were a rich, dark brown like the soil of the forest, and his hands were calloused from years of out-door labor. His skin was tanned, his face lined from the sun, and he wore a simple leather vest over a linen shirt and trousers. "Jirah? You broke the curse?" His voice broke, and he opened his arms.

The two girls leaped from the table and ran to him, flinging their arms around their father. Koi slipped Nagato's chicken from his plate as the family embraced, wiping happy tears from her eyes. Lanni smiled, folding her hands against her chest in joy.

"Eric, what are you doing here? You were supposed to tend to the woodchopping down by the river!" Lanni laughed to see him. "It should have taken you an hour to get back—and you had no reason to come!"

"I was close to the house when I saw the horses pass by. I decided to work up closer to the road today," Eric explained, look-ing uncomfortable for a moment. "I just had a feeling we might have visitors." He knitted his brows with concern.

"Is everything all right, Eric?" Lanni asked.

He nodded, features clearing as he stared down at his daughters with pride. "I knew you'd break the curse, Jirah." Eric squeezed both of his daughters tightly, kissing Jirah's dark head. "I always knew you would."

"I'm so sorry for running away, Da. I know you told me to stay home and wait for you to come back with Mama." Jirah wiped away her tears against his vest. "I didn't want to worry you. It was just . . . with Nearra gone and no trace of her at Cairngorn Keep, someone had to do it. I stole the Trinistyr and I went to find Nearra. And I did find her. She'd been kidnapped—"

"I know, I know," Eric said soothingly, pressing his cheek to Nearra's golden hair. "I searched all over and never did find your mother. I came home, and she was back, but you were gone and so was Nearra. I went to Cairngorn Keep and demanded answers, but Maddoc and Davyn weren't there either. After questioning several of the other servants, I found out that Maddoc had taken Nearra away."

"But Mama, where had you gone? We were so worried," Jirah said, though if she looked back too deeply, she knew she hadn't been as worried back then as she should have been.

"I was really sick then," Lanni answered. "I really don't know, to tell the truth. But as your father said, when he came back, I was home, too, and recovered. Your father dragged me all over this area, from Palanthas to Solanthus, looking for any trace of you girls." Lanni chuckled, obviously relieved. "I think we talked to every wizard in Solamnia, but none had seen you—or even heard of you." She set another place at the table, cutting a plump chicken leg for her husband. "We thought you were lost forever. I for one am so glad to have you back . . . even with golden hands. What happened, Nearra?"

Nearra pulled her father to the table to sit with her friends. Lanni came up to embrace her husband's neck from behind. Nearra told her father the tale of Asvoria—the sorceress's possession of her body and her defeat at the hands of Nearra's friends.

"And then, Nearra and I took the Trinistyr to find Anselm's grave, and the graves of the wizards he had cursed," Jirah continued. "Nearra's hands turned golden during the last fight." She slowed down and took a breath. This was the hard part. "And at the end, I released the magic in the Trinistyr, and the curse was broken." She bit her lip. "But . . . there was . . . a price."

Eric seemed not to hear the last part. "Broken! At last! And you've brought wizards with you, obviously to invite our family back into the fold. Excellent." He puffed up and turned to Nagato and Loreddion. "My family has never forgotten its past, gentlemen. You'll see. I have numerous spells and books of lore, things I've studied. Now that our magic is returned to us, I'll make these two girls into wizards that you can be proud of. I guarantee it!"

He clapped the girls on their backs, shaking them in their chairs with his enthusiasm.

"Your daughter already is a wizard, sir. Self-trained. And I assure you, she's quite powerful on her own." Nagato smiled.

"Please! Call me Eric." He turned to Jirah, clasping both hands on her shoulders. "Already a wizard! Jirah! I knew you had the gift! I'm so very proud of you." He shook her gently.

Jirah paled, but Eric had already turned his attention back to the two wizards at the table. "Da, no, I'm not . . ." She looked over at Nearra, but her sister was also staring aghast at their father.

"My Jirah grew up on stories of wizards! We always assumed Nearra would help her become one, maybe be her apprentice." Eric beamed. "Now it's all come true."

There was an uncomfortable silence at the table. Lanni set down the towel on the table, clearing her throat. "Well, those horses won't stable themselves. I'll take them out to the barn while you—"

Nagato and Loreddion stood up at the table so fast they nearly knocked their chairs over. "I'll go with you," they said in unison. They looked at each other with sidelong glances, Nagato flushing and Loreddion clenching his fists. Koi pushed away her chair and smiled up at Lanni. "We're very protective of our horses," she lied. "They're precious to us. Like sisters and brothers."

Nagato added, "Actually, we want to take a look at your barn."

"Our barn?" Lanni asked. "Whatever for?"

"That's a good idea, actually," Nearra said, stepping in. "We need a minute to talk to Da alone, if you don't mind."

"Well, I suppose so." Lanni and Eric looked at one another, and Lanni shrugged. "After all, I'm sure you girls have a lot to talk about with your father. This magic and all. Perhaps it's better if I entertain our guests with a look around." Lanni came over to

Eric, hugging his shoulders gently. "We can take the horses down to the barn while you talk. Come with me, gentlemen," she said cheerfully, then looked down at Koi. "And lady," she added with a smile.

Koi led the others to the doorway. "Do you have goats? We have goats back in Haymore, and I always liked them. Goat cheese, goat milk, goat bread—"

"There's no such thing," Loreddion said as he followed, pausing to allow Lanni to go before him.

As they untied the horses and led them toward the rear of the little clearing, Jirah heard Koi and Loreddion arguing. "There is so. We had goat bread all the time. We'd take the fruit of the goat tree—"

"Again, no such thing."

". . . and we'd mix it with goat milk, and make goat bread. What kind of stupid are you?" Koi sounded almost cheerfully grouchy.

"The kind that doesn't eat goat bread."

The argument continued as the group walked down the path, the sounds of the horses' clopping hooves slowly drowning out the words.

"Da, about the curse, and the magic—" Jirah started.

"I'm so proud of you, Jirah. I always knew you'd do it." Jirah nodded, choking on the lump in her throat. She knew it was wrong to lead him on like this, but he'd never looked at her that way before. She'd always been the other sister, not quite as pretty or as smart as Nearra. She'd tell him in a minute, Jirah resolved. She didn't want to interrupt him—not while he was so happy. And it was only a little mistake, anyway. The curse had been broken, and Jirah had done it; it was only his assumption that Jirah was a wizard that was wrong.

Eric faced Jirah. "And I have something for you. Something very important. I want you to wait right here." He rose from the table and walked through the house, running up the stairs with the energy of a much younger man.

Nearra whispered to Jirah, "You've got to tell him!"

"I'm trying. He's not listening!" she wailed softly.

Nearra's next comment was cut off by the sound of Eric coming down the stairs. Both girls sat back in their chairs, trying to compose themselves as their father entered the room.

He carried something in a thin leather wrapping. It was as thick as his arm and as long as he was tall. He took his seat at the table again, squaring himself to face them both. "Long ago," he began, caressing the leather of the pouch, "Anselm gave this to his son. It has been passed down through our family, a last memento of the power we once used to have." Eric took the end of the pouch in his hand and slowly pulled it down, unsheathing the item inside.

As the old, brown leather slid away, it revealed whiteness beneath—old wood, shining with care and elegance. It was a staff of great quality and age. The wooden length of it was white like new ivory and intricately carved, but so faintly that the carving was barely visible. The staff seemed to be made of one seamless, softly gnarled branch. Pale white platinum shod the base of it, so closely matching the wood that it was indistinguishable save by touch. Twisted roots capped the staff, arching in complex patterns that replicated themselves within the ball of thinly threaded wood. Like a complex puzzle, the roots formed an eggshell, woven together around emptiness.

"It's beautiful," Jirah whispered, watching the sunlight from the window twinkle softly on the elegant paleness of the wood.

"It's yours." Eric pressed it into Jirah's hands, closing his own over them. "Jirah, I'm so proud of you."

"Da . . ." Jirah's voice failed. "It's not what you think."

"You don't understand." Nearra frowned.

"For years before your birth, I studied ways to break the curse myself. I always failed, as had my father and those before him," Eric continued, paying no heed to his daughters. "Once you two were born, I had to struggle to raise a family, but I never gave up on our family dream. Even after you both were gone, I spent as much time searching for magic as I did searching for you." He looked at them with a father's love, but there was also sternness in is eyes. "I thought that if I could break the curse, I could use spells to locate you and save you both from whatever terrible things might have happened. But you did it. You did it for me." He lowered his head for a moment and smiled. "From the moment you were born, when the wizards looked at the stars and read your future, they said you were born for great things, Jirah. You're very special. I knew they meant that you would break the curse on our family. Nearra is our pretty bird, gentle and kind. You are our thinker, and it was you who came up with a way to break Anselm's curse.

"We've lost centuries, but we can educate ourselves, regain our heritage." He looked up at Jirah sternly. "And you will teach us—me and your sister. We will learn magic, and we will all return to Palanthas together as wizards."

"But . . ." Jirah fumbled. "I don't have any books, anything to teach you from. I don't even know . . . much . . ." She tripped over the word, feeling Nearra's disapproving gaze on her. "I couldn't teach you things I don't know."

"That's all right. I have friends with such texts," their father replied. He noticed the girls' confusion with a frown. "But I thought that's why you've come home."

Nearra and Jirah stared at him blankly. Nearra started, "We came home to tell you about the breaking of the curse, but also because the conclave sent us. They chose us—the whole group—to search out the origin of a magical plague that's affecting Palanthas."

Jirah continued, "The plague's put out all the fires in the city. Magical, normal, everything, and even those in Kenderhome, where Koi comes from. It may be spreading across Krynn. The conclave thinks that someone is tampering with an artifact called the Pillar of Flame."

Eric's frown deepened. "The Pillar of Flame?" He thumbed the little beard on his chin.

"Have you heard of it, Da?" asked Nearra.

He shrugged. "There are many old stories. Especially those dealing with fire. I've read a lot of them, but this one doesn't ring any bells."

"There's a symbol on the old barn. You painted it there a few years ago," Jirah reminded him. Awkwardly, she put the white staff on the table and continued. "We found the same symbol—three crescents, interlocked, all on fire—connected with the men who attacked us in Palanthas."

He nodded. "I painted it to study it. The original is on a slate altar in the woods a few miles to the east of here. You know how travelers come through from time to time. A few years ago, a group of wizards was studying ancient holy sites and mentioned this one to me. I went there and sketched the carvings on the altar, then replicated them here so I could look at them without having to go back and forth." Eric emptied his buttermilk. "You say these men tried to kill you?"

"They attacked us," Jirah replied. "I think they're trying to stop us from finding out more about the Pillar of Flame."

"Let's go have a look, then. If it's the same symbol, I can take you out to the altar tomorrow morning. After your friends have a look at it and get all the information they need, they can return to Palanthas and tell the Wizards' Conclave. I'm eager to get started on our work after they go." Eric set his empty mug on the counter and smiled thinly.

"But we'll have to go back with them," Jirah protested. "The conclave—"

Eric gazed at his daughters sternly. "Your sense of duty is a noble thing, Jirah, but this is your family. Family comes first. Haven't I always taught you that?" The daughters nodded slowly, and Eric's smile returned, though not as joyful as before. "It's settled, then. Tomorrow, we visit the altar, your friends go back to Palanthas, and this family starts down the road to the destiny which has been denied us for so many generations.

"I'm so very proud of my girls."

CHAPTER

10 CARVED IN STONE

"It was amazing. Exactly like the symbol we found on the book in Palanthas, but far more intricate," Nagato said. For once, his voice was bright and excited. "There were runes in that painting that I haven't seen in parchments for hundreds of years!"

"He sounds like a bird," Nearra sighed to her sister. "The Nagato bird! Chirps all day and night, so long as you feed it paper and obscure information." Jirah remained quiet. She had said only a few words all afternoon.

Afternoon sunlight filtered through the trees as they hiked down the path, following in the footsteps of their father and the suddenly talkative Red Robe. They had been walking since lunchtime, spurred on by Nagato's eagerness to see the original carving behind the painting on the barn. Koi and Loreddion had fallen behind some few minutes ago, so for the first time since lunch the girls could speak freely.

Trying to raise Jirah's spirits, Nearra kept talking. "Nagato said that the painting on the barn was still incomplete. Maybe there will be more information on the altar, something carved around the sides that will tell us more about the cabal and the Pillar of Flame."

"And then what? Nagato, Loreddion, and Koi go off on an adventure to find it, and we stay home and study books for the rest of our lives."

"Oh, it's just until Da learns to be a wizard, Jirah." Nearra looked down at her golden hands. "It won't be forever. He's wanted this all his life. You can't expect him not to be excited."

Jirah poked a bush ahead of them with the long white staff. She shifted it in her grip uncomfortably as they walked, the metal-capped end banging against the ground with each step on the forest trail. "I know. But that doesn't mean I want to spend years here in the forest with Mama and Da."

Nearra waited a moment, listening to Nagato and Eric chatter about ancient scripts. "Jirah, you have to tell him. When we get back to the house, he's going to want you to teach him magic."

"You could teach him," Jirah said halfheartedly.

"Jirah, he's going to find out eventually." She softened her tone. "You shouldn't be ashamed of giving up magic, Jirah. You gave up your dreams so that our family could have its heritage back. That's something you should be proud of."

"I *am* proud!" Jirah said in a tone that clearly indicated she wasn't. "It's just that magic is the only thing Da ever thought I could do better than you. If I don't have that anymore, then I don't know what I am in this family."

Exasperated, Nearra grabbed the white staff and forced her sister to halt. "You're his daughter. Even if you can't be a wizard or a cleric, there are still lots of jobs—really important jobs—that you can do."

"Do you think Da would be happy with any of those?" Jirah sighed.

"So what are you planning to do? Fake it for weeks while we teach Da magic?" Shaking her head, Nearra caught Jirah's eye. "He'll figure it out. He always knows when we're lying to him.

PILLAR OF FLAME

93

Remember the time we tried to adopt that badger and keep it in our room?"

"That was different. The badger had to eat, and there wasn't anything to feed him except Mama's potato salad."

"You have to tell him!"

"No, I don't!" Jirah exploded, stamping the staff into the ground. She glared at Nearra for a moment as if she were going to continue the fight, but then she deflated. Jirah sagged against the white staff, her eyes dropping to the ground. "I'll wait until after Nagato and Loreddion leave to find the Pillar, and then I'm going to go after them."

"Run away again?" Nearra could hear Koi and Loreddion coming up behind them on the path, but their shapes were still hidden by overhanging tree limbs. "Like you did with the Trinistyr?"

"Just help me, Nearra. Please?" Tears reddened Jirah's eyes, but she brushed them away quickly. "I don't want Da to think I'm a failure. I'm just not ready to tell him yet."

"I won't tell him, but only if you promise not to run away. Is that a deal?" Nearra placed her hand on the staff. Her sister looked so small and frail.

"All right. I promise." Jirah half-smiled. "They're getting really far ahead of us. We should catch up."

Koi bounded through the bushes. "Aren't we stopping for lunch?"

Nearra hugged her sister, then turned to smile at Koi. "We had lunch before we left the house."

"I know." Koi grinned. "But I can still hope!"

"She sounds like that badger." Jirah chuckled under her breath.

Loreddion walked past sullenly, sparing only the barest of glances for the girls. He pushed through the trees ahead of them, and Nearra caught a glimpse of a small sunlit valley. His black robes seemed out of place against the green and verdant forest. He stopped to glare back at Koi and the others only after he was several paces down the path toward the valley. "Are you coming?"

"What, into the valley of danger? Wouldn't miss it for the world." Koi ran ahead.

Nearra looked past them into the clearing. It was fairly large, marked by a hollow depression in the center where the sun shone through the opening in the trees. A granite slab lay atop two smaller rocks, forming a table of stone. Even at a distance, Nearra could see that the topmost slab was covered in carvings, some still holding faint vestiges of ancient pigments. Atop the main slab were the triple crescents of the cabal, made silver with a metal coating that glinted between patches of moss.

"When the wizards who told me about this place came to my house, they took me with them into the grove. I remember they did something before we went to the altar, some sort of ritual," Eric explained as he rocked back on his heels and considered. "There may be a guardian of the grove—something I don't know about."

"Do you trust these wizards?" Nearra asked. "Have you known them long?"

Eric shifted back and forth, stroking the small beard on his chin. "I have many friends among the wizards of Krynn. I hadn't seen these men before, but they came highly recommended by my contacts in Palanthas."

"Well, only one way to find out." Without hesitation, Koi marched into the glade. Nagato squeaked in surprise, fumbling for spell components at his belt. Nearra and Jirah stood rigid in shock, and Loreddion pushed off from the tree to follow Koi's quick steps. Koi strode forward, looking both ways as she tossed her weapon between her fists. The wind in the tall trees died, and the sound of rustling leaves faded away. "I don't know what you're all so afraid of." Koi shoved the baton back into her belt. "There's nothing here."

A terrible roar shook the clearing, and the trees on the far side of the glade tore open. Limbs snapped and leaves showered down in an explosion of fluttering green. A shuddering, terrifying mass of roots, leaves, and vines ripped up from the ground, all coiling together. Moss and earth merged with balls of twisting vegetation, coming together into a single creature with long arms that scraped the ground. Its wrinkled face was long and bearded with trailing moss over a gaping dark maw. Thick, trunklike legs carried a wide-girthed body, like an old oak tree.

As the vegetation monster roared, Nearra heard Nagato scream. Two more of the leafy plant men tore up from the ground in other places around the clearing. "The forest is alive!" Nagato backed against a tree, only to leap aside when the shambling mound swiped at him, leaving a trail of reddish clay where Nagato had been standing.

Koi shoved in front of Nearra and Jirah, spinning her baton in the air. "Don't you dare!" Nearra said quickly, catching Koi's wrist. "An earthquake will break the altar!" Koi froze.

"Fine, posey breath. We'll do this the hard way." Koi turned the baton sideways in her grip and pulled a small sack of lead shot—a sap—from her pocket. The sack was longer than her hand, weighted and thick, and Koi slapped it on the baton with a solid thud. She winked at Nearra, then quick as a cat, leaped forward to engage the first of the shamblers.

Eric ran toward his daughters, Nagato close at his heels. They gathered around the altar. Jirah held out the white staff awkwardly, her father's hand on her back. "Do something, Jirah," he said as the other two mounds of vegetation shuffled into the clearing toward them.

Koi jumped onto the first monster's knee, launching again

before its roots could snap up and grab her ankle. She landed on the creature's arm and swung her baton toward the beast's head. The steel thumped powerfully but uselessly against the creature's wooden structure. Leaves shook down from the beast's shoulders as Koi continued to leap around. "It's got a head like iron!"

The third creature shuffled slowly toward the group in the center of the clearing. "Nagato!" Jirah yelled, thrusting at the beast with the platinum-shod end of the white staff.

"Me?" Nagato squeaked. He clutched the steel book to his chest, pressing back against the stone altar. "I'm a researcher! A diviner! I can't fight!"

"Loreddion! Cast a fireball!" Koi yelled from a perch on the first monster's shoulder.

The Black Robe growled. He said scathingly, "That's not my kind of magic."

Jirah groaned, waving the staff about erratically. Nearra assessed the situation. Eric had no weapon at all, Nagato didn't know any fighting spells, and Jirah was more likely to hurt herself with the staff than she was to actually defend them. Jirah was good with swords and with bows, but she didn't usually fight with a staff. Vines lashed out from one of the monsters, catching Loreddion's sleeves and twisting eagerly around his forearms.

They were in trouble.

"Loreddion!" Jirah yelled past her sister.

"I'm doing what I can." He muttered a phrase in the language of magic, and a blackness smeared down along the length of the vines that bound him. The greeneries wrapped around Loreddion's wrist shriveled, turning black and tarry. He pulled on them, forcing the beast to come closer. Drawing the dying vines around his arm, Loreddion reached the creature's arm, knocking aside the beast's claws with a vicious slap of his free hand. Reaching back, Loreddion roared a vicious, guttural sound and raised his free hand into the air. *"Keawetannir!"* His bound hand glowed red, then sparks of yellow and black flashed off the fingertips and shot out like lightning, releasing his hand from the vines.

Loreddion pointed at the monster that had held him. *"Capik,"* he snarled, and the vegetable monster froze in place. "Paralysis spell. Won't last long, but it keeps them quiet while I work up a more foul bit of magic." Loreddion cracked his knuckles, preparing a more complex spell. Chanting strange poemlike words, he plunged his hand into the creature's chest, digging past the moss and tree limbs that formed its rib cage. His hand sunk deep as the magic took hold, red and black sparks rising from his skin in small showers of color. The frozen monster shrieked again.

"Jirah, use your magic." Eric's voice finally sank into Nearra's ears. "Stop them!"

"I . . . can't," Jirah cried. Nearra looked at her and saw her sister flailing. "The magical plague from Palanthas. We're still too close. My fire spells won't work."

Eric leveled the same stare at Jirah that he had always used with the girls. That stare said to obey their father's command. When Eric used that look, the girls jumped to do what he asked. "Now, Jirah."

"I . . . I . . ." Jirah swallowed hard, the color draining from her face. She clutched the staff in white-knuckled fingers, hunching back inside herself. It wasn't fear of the shambling vegetation that froze Jirah so thoroughly, Nearra knew. It was fear of her father, of losing Eric's respect. That would break Jirah. Everything she'd done—stealing the Trinistyr, hunting down Nearra, giving up magic in order to break the curse—was for her father's love.

Nearra couldn't let her lose that.

Nearra put her golden hand over Jirah's, where Eric couldn't see. She whispered softly, close to her sister's ear, "Say *perak lingkaran.*"

"Perak ling . . . lingkaran!" Jirah yelled, giving her sister's hand a desperate squeeze. At the same time, Nearra whispered the words again, concentrating on the end of the white staff. A sharp light burst from the tangle of root clusters, shimmering and coalescing into a ball of silvery steel. Jirah stabbed the staff forward as though to shake off rainwater, instinctively swinging it toward the approaching vegetable man.

The light spun off the end of the staff, swirling toward the creature. It flattened into a disk of cutting light, whirring like a fistful of blades. It sank deep into the creature's shoulder, ripping open a wide wound. Sap dripped from the wound in long, oily strands, pooling brackishly on the ground below the creature's rooted feet. Nearra focused on the lights, and the whirling disk pulled back to circle for another strike.

The beast roared and swung, sap flying through the air. Jirah squealed and ducked, trying to block the blow with her staff, but Eric was quicker. He grabbed the plant beast's arm, swinging it to one side and putting the beast off balance. He didn't try to punch it, probably guessing that his fist was softer than the shambler's wooden frame, but instead shoved a heavy, booted foot through the monster's vine-entwined knee. Thin, flexible branches snapped beneath the kick, and the beast stumbled.

"Well done, Jirah! Keep cutting! Try the joints!" Eric yelled gleefully.

Jirah looked at her sister, pleading silently. Nearra sighed.

The disk of silvery light swept down again on the monster that Eric was fighting. It whirred into the monster's thigh joint, chopping violently through leaf and vine. Greenery flew from the cut, sap flying. Combined with Eric's attack on the knee, the creature staggered and fell to the side, arms flailing. The beast made a terrible sound like the wind of a ferocious storm in the branches, and vines shot out of its arms toward them.

Nearra concentrated, making the disk flicker back and forth before them, cutting each vine before it could reach the altar. The beast tried to stand, but its wounded leg would not hold. For now, they were safe.

Across the altar, Loreddion withdrew his hand from the blackened, withered mass of vegetation he faced. It shuffled a half step forward, its sagging vines and rotted wood refusing to give up. But as Loreddion smiled vindictively, the creature fell to the ground in a mulched lump of decay.

Koi still danced on the shoulders of the third vegetable mound, ignoring the vines that shot up toward her. The monster was unable to move fast enough to catch the quick kender girl. "I just got a great idea!" she yelled. "Watch this!"

She pounded the earthquake stick down onto the monster's head. "No!" Jirah yelled. "The altar!"

"I . . . got . . . it . . . cooo . . . ooo . . . ver . . . ed . . ." The monster shuddered instantly, ripples flowing through it with small explosions of leaf and twig. The shambling mound jerked crazily with each massive jolt. Koi slipped and fell, throwing her arms around the creature's thick shoulders. Her fingers jammed into the vine-twisted shoulder, clenching as she flopped about from the monster's erratic steps. "It . . . just . . . shakes . . . him . . . up . . ." she tried to explain, her feet flopping beneath the vegetable man's arm.

Nearra watched the shambling monster jerk about the clearing, walking much like a confused stork. Green explosions of leaves fell in its path, the wooden frame of the monster's body snapping with each violent pulse. Koi screamed, half laughing, banging against the creature's back. There was a sharp crack, then another, and Nearra could see the white flesh of the wood showing where the monster's wooden rib cage and branches were parting from the jolts. "It's working!" she yelled at Koi. The kender merely grinned and held on.

The vegetation monster that Nearra and Jirah fought was closest to the altar, crawling along the ground without the assistance of its wounded leg. Vines spiraled along the ground, edging under the whirling blades of Nearra's spell. One grabbed Nagato by the leg, and he shrieked.

"Nagato!" Nearra yelled. "Can't you do anything?"

The Red Robe fumbled in his sleeve and pulled out a thin golden wand. Shaped like a long serpent with green emerald eyes and an open mouth, the entire branch of it was slightly S-shaped. The metal curved, etched with scales, as though the little snake were slithering on the ground.

"That's wicked looking." Loreddion's eyebrows shot up. "What does it do, summon a giant snake?"

"Well, no, not exactly," Nagato began.

"I don't care what it does!" Jirah yelled, interrupting him. "Use it!"

"*Avatio!*" Nagato squeaked as he pointed the wand. Bubbles streamed from the serpent's mouth, pink and red, shimmering and catching the sunlight in a steady flow.

"Bubbles?" Loreddion's scornful words exploded out of his mouth. "That's the dumbest thing I've ever—"

Before he could finish the sentence, the first of the bubbles struck the monster on the ground. It broke, spattering goo all over the beast. Eric cried out and jumped back as the goo on his pants began to hiss, burning through the light leather of his breeches.

One by one, the stream of bubbles impacted with the wounded monster, exploding in small, acidic splashes. The acid ate through the wood, turning the edges of each wound red with sickly-smelling, bubbling poison. Loreddion gaped, Jirah stepped back, and Nearra let her whirling-blade spell sink through the worst of the area softened by the acid bubbles. It speared through and

PILLAR OF FLAME

101

chopped the monster cleanly in two. The creature crumbled in a pile of quivering branches.

They all looked at Koi, but the kender's monster was faring no better—the magical thumping of her earthquake stick had broken the beast into small pieces, shaking loose every bit of the creature's solidity. Koi sat on the ground watching the last of it. She poked the larger area of moss and bramble that she now sat upon, and sighed. "It might be able to put itself back together, once the earthquake wears off. But I doubt it. Too bad. For a few minutes, it actually had me going. I was almost . . . vaguely . . . concerned." She shrugged and stood up, pushing the metal baton back into her belt.

"That wand is crazy." Loreddion walked across the clearing, shaking black mold from his hands. "Where did you get it?"

"I made it." Nagato sniffed, cramming the golden serpent back into his sleeve. "It was a project when I was an apprentice. I wanted it to be a wand of nature-based power, perhaps some kind of venom, but the spell was flawed. It's kind of uncontrollable."

Loreddion paused and pushed part of his hair back behind one slender, pointed ear. "For a messed-up spell, it's not bad," he said to Nagato with a sharp-toothed smile and a little shrug. "Not bad at all."

Surprised by the compliment, Nagato flashed the Black Robe a hesitant smile.

Jirah lowered the staff, and Eric came over to hug his daughter. "That was amazing, Jirah. I've never seen anything like it. Did you make that spell up yourself?"

"It was nothing, Da, really. Just a little blade spell. I could have done an ice ball, but I didn't think the vegetable men would be too affected by frost."

"Smart girl! I bet you could have done a mass invisibility spell too, except that those creatures don't really have eyes. But you thought of that, didn't you?" Eric clapped his hand on his knee, a thrilled grin breaking across his features. Before she could answer, he rushed on. "I can't wait to learn all these things. You're a tremendously accomplished wizard, Jirah. These spells are going to be useful in any number of situations."

"Da," Nearra said, hesitating.

He turned to hug her as well. "You were very brave, Nearra. You didn't run, even though there was absolutely nothing you could do. I'm sure when you learn magic, you'll be a very good wizard, just like your sister. You just haven't applied yourself. It'll take more dedication and hard work than you've shown to be a wizard. You remember that."

Nearra reddened, anger rising in her stomach, but she ground her teeth and kept silent. Jirah tried to catch her eye and whisper a thank you, but Nearra turned away without answering.

"So what does the table say, Nagato?" Koi asked.

Nagato was already kneeling by the stone slab. He held the steel-covered book in one hand and peered intently at the carving on the stone. Eric crouched down beside him, pointing at a symbol. The two began an earnest debate about the meaning of each rune, while Jirah, Nearra, Koi, and Loreddion gathered to one side.

"He thinks you're a wizard?" Loreddion's eyes flashed. "You?" The Black Robe stared down at Jirah arrogantly. "That's ridiculous. You're no more a wizard than I am a kender."

"You'd be a terrible kender. Leave her alone." Koi pushed between them, keeping her voice down. "You can't even throw a fireball."

"I don't need to throw fireballs. Disease and decay worked just fine against that monster, in case you didn't notice. And I'm not going to let someone pretend to be a wizard when they aren't one," he snapped. "I'm going to tell your father all about your little lies and your fake 'magic.'"

As one, the sisters bristled. "Don't you dare!" Nearra and Jirah both yelled.

Loreddion narrowed his eyes. "One day," he growled. "If you don't tell him by tomorrow, then I'm telling him before I leave."

"Fine," Jirah snapped. A silence fell over the foursome for a long moment. Jirah and Loreddion matched stubborn stares.

Nagato's voice broke the standoff with an excited shout. "Look here! On the stone! I think I've found something!"

CHAPTER

11

Dangerous Knowledge

Outside the cottage, crickets and tree frogs sang a symphony of noises, their music leaking through the kitchen windows. Nagato had pages covered in detailed notes from his study of the stone table that afternoon spread across the kitchen table. He scurried around the table, occasionally pausing to write something or to whisper to himself in encouragement or annoyance.

Lanni washed the last of the dinner dishes, pouring water over them from a bucket to clean away the soap. Koi could see her smiling, humming softly as she wiped the dishes with a rag. Nagato kept talking, the constant babble of his voice carrying through the small cottage. His words faded back into Koi's consciousness: "These symbols aren't a language. They're some kind of code, I'm sure of it. It's just not making sense."

"Well, parts of it make sense," Eric countered. "It just doesn't seem to flow right. Like it's all broken up. Maybe we aren't putting it in the right order."

"This has to be the right order." Nagato tugged at his hair. "We're missing something."

Koi sighed. "I'm tired of messing with it. Minds are fresher 105 with dew and dawn, my mother used to say."

"You're right," Nagato sighed. "We can continue tomorrow."

Eric looked frustrated. Koi watched him, peering beneath one eyelid. At last, he threw up his hands. "Fine. Tomorrow," he conceded. Still, even when Lanni came over and held him close, Eric looked monumentally annoyed.

"The girls have rooms upstairs, and we have one guest room. Loreddion and Nagato can share it, and Koi is welcome down here." Lanni opened a pantry and pulled out a thick blanket and some pillows. Koi sleepily dragged herself away from the fire as the others said their "good nights." The couch was warm where Nearra had been sitting, and the pillows were feathery and plush. The fire continued to crackle cheerily in the hearth, and the soft drone of voices continued upstairs for a while after the lights were extinguished. Koi could hear Nagato going over the last of the combinations of letters with Loreddion even as she slipped into sleep.

It was the creak at the door that awakened Koi deep in the middle of the night. Fearing at first that more thieves had come to attack them, the kender rolled to the ground and groped in the dark for her metal baton. Sleep clouded her senses, and she shook her head to clear it. Voices—outside, not inside—whispered in hurried annoyance.

"Come on," a low and unrecognizable voice said. Koi perked up her ears and tried to hear more.

"This is ridiculous." Koi recognized that grumpy tone. It was Loreddion. "Why can't we go in the morning?"

Nagato—it had to be Nagato—answered with a whisper, "I told you that you could stay. If I copied that text wrong, we could spend days trying to fix my error. I can't sleep without knowing I was right. The barn is only a little bit down the path. We can be there and back in less than a candlemark."

"Well, at least you aren't taking me all the way to the stone table." Loreddion yawned, tugging his thick hair back and scratching his neck.

Koi slunk to the door, peering out into the yard. The moons, a slim silver crescent and a wide red one, shone down on two figures crossing the yard. One wore red robes, brilliantly scarlet under Lunitari's light, the other had a long, white blanket pulled over his black clothing. He tugged it close around his shoulders, the edge arching up over his head like a white, pointed hood.

Koi stepped out into the night, keeping close to the bushes and trees near the house as she followed the two wizards. Nagato continued to talk, and even when she couldn't see them, she followed the sound of his voice. The woods were dark, and the crickets and chirping frogs of early evening had faded into silence. The wizards were a bit ahead of her, their voices softly rising and falling with sleepy argument.

"Crazy elves." She yawned, scratching her head with the tip of her baton. "They don't even take the time to light a candle or a torch or something because of their weird night eyes." Koi blithely ignored her own excellent vision, following the path easily even when the moons were blocked by thick tree limbs. She envied Loreddion his blanket; the night was cold, and a stiff breeze rustled the forest from time to time, cutting through her sleeping shirt and chilling her bare toes. The walk took only a few minutes before the path widened at a small, open gate.

Koi turned a corner in the path and saw ahead the huge, ghostly image of the gray barn against the darkness of the forest. As it had been when they brought the horses to the stable yesterday, the side of the barn was covered by a large painting—a symbol visible from the forest path and beyond, the same symbol carved into the stone table. Koi sighed. How boring. Maybe a wild animal would come along out of the darkness and attack them. Maybe the horses would stampede and crush their skulls beneath pounding hooves.

She sighed again. Even that wouldn't be very scary. She needed to think of something more dangerous. That might help get her in the mood to be frightened. Koi frowned. Ghosts and goblins? Mad, rabid tentacled monsters? She crouched down by the path and watched as Nagato dragged the white-swaddled Loreddion back and forth in front of the barn. They were too far away for Koi to hear the words, but the sound of their voices was comforting in the darkness. Maybe if she thought about it very hard, some monster would come raging out of the woods and viciously attack them all. Or maybe a demon!

Koi put her head on her hands. She'd never be that lucky.

There was a rustle in the woods, and Koi saw movement close to the barn. She shot up, eyes wide. Maybe she *was* that lucky! "Demon, demon, demon?" she chanted hopefully, balling her fists together and crawling up on her knees to see around a wide bush. "Aw, nuts." She grimaced. "Those aren't demons. Those are just humans. And here I thought I was getting somewhere."

Three figures slipped out of the woods, moving swiftly toward the barn. They carried strange weapons, tucking them close to their bodies. Dressed in black outfits with silver-threaded belts that twinkled in the moonlight, these intruders were much the same as the ones that attacked them at Nagato's house. "These guys just don't give up, do they?" She drew her baton from her belt. Koi wasn't too worried—she'd seen what Loreddion did to those plant monsters. He could handle these jokers.

And indeed, out in the clearing, Loreddion began to chant in a cruel tongue, spreading his fingers toward the three men who rushed toward them. But as spell power circled his fingers and coalesced around the dark elf's palm, one of the three men struck him lightly with a long, narrow rod. The rod was nearly twice as long as Koi's baton, but still only half the size of a wizard's staff. It was a coppery color, and the tip was a dark scarlet gem, roughly the size of a hen's egg. The gem flashed as it struck Loreddion.

The magic around Loreddion's hand swelled, as if uncontrolled. Then, as the gem faded, the magic died as well. The Black Robe looked stunned, pale blanket falling from his rigid shoulders. As it crumpled to the ground in a pallid heap, Loreddion drew his hand back and stared at his fingers. "My spell!" Koi heard him say. "What happened to my spell?"

"I know a speed incantation. Quickly! We need to warn the others!" Nagato clapped Loreddion on the shoulder and shouted something in the same magical tongue. A warm green glow encased them both, lifting them slightly off the ground. Nagato started to yell, but before he could get another word out, another intruder struck him with a copper rod. The green aura blinked twice and then faded, and the two wizards were dumped unceremoniously to the ground.

"Those rods steal magic!" Koi's jaw dropped.

Nagato reached quickly for his wand. The assailant closest lashed out, rod striking Nagato hard enough that Koi heard it crack against the bone. Nagato dropped the wand, clutching his arm. He flexed his fingers gingerly, as if hoping they still moved. Loreddion dived, lashing out at the closest man with one foot. He knocked the thief over, hurling him to the ground, and the two scrabbled for Nagato's wand. One of the other two grabbed Nagato, placing the red gem of the copper rod beneath the thin wizard's chin. It pressed against his throat, pulsing the color of blood, and Nagato slumped to the ground.

"Loreddion!" Koi dashed forward, but even as she readied her baton, she saw the third man bearing down on Loreddion. While the Black Robe wrestled on the ground with his opponent, the second of the three thieves jammed his rod against Loreddion's ribs. The elf howled, snapping back to attack his opponent. The gem flashed red and pulsed as the other had, and Loreddion's eyes widened in pain. As the light from the gem faded, the dark elf sank down, unconscious.

Koi pulled up short as the three enemies turned toward her. They held their rods at the ready, the silver and red light of the crescent moons casting strange double shadows on the ground where Loreddion and Nagato lay. She spun her baton in a circle, readying it for a jump attack. Before she even got to activate it, they struck her. The gem flashed like glistening blood, and Koi felt a strange, uncertain feeling rush over her. The copper rod caught her attention, and she felt herself sinking into the red glow. She could feel her body slump, her eyes closing. The ground rose cold and hard to meet her fall.

She struggled against the darkness. Every bone in her being screamed to wake up, get her friends out of trouble, defend the people still sleeping peacefully in the cottage. Koi felt herself crawl forward, still clutching her metal baton. Voices whispered over her, and she listened to them as she fought her way back to consciousness.

"Yzor will want all the magic-users," one of the men said. His voice was clearly human, but without remorse. "There is one more wizard in the house who must be captured."

"Then we go to the house," the second man said in a harsher voice. "Capture the magic-user."

"And the others?" asked the third.

"If they resist"—the second thief's voice turned cold—"kill them. And take the kender's little stick. It's obviously magical."

As one of them slid the rod out of Koi's hand, she focused her attention instead on Loreddion and Nagato, who were lying beside the barn. Nagato's eyelids fluttered, his fingers twitching slightly. Loreddion seemed a bit more aware, the Silvanesti's dark eyes narrowed with anger. "Lor," Koi whispered, forcing the sound out through her clenched throat muscles. "I won't let them hurt anybody. You hear me?"

Whether he did or not, Koi couldn't tell. He'd probably be angry either way, she reasoned, so his expression wouldn't change. One of the thieves came over to them and lifted Nagato under one arm and Loreddion under the other. He stared down at Koi for a moment and shrugged. "Not a magic-user," he muttered. "And I can't carry three to the table."

Behind her, Koi heard the other two men heading down the path toward the cottage. Everyone there was asleep. The door was unlocked and open. Her friends were helpless. Koi pushed herself to her knees. She felt her body resisting and turned her head. Her stomach clenched, and she vomited. "Can't stop . . ." she groaned, resisting the urge to sink back down into darkness.

Staggering to her feet, Koi leaned back against the barn. To the left, the faint echoes of breaking branches told her where Nagato and Loreddion were. To the right was the path that led to the cottage. "All right, Loreddion," she mumbled, wiping her mouth. "I'm going to trust you to take care of Nagato. I've got to go back for the girls. Whoever this Yzor is, they're no match for you."

She pushed off against the barn, staggering toward the trail. Each step set her body on fire, pain searing through her muscles with each flex. Her body was in agony, but Koi wouldn't stop or slow down. She shoved one foot in front of the other, stumbling over stones in the hardened mud. One step. Two. More.

Stumbling, Koi almost fell into the yard, leaning on the last of the trees. Koi noted that the front door was open and that someone had poured some sort of foul-smelling liquid across the porch. She leaned down to touch a pool of it that had trickled down the hill from the house. It was sticky and smelled of oil and brine.

"Fertilizer from the barn." Koi leaned against the doorway. "I wonder what that's about?" She straightened, leaning against the tree just a moment more. "All right, you cabal. You just wait one second. I'm coming for you. Even your crazy pain stick doesn't scare me." Her shoulders drooped. "I really expected more from a thousand-year-old cult."

There was a scream inside the house and a rush of flame from the kitchen. "Oh!" Koi straightened, blinking rapidly. "I guess that's what the fertilizer is for!" Fire licked against the walls of the little cottage, and a sudden hot wind rushed through the yard. Koi stared in morbid delight, muttering to herself. "Isn't that just typical. It'll probably burn up the entire house, the barn, maybe the woods around here for miles. Thousands of acres of wildlife displaced, little bird nests turned to cinders, and all my friends . . ." She jolted back to herself. "Oi! My friends are in that house!"

Koi tried to run, but her stiff legs wouldn't hold her. She half stumbled, half fell toward the front door of the cottage. One of the cultists saw her and turned toward her with his copper rod in hand. "Get the wizard out of the house!" he snarled to the other. "I'll handle this bug."

Koi rolled the last few feet, coming up under the human's guard with a quick strike of her sap, the small bag of lead shot. It thumped hard against his hand, and the cultist yelped. Koi grabbed the lower part of the copper rod and jerked it away. The cultist connected a punch with her chin, but she had a very short distance to fall. Rolling with the punch, Koi hit the ground again, twisting like a cat with the copper rod under her.

"You don't have the slightest idea how to use that." The man in black grabbed her by the collar of her leather jerkin, dragging Koi to her feet.

She grinned wickedly. "I may not know how to make the magic work, but I sure know how to use this." She spun the rod in her hand like a baton, striking rapidly with either end. It flew across her knuckles, connecting with his knees, his thighs, and then she sank the end into his stomach in a sudden strong blow. The man gasped for air, sinking to his knees, and Koi reached to grab his collar. "See what I mean, bub?" She raised the copper rod to strike him again, but paused. It had bent exactly the width of his knee with the force of her blows, the gem cracking and hanging loosely in its setting.

A scream in the house caught Koi's attention. "They just don't make magic items like they used to." Raising it above her head, she brought it down on his head with another massive thump. The copper rod bent almost in half, and the man's eyes glazed over. He fell forward, face-first into the grass.

Koi dropped the ruined copper rod and dug into the man's belt for her own steel baton. "Now this is a quality weapon," she said, flipping it between her hands expertly. "And I thank you for giving it back to me. I've got work to do."

By this time, the fire had spread through the lower parts of the house, and Koi heard a great deal of shouting upstairs. It seemed that the family had awakened too early, catching the other cultist before he could subdue Nearra—and now they were all trapped inside.

"House on fire. Everyone trapped inside, about to be burned alive. Two of the wizards kidnapped, dragged off to—who knows— be sacrificed in the woods somewhere. The rest of us about to be roasted like chickens. And here I am, going to run right into the heart of the flame, sacrificing myself uselessly in a hopeless situation." She considered that, chewing her bottom lip, then sighed from the depths of her heart. "Nope. Still nothing."

With that, Koi leaped through the flames in the front doorway, her baton in one hand and her sap in the other. The entire front room was on fire, but Koi danced between burning lumps of furniture toward the stairwell. She could hear fighting upstairs, and Eric's angry shout. Koi jumped over the couch, right through a puff of fire so close she could smell her hair singeing. She charged up the stairs, feeling a strange sense of déjà vu, and stood in the hallway above. "Well, this has got to go better than at Nagato's house." She readied her baton and looked for an enemy. "Or at least . . . it'll be shorter."

There were sounds of fighting in the rooms, the ones against the overhanging sod ledge. No windows here, though, so the smoke was thicker, and the heat from the fire in the kitchen below made the floorboards warm to Koi's bare feet.

The room at the end of the hall was a big chamber with a single large bed pushed against the rear wall. She saw Lanni holding a candelabrum to fight with while Eric raised a woodsman's axe that glowed with a faint bluish light. Behind them stood Nearra and Jirah, the latter clutching the long white staff. The Crescent Cabal member drew back his copper rod, and the red gem on the tip of his weapon flashed menacingly. Dazed by the rod, Nearra sagged and collapsed, landing on the floor heavily. Her eyes were glassy and confused, her mouth moving softly as though to form words that Koi couldn't hear.

"No spells for you." The Cabal thief grinned behind his black bandanna. "Give me the wizard, and I'll let you go."

"You can't have Jirah!" Eric cried, stepping in front of his younger daughter. The cabal thief looked confused, but Eric didn't hear him out. "Jirah! Use your magic. Put out the fire and trap this man in a cage of magical force!"

Jirah flushed. "I . . . uh . . ."

"Don't know that spell yet? Well, that's all right. Use the one you mentioned before—the ice ball. That'll cool down this fire!" Eric grinned proudly. "You'll see! My daughter's a powerful wizard! She'll deal with you!"

Lanni knelt on the floor beside Nearra, gently shaking her daughter's limp form. "What have you done to her?"

Jirah clutched the white staff, stepping up beside her father. "I won't let you hurt my family."

"Cast something!" Eric reached out and grabbed his daughter's shoulder. She shook him off angrily. "Jirah?"

"I can't," she spat bitterly. He stared at her in shock, expression blank with disbelief. She continued remorsefully, staring at the ground with hands balled. "I'm not a wizard."

Leaping forward, the thief gave Jirah no further chance to explain. He lunged for her staff, rod extended, but Jirah twisted to the side and brought the length of the staff down against the thief's back. There was a solid thunk, and the man fell sideways, staggering to regain his feet. Though the staff was clearly too big and heavy for such fighting, Jirah nevertheless refused to give up and pounded after him in bare feet. Eric simply stared while Lanni helped Nearra back to her feet. Koi could tell that the rod's magic weakened Nearra as it had done to herself, Nagato, and Loreddion.

The thief recoiled and struck at Jirah, the rod landing a heavy stroke against her rib cage. But he must not have been using the strength-stealing rod's magic, Koi realized, because though Jirah was shoved back by the force of it, she did not collapse. As if just remembering the axe in his hands, Eric moved forward to swing. He connected with a two-handed blow that hit the copper rod, twisting the soft metal against the blade of the axe. Although the blue glow on the weapon faded, the axe was still extremely sharp. When Eric pulled it back, there was a chunk missing in the copper rod.

Lanni pulled Nearra's arm over her shoulder and half dragged her daughter toward the doorway. Jirah moved to stay between them and the thief. The man drew something else from his belt and hurled it at Lanni and Nearra. Metal swept through the air, landing with multiple thuds in the doorframe—darts, their tips glistening with something sticky. Lanni clutched Nearra to her chest.

Koi yelled, "Eric! Go with Lanni! Nearra's too heavy for her to carry alone!" When the woodsman faltered, Koi yelped, "Jirah and I can handle him!"

The thief struck out again, finding an open avenue toward Nearra as Eric was trying to decide. The man grabbed Nearra's nightgown and jerked her from her mother's shoulder. Koi flung herself forward and collided with the thief, knocking him to the ground again. He grabbed her baton in one hand, trying to bring the copper rod around to strike her, but she ducked the blow and rolled.

Eric jolted into action. He grabbed Nearra's elbow, reached for Lanni's shoulder, and pushed them both through the flames in the doorway. He shielded them as best he could, but the fires were spreading down the hallway, and Lanni screamed. As they vanished down the stairs, Koi saw fire engulf the hallway. She could only pray to Fizban that they made it out through the front door.

Seeing his quarry escaping, the cabal agent turned and leaped through the doorway, screaming as his clothing caught fire. He ran toward a window in the front, the part of the house that wasn't against the hillside. Koi heard glass shatter and a shout, and saw the man hurl himself out the window, completely on fire.

Beside her, Jirah gulped. "I don't think he made it. Koi, I'm scared."

"Lucky you." Koi grabbed Jirah's hand and jerked her forward. "Time to go." Koi made the only choice she could. She followed the man's path, leaping through the doorway and trying to shield Jirah as much as she could from the fire. Jirah screamed, holding the white staff close. Fire dropped from the ceiling in clumps, threatening to set their hair and clothing alight, but Koi didn't stop. She held Jirah close, bulling through with her shoulders and ignoring the pain.

They reached the window. Jirah looked over the edge and blanched. It was nearly fifteen feet down, then a slope of grass. There was no padding below, nothing soft to land on, and the fire downstairs licked out the windows of the house with bursts of hot air. The thief's body lay sprawled below them, arms and legs akimbo, clothing blazing with flame.

"He didn't make it," Jirah whimpered. "I've got to at least throw Nearra her staff. Even if I die—"

"We aren't going to die." Koi bodily picked up Jirah and pulled herself up into the window.

"Didn't you hear me?" Jirah clung to the strong little kender, staff wedged between them. "He didn't make it!"

"But we will." Koi's face was hard as granite, her green eyes as solid as emerald chips. Fire in her hair, her clothing charring against her skin, the kender leaped out into space with a roar.

CHAPTER

12   FALLING

"Jirah?" The voice was familiar, but it didn't quite penetrate her consciousness. She had a vague memory of falling, a sensation of hot wind against her skin. "Jirah!" Slowly, she opened her eyes.

She was hovering just a few feet off the ground, Koi beside her. The kender writhed behind her like a cat trying to find its footing in the air. "Aw, Nearra," Koi said with a frown. "And here I thought that seeing the ground rush up at us might make me . . . I don't know . . . a little nervous, maybe? Or just a tiny bit scared?"

Jirah looked down at the grass beneath her, slowly rising up to touch her bare toes. Nearra, Lanni, and Eric stood outside the light of the burning house. Nearra's golden hand lowered as they softly floated down, and Nearra's whispering faded. Jirah stood rigidly, staff clutched to her chest. Koi stuffed her hands in her pockets and shuffled forward. "Party pooper," the kender muttered.

Nearra looked wan and pale, but she drew a long, shuddering breath and raised her hands again. She pointed at the house and said, *"Berair."* Water spouted from the earth, welling up in great fountains all around the house. Tremendous spurts of clear, cool liquid sprayed over the house and the yard, immediately drenching the fire. Smoke boiled up from the house as the flames hissed and died. Once they were gone, Nearra lowered her hand, and the water sank back into the earth.

The house stood intact but badly seared, all the furniture blackened with the heat of the blaze. The upper window was shattered, the stairwell completely gone, and both the front room and the kitchen were charred. Lanni grabbed her daughters one at a time, hugging them tightly and looking them up and down for any wounds. They both reassured her that they were fine. At last certain that both girls were all right, Lanni turned her attention toward the house. She placed her hand on the charred front door, tears in her eyes. "Thank Paladine none of us were hurt. Oh, that poor man."

That was just like her mother, Jirah thought. Lanni was always gentle, quiet. Nearra took after her in that, the same way that Jirah inherited her father's stubbornness. She shook herself, trying to get the smell of the fire out of her hair. Jirah's nightclothes were covered in soot, and she had to pat out small areas that were still smoldering when she landed. Beneath it, her skin was red and tender from the flames. She stared in envy at Koi, who seemed not at all hurt by the fire.

Koi was rolling on the grass, enjoying the dampness after the warmth of the fire. "Where did the other one go?" she called. "Must have woke up and run off, I suppose."

"That man is dead." Eric pointed at the body. "Someone tell me who he is and why he was attacking my family."

The kender looked up at Eric and answered his question. "They came for the wizards. Nagato and Loreddion went out to the barn to look at something on your mural, something Nagato thought he'd missed on the stone table. Three of these men—agents of the Crescent Cabal, like the ones who attacked us in Palanthas—came out of the woods and knocked them out with those copper rods. They dragged the wizards off and came up here to finish the job."

"They wanted the wizards?" Lanni asked, her voice quiet.

"Loreddion, Nagato," Koi kept talking, completely unashamed, "and Nearra."

"Nearra," Eric repeated bitterly. "Not Jirah."

"Yes, Da." Nearra looked pale, but she raised her chin. "Everything else that Jirah and I told you was true. Jirah stole the Trinistyr. She traveled across Krynn to find me and to free me from the sorceress Asvoria. She risked her life. We took the Trinistyr to the tombs of Anselm's friends, relived Anselm's deeds, and then Jirah broke the curse. She did it. Not me. Jirah."

Jirah couldn't let her sister face him alone. "I made the choice. When I used the Trinistyr, Paladine spoke to me. He asked me to pay a price to lift the curse. And I"—Jirah felt a lump growing in her throat—"I paid it."

"What kind of price?" Lanni fixed her gaze on her younger daughter. The wind ruffled her grayish blonde hair. "Jirah, are you all right?"

"I'm fine, Mama. I gave up magic. That's what Paladine wanted in exchange for lifting the curse. I'll never be a wizard." Jirah stared her father down, trying to force the fear in her stomach back into its tight little ball. "And there's nothing anyone can do about it."

Eric's muscles clenched as though he might lash out at something. Jirah flinched. She'd never known her father to strike her, to strike anyone, but he was enraged. His eyes bulged slightly, and he raised one shaking hand to point at Jirah. "You lied to me." Disappointment colored his tone, cold as a snake.

Jirah stood there feeling mutinous. She had broken the curse, given them all back their magic, something Eric could never have done—or all the generations between him and Anselm! And this was how she was treated? "I tried to tell you the moment we arrived."

Eric glared, then barked, "Not hard enough to actually *say the words*, though, did you?"

"Hang on," said Koi. "You can't still be mad at Jirah, can you?" She hesitated for a moment, then the morose kender slumped. "Isn't that just typical? Spend all your life looking for something, and then when you get it, blame the person who brought it to you. I hope I'm not as ungrateful when I feel fear for the first time."

If Eric had been angry before, he was livid now. "I expected things from you, Jirah. Better things than lies. You were going to be the greatest wizard in Krynn. You had a destiny. You were going to be someone important. Now you're nothing." Dismissing her with a gesture, Eric stared down at her with fire in his brown eyes.

Before Jirah could say anything, he turned to Nearra. "How far along are your studies of magic?"

She stammered, "I-I-I was to take my Test of High Sorcery in Palanthas before this issue with the Pillar of Flame. When we return—"

He cut her off. "When we find Loreddion and Nagato, we'll help them. Then Jirah will return to Palanthas and tell the wizards what they want to know. You'll stay here."

"But—" Nearra began.

"Together, we'll learn. You will instruct me in magic, and when we're both ready, we'll go take the test together." Eric didn't slow down. He put his hand on Nearra's shoulder, a faint smile returning to his face as if he'd completely forgotten about Jirah.

A quizzical frown touched Nearra's features. "But Jirah—"

Eric crossed the yard to the front door. "Lanni, see if you can scrounge up food from the kitchen—anything that's not burned or wet. Something we can travel with. Nearra, Koi, and I will go after the wizards."

"I know where they're going." Koi grabbed her toes and rocked back and forth. "They've gone to the southeast, toward the stone table. I bet they're going to sacrifice the wizards to some dark god. Or maybe throw them into the Pillar of Flame after they do terrible things to them on the ancient altar." She pouted. "Some people have all the luck."

Lanni slipped into the house, stepping gingerly through the burned furniture toward the ruined kitchen. Jirah could hear her banging about, moving aside charred pantry doors, searching the storeroom beneath the house for anything that made it through the fire. At last, Jirah found her voice. "I want to go too."

Instead of denying her right away, Eric turned to face Jirah. "And do what? Throw rocks at them? You have no magic, you're too young to be effective in combat, and you've already lied to me once." The words felt like blows to Jirah, who gasped for breath as her father continued. "You will stay with your mother and pack up anything of value that survived the fire. After we get back, the family will take the horses and move away. Lanni?" He turned to call into the house.

His wife walked back toward them, carrying a basket. She tucked a blue-and-white-checked towel into the corners, covering the small mound of food and water inside. In her other hand, she held a pile of clothing for Nearra—breeches, tunics, and a silver dress. "I found enough for a few days, at most, and both Nearra and Jirah had some old clothes stored downstairs. You had clothes on the line, Eric, so dress yourself from those. As for the food, well, if you hunt while you travel, you may make it last a week. And I found the kender's armor right where she left it—in the pantry. Don't ask me why it was there."

"The buckles were too tight." Koi reached up and grasped her leather breastplate and helmet, thanking Lanni profusely.

"Due to that blueberry pie you ate all by yourself while we were studying the runes, no doubt." Lanni shook her head.

Eric took his wife in his arms and kissed her gently. "Thank you. We have to leave immediately. Koi, Nearra, come on." Eric handed Koi the basket and turned away. He fingered the axe at his belt, which had regained its blue glow. "It seemed the copper rods only steal magic for a few moments. That's good news."

"Da?" Jirah tried once more. Even to her own ears, her voice sounded weak and shaking. "I want to come with you. I can fight. I know how to use a sword."

Koi tossed her metal baton from hand to hand. "I think the copper rods can steal non-magic users' strength, too. They hit me a while back. And there might be reinforcements at the stone table. They'll be waiting for their friends to meet up with them, after they got Nearra. There could be ten, twenty, even fifty men. That sounds pretty desperate, a real standoff. And those vegetable men will be back again, of course. That'll make it even more against us. We'll die in a blaze of glory."

"What Koi's trying to say is that we could use the help," Nearra said hesitantly.

Eric reached out toward Jirah, and for a moment, Jirah thought her father was going to rustle her hair as he'd done when she was a child. She leaned forward into his touch, but his hand stopped just short of her face. His fingers wrapped around the white staff of Anselm, jerking it from Jirah's grasp with a savage tug. Without its support, Jirah staggered forward, and only Lanni's supporting arm saved her from a fall.

"That belongs to your sister." Eric coldly handed the white staff to a shocked Nearra.

Jirah watched her father and the others leave without even

changing their smoky clothes. Nearra carried the white staff and Koi twirled her metal baton around one finger by its leather strap. Eric never slowed down, vanishing into the trees without a backward glance. At the edge of the woods, Nearra turned to look at her sister, a pained expression on her lovely features. Jirah wanted to yell at her, beg her to talk to their father, but she knew it was no use. Nearra obviously didn't want to go without her, and that raised Jirah's spirits just a little bit. Although she wanted her sister to stay, she wanted the mission to succeed. Loreddion and Nagato were in danger.

She raised her hand and waved in farewell. Nearra waved back before she slipped into the dark forest. Jirah felt her mother's hand around her shoulders.

"I didn't want to lie to him, Mama," Jirah whispered. "I just didn't want to disappoint him."

"I know, sweetie." Lanni pressed something into Jirah's hand. It was a small bundle, a blue-checked towel like the first. She unfolded the corner, and inside were sandwiches of brown bread, smoked ham sticking out appetizingly from the side.

"What's this?" asked Jirah, confused.

"Enough food so we can follow them, and some clothing for you and me."

"Follow them?"

Lanni did not answer at once, but remained quietly smiling at Jirah's side. "Magic doesn't make the world go around, Jirah. Not everyone is a wizard. Some people are warriors, rangers, or simple craftsmen. And Krynn needs every one of them."

"But Da said for you and me to stay here."

"I've never obeyed everything your father said, Jirah. That must be where you get it from. Stealing the Trinistyr worked out pretty well, didn't it?" When Jirah nodded numbly, her mother smiled. "I have a couple of bows in the barn, and some knives survived the fire in the kitchen. We'll be fine."

"We?" Jirah blinked. "You're going with me?"

"Eric thinks that wizards are the only people in the world who are worth anything at all. He hasn't only insulted you, Jirah, he's insulted me too. I'm not a wizard."

"No, you're not." Jirah brightened with the realization. "But you're definitely worthwhile."

"I should hope I am." Lanni hugged her. "And so is my daughter." She lifted Jirah's chin with her hand, smiling proudly down at her. "Your father and the others are walking straight into danger. They're going to need us, whether he believes it or not. Let's go show Eric what we're made of."

CHAPTER

13   Division in the Ranks

"K eep going." The agent shoved Nagato from behind, and he stumbled. He regained his balance quickly, his elf dexterity helping him manage even over twisted roots. Nagato's hands were tied behind his back with a chafing piece of cord. His velvet sleeves kept getting twisted together, catching on everything as he tried to keep up with the man's pace. Loreddion walked behind him, tied to the same cord. Each step jerked Nagato back and forth as the rope cut painfully into his skin.

Every once in a while, the cabal agent poked them both with the copper rod. He didn't leave it against their skin very long, only tapped them lightly. The sensation tingled, setting Nagato's blood on fire. Each time he did it, Nagato felt sick and weak. They were stealing his magic, tamping it down so he couldn't use it. And without it, he was helpless.

Loreddion grunted, and Nagato knew that the agent struck the other wizard as well. That was worse. While Nagato's magic was primarily divinatory, Loreddion had already proved to be a monster in a fight. Taking away Loreddion's spells ruined their best hope for escape.

At last, the woods parted in front of them. As soon as he stepped past the treeline, Nagato knew where they were. "The stone table," he breathed, seeing it by moonlight. Solinari's last few rays sparkled on the lettering on the side of the granite slab, catching silvery mica that outlined several of the characters.

The agent lifted something from his boot that looked like a small padlock. He held it in the air, chanted a few words, then turned the top of it away from the bottom, nearly twisting it in two. There was an audible snap, and the air in the grove lightened. A wind suddenly started blowing through the area, only now making Nagato aware of how still the little clearing had been before. The black-garbed agent smiled and put away the little device.

"So that's how you do magic." Nagato said. "You're not a wizard at all."

"Shut up." The man shoved Nagato forward so hard that he tumbled to the ground, the rope jerking into his skin hard enough to draw blood. Unable to stop himself, Loreddion fell too and landed hard on top of Nagato. Nagato felt an elbow in his rib cage as they rolled down the slight slope toward the table. Loreddion cursed, elbows and knees going everywhere, and the two of them ended up in a pile against the stone.

"You're late." The voice didn't come from their captor, but from another man emerging from the far side of the woods.

Loreddion only growled deep in his throat. "You shouldn't anger them," Nagato whispered.

"What, play the sheep like you do?" Loreddion's scorn was obvious.

"Aruk and Darex are still behind me. There was a third wizard." Their captor went to greet the other man with a strange handshake. "They'll catch up in a little while. I was sent on ahead."

"Two wizards? Are either of them capable of creating magic items, Zann?"

PILLAR OF FLAME

127

"Yzor will question them when we arrive at the Pillar of Flame. They know much of what was occurring in Palanthas. If they cannot serve us and they have no information for Yzor, they will have to be destroyed," their captor, Zann, said in an emotionless tone. Nagato shuddered. Loreddion didn't flinch, move, or even seem to hear the conversation around them. His eyes were half closed, and he was testing the ropes around his hands. He flexed them behind his back, keeping the motions small and quiet.

"We're late already," the man in the clearing snarled. He wore no mask, and Nagato could tell he was human. His features were pinched and dark hair flopped about his forehead. "We can't afford to wait more than a few minutes for the others."

"Yes, Feren." Zann nodded willingly, not asking any questions.

"What do they want?" Loreddion shook his head. "Why are they waiting to kill us? Are they going to steal our spells and leave us husks?"

"You're starting to sound like Koi. If they were going to kill us, they already would have done so. They aren't wizards," Nagato whispered, taking advantage of the conversation to mutter a few words into Loreddion's ear. "If we can get a bit of our power back, we should be able to best them."

The dark elf rolled his eyes beneath the long mane of silver hair. "You said the cabal collects magic items and spells."

"Yes, well, this is obviously how they keep them. They employ nonwizards as thugs, ensuring that they know only enough about magic to fight wizards, not enough to use spells themselves."

"Well, whoever is leading them has a lot more magic than that. Someone had to enchant those rods they use," Loreddion grunted. "This Yzor they're talking about. Could that be a leader?'

"Yzor . . . that's so familiar." Nagato wriggled in his bonds, trying to think harder. "What is it about that name?"

The two men walked back toward them, and both wizards fell silent. As Solinari slipped farther and farther into darkness, the outlines of the two men grew vague, blackness blending with the shadows around them.

"You're certain they're coming?" Feren asked.

"Yes, of course. Right behind me," Zann simpered, clearly concerned.

Feren gauged the other man for a moment, and then turned away. He spun back with a burst of energy, fist lashing out to strike the other man across the jaw. His hand met the man's bone with a cracking sound, and Zann fell on his knees. "You're lying," Feren spat, grabbing him by the collar.

"I swear I'm not!" Zann panted, blood trickling from a split lip.

"Yzor will have your tongue if you're a traitor."

"I know! Don't you think I know that?" Zann cried, genuinely frightened.

Feren's face was white in the last rays of the silver moon. "I don't think you know it well enough. Someone told the wizards in Palanthas that we were still active. Someone planted information in Viridia's office, telling her that cabal agents used this area as a drop-off point. Why do you think she chose that silly girl to represent her order? The girl was born in this area. She knows these woods. She could find us," Feren said, shaking Zann hard enough that Nagato could hear the man's bones cracking together.

"I didn't tell them anything. I just brought them here." Zann gestured at the two wizards.

Feren glared at Zann fiercely, then let him go with a shove. "Yzor has no conscience, no mercy, and no fear. Someone in this organization is helping the wizards in Palanthas, and Chemosh help whoever that is when Yzor finds them." Zann shrank back, scuttling on the ground like a crab.

"I've got my hand free," Loreddion whispered. Nagato nearly jumped out of his skin. He'd been concentrating so hard on Zann and Feren's conversation, he'd forgotten all about the other elf. The ropes around Loreddion's wrist were loose, and he slipped his palm past them easily, then pushed it back into place. He gripped the ropes between his fingers, hiding the slack in his hands. "When they come back over here, we'll try to overpower them. I don't just rely on spells. I know how to fight."

"You heard what they said about Yzor," Nagato protested. "They could be here any second and you want to fight?"

Nagato saw Feren walking toward them. When they got close, Loreddion leaped up, drawing the rope between his hands and wrapping it over Feren's head. Feren struggled, but the elf drew the rope tight, kicking the cabal agent around so that he could close his hands against the back of the man's neck.

Zann rushed forward, drawing his copper rod. Loreddion snarled as he jerked Feren to face the him so that the man's body was between Loreddion and any hurled knives.

Following Loreddion's lead, Nagato tottered to his feet timidly. He wrestled with the ropes on his arms, trying to free himself but to no avail. Nagato didn't have Loreddion's strength—didn't have much courage either, the Red Robe gulped, so thank goodness Loreddion did.

Zann froze, unsure what to do. Loreddion jerked the cabal leader back and forth, his ropes cutting into the man's neck. Feren choked, gasping for air. His hands scrabbled at the cords, but Loreddion was stronger. Nagato saw the man's face turning purple, his eyes rolling back behind their lids.

"You're going to kill him!" Nagato yelled.

"That," Loreddion grunted, "is the point." He twisted the ropes tighter, and Feren started to go slack.

Zann finally found his courage, rushing toward them with his rod in his hand. Before Loreddion had a chance to notice, Zann hit him. The copper rod struck Loreddion in the chest, and he screamed. The ropes went slack around Feren's neck for a moment, and the leader managed to scream out a hoarse, "Subdue them!"

"Nagato!" Loreddion yelled, trying to tighten the ropes again despite the pain of the copper rod's nullifying magic. "Do something!" Feren was choking again, but he had gotten one hand beneath the rope while Loreddion was stunned. He tugged wildly on the cord, trying to get it away from his neck so he could draw breath.

Running was difficult with his hands tied behind his back. Nagato had never really thought about how much he used his arms to balance himself until he no longer had the use of them. He threw himself at the charging man, hoping to block his assault.

It worked, but not exactly as he'd planned. Nagato half ran, half fell into his opponent, kicking his feet as he tripped over brush on the ground. Zann yelled, falling with him, and Nagato worked to tangle his legs about the other man's knees. The man yelped, twisting about until his copper rod could reach the wizard, then shoved the end with the red gem into Nagato's rib cage. The pain this time was even sharper than before. He felt, as well as saw, the scarlet glow envelop him. Screams tore from his throat.

The fight was two against one, and Loreddion could no longer control Feren with the rope. Feren arched his back, driving an elbow into Loreddion's stomach. As Loreddion coughed up all the air in his lungs, Feren hunched forward and threw the Black Robe over his back. Loreddion landed on his back, thudding roughly against the hard ground. Free of the cords at last, Feren backhanded Loreddion. Zann and Feren drove their copper rods into Loreddion's flesh, and two bright flashes of red light illuminated the clearing.

"You were foolish to try to escape." Feren rubbed his neck.

Sharp purple bruises were beginning to blossom. "Yzor will see you both tortured for that, I promise you."

"We caught them!" Zann said feverishly. "We stopped them."

"We?" Feren's gaze was icy. He turned to face Zann. He didn't say anything more, but the cold rage on his face spoke volumes. Zann fell back, waving his hands in protest.

Feren didn't have to say anything else, and Zann never saw the knife coming. Zann fell to his knees, and the knife slid out with a thick, squishy noise. "You almost let them escape," Feren said. Zann fell forward on his face, his fingers twitching with the last impulses of his life.

Feren looked away from the body on the ground.

At the edge of the clearing came a soft sound—footsteps. Nagato could tell that they were hurried, breaking through the twigs on the ground with no thought for silence. He rolled toward Loreddion, muscles still spasming in pain. "Loreddion?" he whispered.

Loreddion's eyes did not flutter. He was in terrible shape. Blood trickled from a cut in his cheek where Feren had struck him, and his hands were raw and bloody where they held the rope.

A man dressed in the same black clothing of the cabal agents broke through the clearing, his steps faltering to a halt while he surveyed the scene. Nagato recognized the man at the edge of the clearing as one of the three who attacked him by the barn.

"What happened?" Feren snarled. "Darex, where have you been?"

"Trying to capture the girl wizard. Aruk's dead—he fell out a window trying to escape the flames. Zann was supposed to meet us here, so I came as quickly as I could . . ." Nagato saw the man's eyes fall to the body on the ground. He drew in a deep, shuddering breath and fell silent.

Feren nodded impassively. "I trust you were not followed?"

The man was slow to answer, tearing his eyes up from the corpse of his friend. "No. But they'll come here. They're not stupid," the man panted. "We have to keep moving. There isn't much time."

Feren put his weapon away. "Yzor will be waiting. There's a second team just past the edge of the forest, in the mountains. They'll escort us to the portal."

Nagato stared up at the stone table. It was right in front of him, only inches away, staring him in the face. Suddenly, his eyes fixed upon four letters in the carving. "Oh my goodness," Nagato breathed, inching closer. "That's why the name seemed so familiar. Those letters are scattered through the writing randomly, mixing up the code. If you take those letters out, it makes sense. Loreddion! I get it!"

Loreddion didn't move, still stunned and semiconscious. That didn't dim Nagato's excitement. "If you take out the letters in Yzor's name wherever they appear, the rest of this becomes a description—directions, like a map. You could follow those directions right to the Pillar of Flame." Nagato's keen elf eyes scoured the writing, picking out small details he hadn't noticed before. "Anyone who knew Yzor's name could figure this out."

The Black Robe groaned beside him. Any minute now, Feren and his friend would come for them.

"Loreddion, I need your help." Without his arms, Nagato had little leverage. He nudged Loreddion's limp form with his shoulder, trying to push him closer to the stone. "Loreddion!"

"I feel like I ate sand," Loreddion grunted. "Leave me alone. I'm trying to die."

"You can't die, Loreddion. I need you."

The Silvanesti opened one dark eye. "There's nothing wrong with dying. A lot of people are friendlier after death."

"Loreddion!" Nagato shifted around and kicked him in the leg. "Your hands are free. I need you to touch the stone table. I have to mark these letters on the stone. If Nearra finds it, she'll put together that these letters shouldn't be in the pattern. She'll be able to follow the directions encoded in the rest of the pattern and come after us."

"You've got to be kidding." Loreddion looked down at his chewed and bloody palms. "I can't even move." He groaned, struggling to sit up, but failing miserably. "I feel like someone ran over me with an elephant."

"Touch the stone!"

"What are you talking about?" Loreddion lifted his blood-covered hand, and Nagato grabbed the wizard's black sleeve in his teeth.

Through his teeth, Nagato growled, "Just keep your hand up." He pulled the other elf's arm forward with the strength of his teeth, positioning the fingers over a character on the stone. Then, with his forehead, Nagato knocked Loreddion's hand toward the granite. His palm slapped against a character, drawing out a small cry from the other elf.

"Ow!"

"Shut up! They'll hear you."

"They're almost done." Loreddion muffled another cry as Nagato pushed his hand against the stone again. "What are you doing?"

"Two more, just two more." Nagato marked a third letter in Loreddion's blood.

Loreddion wrestled his hand away. "They're coming."

It was true. Feren crossed the clearing toward them, rod in his hand. He stood in front of the two fallen wizards. "Get them up."

"The Z," Nagato hissed out of the corner of his mouth. "I couldn't reach it. Loreddion, I need you to mark the Z." Forced to fall silent by the approach of the agents, Nagato bit his lip in frustration. The two men grabbed Nagato's arms and hauled him to a very shaky stand. Nagato looked down at Loreddion, but he couldn't tell if Loreddion heard his desperate plea. The Black Robe's head lolled on his shoulders as two others jerked him up. His knees collapsed, and he fell forward onto the table with a sickly-sounding thud.

"This one can hardly walk," Darex said to Feren. "Should I carry him?"

"Tie his hands again, and drag him if you need to," Feren answered. "The Silvanesti dog deserves no better." Feren rubbed his bruised neck again, scowling. His lieutenant did as he was told, tying Loreddion's arms together and attaching a length of cord under his shoulders to drag him along the ground.

Nagato was shoved forward. "Get moving," Darex growled. Dejectedly, Nagato took a step, watching as they dragged Loreddion from the stone table to the floor. The Black Robe was pulled past him. Nagato followed to the edge of the clearing, glancing back to catch a glimpse of the stone table as the last rays of Solinari faded from the black sky.

There, where Loreddion had lain against the stone, Nagato could see blood trickling from a letter.

Z.

CHAPTER

14   Explosions

"That was incredibly clever of you, Nearra," Koi sighed, kicking an acorn along the ground. The gray skies suited the depressed little kender. "Figuring out that pattern on the stone table."

"It wasn't me," Nearra blushed slightly. She walked with her white staff in hand, stepping through the trees lightly. "Whoever marked that name on the stone gave me the leg up I needed to decode the table's pattern."

"I bet that was Nagato. He's smart."

"I don't like to think of Nagato wounded like that. Those letters were marked in blood, Koi. That's definitely not good." Nearra kept the staff close. Morning fog had given way to early afternoon sunlight, which was coming down in slim shafts of gold.

Koi paused and shook her head. "It might have been Loreddion. He's a real fighter, Nearra. He'd have given those cabal agents what for!" She raised her fists and pretended to box one of the trees. "Even without his magic, I doubt he'd give up easy."

Ahead of them, Nearra saw Eric looking back through the trees. "You two keep up." Eric had said little since they'd left the stone table. Koi wasn't much of a travel companion either, with her depressing comments.

Nearra shook her head, blonde hair falling from her loose ponytail. "Some adventure I'm on. Me, my father, and a suicidal kender. I'm up to my ears in 'whee.'"

"Yeah, but at least we sort of know where they're going. We can find them and give our lives in noble sacrifice." Koi considered, kicking an acorn into the deep woods. "Do you think death feels a little like fear? I'm only asking because I'd like to think that at the end, maybe I'd be able to get just the teeniest glimpse of it. Just a look, you know?"

"Why are you so obsessed with fear, Koi?" Nearra asked. "It just seems to depress you."

"Haven't you ever wanted something you couldn't have? Wanted it so badly that it feels like your whole life is empty without it? I think kender are cursed. Thousands of us have died in all kinds of stupid ways just because we don't feel fear. Have I told you about my Uncle Beng? He went to see what a gorgon's face really looks like. We never heard from him again. Or Cousin Jokeeda? She was a tailor. Sounds safe enough, doesn't it? Took a job doing robes for a lich, and now she's a zombie in the Hollowlands." Koi spread her arms in exasperation. "There was another kender in my village by the name of Fiddek Trolltaster. He had a theory that if he ate a piece of a troll, he'd never be hungry again. You don't want to know what happened to him."

Nearra was caught between a laugh and nausea. "That's terrible!"

"It's all terrible. I don't want to end up like that. If I'm going to die, I want it to be on my terms, not because I don't have self-control. Fear is necessary, Nearra. It saves lives—but not kender lives. Do you see why I said that my race is cursed?"

The woods around them were bright with early afternoon

sunlight, and the little path Eric led them down was soft and dark amid green moss. It seemed a happy place, a lovely pastoral setting, but Nearra couldn't help but feel a twinge of sadness.

"Is it really like that in Kenderhome?"

"Yes," Koi sighed, her voice falling. "It's a happy place, Nearra. Wars? We don't care about them. Ogres ravaging Southern Ergoth? Ooh, that's fun! Let's go there! Undead marching in big armies from lost cities, threatening to destroy civilization. 'How interesting.' That's what they say. 'Interesting.' Loreddion was right—it's the kender battle cry." A sad furrow locked the kender's brows. "If fire never returns to Kenderhome, 'interesting' will be all that's left of them. They'll all become wanderers, go off and have dangerous adventures—and die in droves."

"Koi, don't say that. We'll fix this." Nearra patted Koi's shoulder.

Catching sight of her friend's golden hands, Koi paused and managed a rare half smile. "Now that's interesting—your hands. Where did you say that happened?"

"I didn't say. It was a side effect of breaking the curse. One of the wizards who fought us used a pair of magical gauntlets. When the curse was broken, his death revived me, and somehow, his gauntlets were changed by that spell and they sank into my flesh. They don't seem to do anything." Nearra raised her hand and flexed her fingers. "They're just strange."

"Nothing wrong with strange." Koi looked ahead. "Eric's slowing down. I wonder why?"

Nearra's father walked through the trees toward them. "There are clear signs of passage ahead, and I think we have a moment to take a rest. If Nearra's directions are correct, they're going to head into the mountains from here."

"There are a lot of small villages in those mountains. This Yzor might have a hideout in any one of them. It's kind of odd," Nearra mused. "That table was decades old. Maybe older. The carving on the stone was deeply worn."

Koi was taken aback. "That name was on it too, wasn't it? I mean, it was part of the code that hid the directions. Huh. Yzor must be an elf, then. Humans don't live that long."

That night, they slept for only a few hours. Eric woke the two girls before dawn, encouraging them to hurry. Lunch was the only break they got, and all through it, Eric harassed them to make speed. By the time evening rolled around again, Koi was complaining about her sore feet so loudly that Nearra thought the men they were chasing must surely hear them. Still, Eric allowed only a slight rest that night, pulling them from sleep before the two moons were fully in the sky.

Just after dawn, Eric stopped them. They stood in a light mist, the sun igniting the horizon through a thick fog. The forest was still mostly dark, shafts of light fighting their way through to touch the occasional bush or tree. They had entered the mountains, and the ground turned from soft earth to stone. The trees that grew here clustered close together, huddling against the winds that swept the mountain passes. Long vines crawled to the sunlit side of sharp-edged boulders. Koi grabbed one of these vines, holding herself still.

"There's a group down there." Eric pointed to a spark that glimmered in the fog. "I think it's them."

Below them, in a small valley no bigger than a city street, the spark twinkled again. Nearra squinted, trying to get a better view. Several dark forms lay near the twinkling fire. She tried to count them, but the mist faded the shapes in and out of her view. "Four?" she guessed. "Maybe five?"

"Nope. Looks like at least eight to me," Koi corrected her. The kender's vision was sharper than Nearra's. "I see two moving around, but the rest are asleep. It looks like there's some kind of a crate down there with them. I wonder what's in it?"

"Eight. Even if we guess that two are Loreddion and Nagato, that's still six people we'll have to fight to get to them," said Eric the moment Koi stopped talking.

"I can take at least four," the kender declared. Pushing her helmet down squarely, Koi grinned. "More, if I can use my boomstick."

Nearra reached out and tugged the vine that Koi was hanging on. The stone it was attached to shivered, and little puffs of dirt fluttered down. "I don't think that's a good idea. This shelf isn't stable. If you start an earthquake, it might collapse on everyone in that valley."

"Poo." There was a pause, then Koi drew the sap from her belt. She held it in one hand and the baton in the other. "All right, then. Four it is. Can you handle the rest?"

Eric pulled his axe from the sheath on his back, checking the blade for sharpness. "All right. Nearra, we'll have to make the best use of your magic that we can. Those men are certain to have more of those copper rods. We can't allow them to touch you with one, so you need to stay back. Koi and I will move out in front. I can't see well in this mist, but these valleys aren't much more than open cracks in the ground. There will be two sides and two openings, one at either end. The cabal agents can climb this side easily, we can see that it's just shale and rock. The other side is probably the same. Unless there are large rocks down there, this mist will be their only cover."

"I'll stay back here, try to keep behind this boulder, and use my magic from above while you and Koi go in." Nearra tried to sound casual, as if this kind of fight were an everyday occurrence.

"Right." Eric patted her on the shoulder. "Koi, do you know what to do?"

There was a long pause.

"Koi?" Eric and Nearra looked around. The fog was beginning

to clear, and Koi was nowhere to be found. Nearra ducked behind the boulder, checking the vines, looking down the hill. Suddenly, she heard the kender's voice rising out of the little valley.

It took Nearra several moments to recognize Koi's words. She stared over the edge of the valley, down past the boulder to the forms of sleeping men—men who suddenly sat upright, as stunned as Nearra.

"What do you think you're doing, sleeping? Don't you know Yzor's on the way?" Koi yelled. "Yzor could be here any moment! Get up, you lousy dunderheads!" Nearra heard Koi's stick land with a thud against someone's back. "You! Over there! Clean up that mess! You! Run and get some water from the stream! Yzor will be thirsty! And what do you think you're doing, you layabout!"

Thud! Thud! Thud!

"Mishakal, have mercy," Eric choked softly.

"On Koi?" Nearra asked her father. "Or on them?"

In the few heartbeats as the mist was clearing, Nearra could see down into the valley. Two men ran in circles, one grabbing up an empty waterskin while the other desperately piled up blankets and packs. A third stoked the fire frantically, dumping twigs on it as quickly as he could to start the flames. By its light, Nearra could make out two figures near the fire, tied back to back with their hands together. "Nagato and Loreddion."

"Who in the Abyss are you?" A sandy-haired man with the attitude of a leader faced Koi. Just awakened from sleep, he shook his blankets off and reached for his copper rod. "I've never seen you before."

"I'm Yzor's lieutenant! The right-hand man!" Koi edged toward the crate, bustling through the crowd of men. The crate was half her size, made of light balsa wood but reinforced with copper. Without pausing, Koi shoved one hapless fellow forward. She jerked another one by the belt and set him running toward the dying fire. "Yzor's going to be very angry when—"

"*I'm* Yzor's lieutenant!" the man yelled in outrage. He swung his rod at Koi, and she was forced to dive out of its way. "Get her!"

The camp was in complete disarray. Some of the agents, still sleepy and uncertain, froze in place. Two continued running about on Koi's orders. Two more scrambled for their weapons, leaping to fight her. Koi grabbed the edge of the crate at her side, lifting it with a mighty effort. "Well, it was a good try." She shrugged despondently as she jerked the box into the air. "Maybe this is a better idea."

The crate flew past the cabal agents before they could react, whizzing over Nagato's head with barely an inch to spare. It landed squarely in the fire just as the man she'd ordered to tend it dumped another load of brush into the flames. The twigs caught instantly, the dry balsa of the crate only half a heartbeat behind.

"No!" Nagato yelled, rolling to the side and taking Loreddion with him. "Koi!"

But it was too late. The crate split open in the fire, spilling out a load of books and paper, a few odd trinkets, some jewelry, a strange black wand, a helmet made of vallenwood that glowed greenly in the firelight, and several small weapons, and the only thing Nearra recognized in the pile—Nagato's golden wand. The fire burned high, catching the papers and books immediately. The black wand sputtered and flamed, shooting sparks into the air above the fire.

"Be careful! That wand is—" Nagato never finished his sentence. The fire leaped up, swallowing the black wand. The sparks whooshed into a fountain, and the fire exploded in a burst of many-colored light. Yellow and red streams shot past Nearra, blue and green exploding by Eric as he leaped out of the way. Like fireworks, the sparks continued flying up into the air, whirling and shrieking. One of the books in the fire detonated with a thumping sound, thick coils of purple smoke pouring out between the pages. The helmet was the next to go. Struck by a random orange ray of light, it cracked in half. Hissing lightning shot out from the helmet as it broke open, striking the ground and blackening the earth around the fire.

The men in the valley were shaken, but as their leader barked commands over the sounds of the exploding magic items, they started to pull themselves together. One jumped Koi, and she ducked out of the way of his copper rod. Eric charged down the hill toward her, axe in his hand. He swung at one man, chopping toward him the same way he'd chop down a sturdy tree. The man met Eric's blow with his copper rod, and there was a flash. Eric's axe faded, its soft glow dimming as the gem on the rod flashed.

"It may not be magic anymore," Eric said over the hisses and bangs. He twisted the axe in his hand, striking the man across the face with the hilt. "But it's still an axe."

Koi took on the leader and one of his men, dodging back and forth to keep her boomstick away from the swinging copper rods. Another ray of light shot from the fire, nearly striking her, and turned a small tree behind her to stone. "Gah!" Koi yelled, pausing half a second to stare at it.

Standing up behind the boulder, Nearra seized the opportunity. She held out her white staff, chanting words of power as she pointed the end down toward the valley. Anselm's staff made her spell feel different than any spell she'd ever cast. Magic coursed down its length, tingling through her hand, her bones, her body. It was like the staff was an amplifier.

Magic spilled out of the staff, covering the little valley in white mist. The mist coalesced into ice, raining down on everyone in range. Nearra hoped the icy rain would put out the magical fire, but it did little good there. It did coat the ground with a thick coat of ice, slowing the movements of the cabal agents and making every step treacherous.

As more items in the fire broke or caught, stranger and stranger things happened in the valley. Koi saw Loreddion shove off from the ground, hurling himself and Nagato three feet to the side as a ray of green light struck the ground. The earth turned a sickly green, and mossy tendrils shot up through the soil. It spread across part of the campsite, catching Eric by the leg. Vines twisted about the woodsman's trousers, clamping down on his boot and holding him tight. "Nearra!" he yelled, swinging his axe to cut through the vines before they could grow further up his leg. "Can you put out the fire?"

"Cut us free!" Loreddion jerked wildly at the ropes that bound him to Nagato. "We can help!" He glanced back at Nagato scathingly and amended, "I can help!"

Eric turned his next blow toward them, his axe hurtling toward the Black Robe's wrists. It chopped through their bonds, cutting long tears in the velvet sleeves of their robes. At last, they were free, but before the last cord fell away, there was another explosion in the fire. The smoke shifted and took a more solid form. "Something's happening!" Eric yelled, readying his axe again. "Nearra!"

On the hilltop, Nearra struggled to remember more magic, more spells. She felt the old memories rising—memories that weren't hers. Thoughts of blood and fire swept through her mind, encouraging her to unleash a torrent of magic that would destroy everyone in the valley—friend and foe alike. "I'm not that person," she said through gritted teeth, clutching the solid wood of the white staff. "I'm not Asvoria." Nearra tried to force her mind to think of another spell, something less violent and destructive. She chanted a short spell, praying that she could guide the magic before it became too cruel—and felt the white staff responding.

Like an old friend, it lent an unknown strength to her will.

Four small white darts of light flew from Nearra's hand, striking the ground and the vines that entrapped her father's leg. The vines tore into shreds, releasing him. More light exploded from the fire, but it could not pierce the creature of smoke that now stood raging over the explosions. It coalesced into a form ten feet tall, with thick, ropy arms and a mouth filled with ash. The creature roared, howling into the wind of Nearra's ice storm, and the cabal agents scattered before it.

"Oh." Koi jerked to a halt. "Magical explosions, smoke monsters, and assassins." Her eyes widened for a moment, then hardened to a glare. "Why do I still think this is neat!? This is not neat!" Koi shrieked, plowing her metal baton into the stomach of a nearby cabal agent. "Do you hear me? This is terrible! Awful! Completely *uninteresting!*" The kender launched into a frenzy, taking two of the agents by surprise with the ferocity of her assault.

Nagato staggered to his feet, but Loreddion was quicker. Nearra could tell the two wizards were weak from their travel, and more, from the copper rods that had been used unflinchingly on them for days. Nagato rushed toward the fire, scrabbling at the logs and ashes of the broken box while Loreddion backhanded one of the agents who came too close. The Black Robe grabbed the man's rod and plunged it into his side, screaming vengefully, "Now it's your turn!" The man collapsed, and Loreddion clocked him over the head with the rod, sending him to the ground.

Magic continued to explode around them, strange colored rays and sickly looking smoke whirling through the valley. There were still six agents running amok, and the smoke creature roared again with thunderous might. The thought that they were going to lose flashed through Nearra's mind like a lightning bolt, and she couldn't push it away.

Nearra saw the two men fighting Koi joined by a third, while

Eric fought two cabal agents one-on-one. Eric's first opponent bested him, knocking aside the woodsman's axe and shoving him to the ground. Before Eric could reach his weapon, the man was on him, a long dagger twisting in the agent's hand. Above them, the second attacker fighting Nearra's father grinned and watched, readying his weapon.

In the fire, the smoke creature's ropy hands swept down and caught up Nagato and Loreddion, lifting them into the air. Nagato screamed, and Nearra saw what he had been scrabbling through the fire to retrieve—his small golden wand. He spoke a word, and bubbles came out, pouring all over the smoke monster. They burst into small pockets of water, but not nearly enough to put out the fire that spawned the beast.

The smoke beast roared again, and Nearra saw the hem of Nagato's red robe begin to glow and smoke from the flame just below his feet. Two spells leaped into Nearra's mind. One would send the smoke monster back to wherever it came, freeing Nagato and Loreddion before they were burned alive. The other was a stun spell that affected an area, blinding or disabling every-one on the ground around Eric and Koi. She thought she could aim it carefully enough that it would affect only the six cabal members they were fighting, and they might gain an advantage for at least a few moments. Neither spell was perfect, but both offered an opportunity to survive—for half of her friends.

Nearra looked down and made her decision. She raised the staff high and shouted, *"Amon azur!"* White light poured from her staff, radiating across the valley. It struck the creature of smoke, piercing the beast's solid smog and tearing it apart the way mist breaks before the sun. The monster screamed, its corporeal form shredding piece by piece as the fire dimmed. Loreddion struck out with the copper rod, and it roared again, but this time the sound was tiny and weak. Nearra kept her staff pointed down toward the creature, praying that the spell would hold. Nagato's robe puffed into flame, the edge of it catching fire as the monster waved him over the blazing wood below. The Red Robe screeched and kicked desperately, trying to put out the flames.

She spared a glance for her father, expecting to see him in dire straits, and something caught her eye. An arrow, launched from the other edge of the valley, came shooting out of nowhere to strike the cabal agent before he could harm Eric. The man dropped his dagger and clutched at the arrow, his mouth moving in surprise. He reared up, eyes searching futilely for the archer, then fell dead at Eric's feet. The second attacker facing Eric backed away in surprise. Nearra saw her father gasp in relief, scrabbling for his axe. Nearra felt cold, realizing what her choice had almost meant. She had nearly lost him.

Nearra saw two figures through the haze of morning fog and the billowing clouds of the smoke monster. One of them nocked another arrow into her bow, taking aim at Koi's targets. Nearra recognized her mother's distinctive grayish blonde hair, the pull of her muscular arms against the string of the hunting bow. But there was also a second figure atop the little ravine. Jirah charged forward, a knife in one hand and a makeshift shield in the other—just like their days on Icefire's ship.

Jirah leaped down onto Koi's four attackers, taking one on herself with a flashing clang of her shield. She slammed the solid wall of it directly into the man's face, watching as he fell to the side, stunned and half conscious. Koi was still screaming as she fought, not noticing Jirah's presence at all. Nearra saw the kender falter, even with Jirah's help. One of her opponents took advantage of this, leaping past Jirah and plunging a short dagger into the kender's side.

Koi's falling arm trapped the dagger before the man could pull it out. Jirah lashed him with the edge of her knife, cutting cleanly through his tunic. Blood tinged the man's chest a terrible scarlet red, and he staggered away, hands empty. Koi stumbled, still growling, and waved her baton at the other two men. She smiled as though pleased about something despite the blood running down her side.

Seeing what happened to his friend, a second man turned from the group attacking Koi and fled. Nearra could hear him yelling to the others to follow. One did, leaving only the sandy-haired man facing Koi and Jirah, and Eric's sole remaining attacker.

With a graceful movement, Jirah blocked the sandy-haired man's quickly thrusting dagger. The copper rod in his other hand shimmered, gem twinkling, but Jirah paid it no mind. Jirah blocked his every thrust with her shield and twisted her knife through each opening in his guard. She had the better of him—for now.

The smoke demon roared again, but the sound was a pale shadow of its earlier rage. As Nearra held her spell on it, it shrank into thin wisps. Smoke poured from its open mouth. Loreddion's feet struck the ground roughly, the arm holding him losing the power to keep him aloft. Thinking quickly, he grabbed a bucket of water standing nearby and dumped it over the dying fire. As the fire hissed into nothingness, the monster whimpered and sank lower. The last strands of its essence dissipated in soft poofs of smoke, dumping Nagato unceremoniously onto the now damp pile of wood and ash.

Lanni's arrow pierced the sandy-haired man's shoulder. He cried out in pain, grasping his companion and thrusting the man between himself and Lanni. Another arrow flew with amazing accuracy and caught the man in the chest. Tugging lightly at it, the man staggered and fell to the ground. Frightened at last, the sandy-haired man turned and ran.

"Go after him, Jirah!" Lanni cried.

"No!" Eric roared, grabbing his daughter roughly. "What are you doing here? I told you to stay home!"

Nearra rushed forward, tripping hurriedly down the hill toward her sister.

"I'm not feeling too well," Koi muttered. The kender touched her side, where the hilt of the dagger still protruded from the leather and mail of her chestplate. Koi's legs lost their strength, tipping her toward the ground, but Nearra caught her. She lowered the kender gently.

"You did great," Nearra said reassuringly.

"I was terrible," Koi contradicted her. "Not a single scrap of fear. I tried so hard to find it." She coughed, wincing as it jarred the dagger that was thrust through her armor. "So hard. But there was nothing at all inside me. Just an emptiness. It all just seemed really curious, the explosions and that tremendous smoke monster. Fascinating. Awful." A slow tear ran down her nose.

Loreddion and Nagato came over from the fire, the Red Robe trying desperately to brush the wet ash stains from his clothing. Eric shook Jirah again, and the knife fell from her hand. "What are you doing here?" He was angry, his face turning as red as Koi's blood. Nearra tore Jirah out of his hands, pulling her sister into a tight hug. She could feel Jirah trembling, her face as white as chalk.

"She came with me." Lanni walked down the ravine, stringing her bow over her shoulder. Eric's fury turned on his wife, but Lanni stood as tall and straight. She faced Eric's wrath easily, crossing her arms in front of her chest. "You needed us, and we came. If we hadn't, Koi would be lying there with much worse than a wound. And you probably wouldn't be getting up again either." Lanni's eyes flashed. "We are both part of this family as much as you and Nearra are, Eric. You're not leaving us behind."

Eric rumbled, opening and closing his mouth without saying anything, but also not admitting his defeat.

"One got away," Lanni said. "We cannot stay here. They will bring reinforcements, and we do not have the capacity to handle another group. Not with Koi injured and two of our wizards still affected by those copper rods."

Eric nodded. "There's a village over that rise. We'll take Koi there and see if we can find a healer."

"What if that's where the cabal was going?" Nearra asked, holding her sister close.

"We'll deal with that," he answered, "when we get there."

CHAPTER

15   A Light in the Darkness

Jirah brushed hot tears from her eyes, struggling to see the ground on which she was walking. If it wasn't for Nearra's arm around her shoulder, she might not be walking at all. Eric's voice still rang in her mind, muddled somehow with the voice of Macus, the fat cleric at the Temple of Paladine. *Useless. Worthless.*

"Are you all right?" Nearra asked her softly. The white staff flashed back and forth in Nearra's other hand as they walked, thumping softly on the earth beneath them.

"I will be," Jirah lied. She looked up into her sister's familiar blue eyes. "Thanks for sticking up for me."

"I'm your sister, remember?" Nearra chided. She squeezed Jirah and looked ahead of them toward Eric and Lanni. The woodsman walked with his axe in his hands, his face dark with suppressed anger. Lanni strode between him and his daughters, bow over her shoulder and hands stuffed in her pockets with an attitude of uncaring ease.

In front of them, Nagato walked beside Loreddion. The Red Robe fussed softly, occasionally turning to Eric to check his directions. Loreddion neither asked nor wavered, carrying the wounded kender in his arms as if she were a child. Koi curled against his chest. Any offers to help him were met with a snarl.

The trees had returned on the other side of the mountain rise, building to thick valleys of evergreens and wide swaths of grass as high as Jirah's waist. The path they had been following twisted onto a broken and ancient road. Rocks stuck out between trampled grasses, showing that someone occasionally used this route for travel. That didn't make Jirah feel any safer.

"There's a building ahead, up through those trees," Nagato said. He led them off the path, out of the bright noon sunshine. He was right, of course. Though as they approached, Jirah thought it looked less like a building and more like a pile of rocks with the remnants of a roof attached. A small stone fence still encircled the building, though parts were collapsed and easy to step over. The iron gate was rusty and immobile, and any trace of a cobblestone path had long ago vanished into moss and weeds. The stone fence continued into the woods, circling something that may have once been a gigantic yard, but was now swallowed up in thick forest. "I think the road leads toward the village. If we follow it, we'll find people."

"Then we'll stop here." Loreddion stepped over a low part of the stone, treading up to the crumbling house. Eric followed, and slowly, the others did so as well. They walked around the ivy-covered walls, searching for a way inside. At last, Jirah caught sight of a door underneath some of the foliage. Loreddion showed absolutely no fear of the place, kicking in the shoddy door with one booted foot. Koi shivered in his grasp, and the Black Robe paused to adjust her against his chest. "She can't be carried any further. She's getting weak. Hasn't cursed at me for nearly an hour."

Afternoon sun slanted down through the cracks and gaping holes in the old ceiling, patterning the floor in wide circles of light. Dust reflected these shafts, making them solid. The room was large, a fallen wall widening it even more through the rear of the house. The floor, built with thick wood, was rotting in places and covered with mold where rain weakened it over the years. "Walk carefully," Lanni nagged, frowning. She tested each step gingerly, then made her way to a sheltered area beneath a partially collapsed wall. "The floor is sturdy here. We can make camp." She spread out a blanket.

Loreddion sank to one knee, gently placing Koi on the blanket. Checking the wrapping on her wound, Loreddion snuggled Koi's cloak about her like a cocoon. He caught Lanni's dark eyes. "Watch her." It was as much a plea as a threat. Lanni seemed to understand, and patted the dark elf's hand before he withdrew it..

Eric walked from window to window, testing the soundness of the structure. Nagato stood by the doorway, wrapping his arms around himself and shivering lightly. Nearra stayed with him, waiting for Eric to beckon them in. Jirah didn't hesitate—she walked to her mother's side and knelt beside the wounded kender. Something held her attention, drew her closer. Jirah didn't understand why, but she felt a need to be there.

Jirah heard the others talking, making plans to go to the village and seek help. Eric was telling Loreddion to remain here and protect Koi, and the Black Robe was arguing. Everyone, it seemed, was arguing—except Koi, who lay still and silent beneath her blue cloak. The kender's eyes were closed, her face pale. Jirah pulled aside the cloak and looked down at the blood-touched cloth that staunched Koi's wound. Jirah explored it hesitantly with her fingers, feeling the dampness of the rag and the stiffness where the blood was dry.

The others were still picking at one another, trying to decide who would stay and who would leave, but Jirah didn't hear any of it. Her hand was tingling. The sensation flickered across her fingertips. She flexed her muscles, pressing her hand to the wound, and tried to reach whatever the feeling was that drew her there. "Please," Jirah whispered, looking down at pale, silent Koi. "Help her. Help—"

She never finished the thought. A rough hand on her shoulder jerked her back. "What are you doing?" Eric glared down at her. Jirah could see Lanni right behind him.

"I was just . . . checking the wound."

"Eric, leave her alone." Lanni pushed past her husband. "Jirah, you had such a strange look on your face. Were you trying to heal her?" She knelt down and touched her daughter's face.

"Lanni, don't be ridiculous. She's not a priestess," Eric scoffed.

"Leave her alone," Lanni repeated. She kept her eyes locked with her daughter. "Try again, Jirah."

Tentatively, Jirah reached out to touch the wound again. She heard Nearra and Nagato come closer, their footsteps light on the rotting boards. She could feel their eyes staring down at her, but most of all, she could fee her father's disapproval, a fire just waiting for a spark.

She closed her eyes, trying to find that strange tingle again. Jirah held her breath, reaching deep into herself. Where was it? What had drawn her there? What was it that had almost spoken inside her soul?

Nothing answered. After a long moment, Jirah opened her eyes. She didn't have to say anything. They already knew.

Eric snorted, eyes flashing. "See, Lanni? You shouldn't encourage the girl. It's a waste of time."

Lanni colored, lowering her head. She reached to pull Koi's cloak back around the kender, tucking it beneath the small girl's arms to keep her warm. Loreddion, Nearra, and Nagato simply turned their attention away, continuing the argument over who should go into the village. Eric grabbed Jirah and pulled her to her feet.

REE SOESBEE

"Help your mother. Don't waste her time or mine with these flights of fancy, Jirah. You gave up your magic. You'll never be a wizard, or a priestess, for that matter. If you have a destiny anymore, it's going to have to be something else." Eric's frown deepened from anger to pity, which was far worse. "You don't have to lie anymore."

She fought back the tears. "I wasn't lying."

"Jirah," Eric said, his voice stern again. "Enough."

Loreddion knelt down beside Koi, taking the kender's hand in his. "Koi?" The kender roused slightly, eyes fluttering. When she smiled, Loreddion lowered his head to stare ferociously down at his friend. "You listen to me. I'm going to the village now, and I'm going to bring help if I have to turn them into toads and carry them here."

Koi chuckled. The sound had a burble of blood in it. "Why do you care?"

Silver hair fell into his eyes. "You saved my life when we were the captives of the cabal. If it hadn't been for you, I might be dead. I don't want to owe anything to a kender, see. Now, to make sure you don't die before I get back, I want you to make a deal with me. You stay here, and you stay alive, and I'll repay the saving of my life. I will find a way to make you feel fear, Koi. Genuine, real fear."

The kender started to sit up, then tensed in pain and fell back again. "You can do that?" she whispered.

The Black Robe clenched his fist. "If you trust me and do what I tell you to do when I tell you to do it, yes."

"Done," the kender said immediately, reaching to shake his hand.

Loreddion rose in a swirl of black robes and headed for the door.

"Wait," Eric called to him. "We haven't decided who's going yet."

"Like I actually care what you decide, Eric." Loreddion stalked out the broken door into the sunlight, leaving the others to scurry in his wake. Koi sighed and closed her eyes again, but her face was rosier, and her cheeks didn't seem as waxy.

Lanni pushed an empty waterskin into Jirah's grasp, and her attention snapped back. "I'm sure there's water here somewhere. See if you can find a stream or a well, and bring some back to me."

Jirah clutched the empty skin to her chest, feeling a hole in her heart. She walked slowly toward the rear of the building. A glance told her that no one was paying any attention at all. Why should they be? Koi was seriously hurt. She might die. And there was nothing she could do about it. Her father was right. She might as well accept it; she'd given up any chance of ever having magic. Paladine didn't want her, and she had no talent at all. Still, the thought kept niggling in the back of her mind: What had that tingly feeling been when she looked down at Koi?

The more Jirah explored, the more she thought this might not be a house at all. There was no upper story other than one small tower to the west. Owls and other birds made their roosts there, covering the stairwell in sticky white droppings. Jirah didn't do much exploring there, other than sticking her head up through the trapdoor to peer into the rooftop chamber. A broken bell lay against the wall, its brass clapper stuck in a thickly built raccoon's nest. Jirah tromped back down the stairs.

She found one room that might have been a pantry, but a mudslide had covered the floor in thick layers of earth. If there had ever been a well there, it long ago overflowed and covered itself in debris and mud. Jirah dug about a bit with a stick, but she couldn't find the well among the mire.

Not wanting to go back and face her parents so soon, Jirah continued wandering through the house. She entered a back room through a fallen oak door that looked as though it had been chewed on by generations of rats. The small room looked as though it might have been an office long ago, with a square desk broken and covered in mold. Jirah walked to the arch-shaped window and looked out at the forest beyond. Trees clustered up against the back wall, thrusting their branches against the stone. One had even broken the window long ago and grown into the room. There were leaves piled up under the window, and it looked like a squirrel used the area under the desk as a temporary storage bin for nuts. Jirah knelt down to look at the little nest, then chuckled and stood, leaning slightly on the desk to catch her balance.

The desk shifted under her weight, and Jirah felt the floor move dangerously. She grabbed at the desk, but the top of it crumbled away even as there was a sharp crack from the floorboards underneath. There was a terrible ripping sound and the floor gave way. Jirah felt herself suddenly hurled downward into the unknown. She grabbed for the overhanging branch and caught it with one hand.

The crash echoed through the room. Jirah found herself swinging precariously over a dark hole, staring down at the remnants of the broken desk and moldy floorboards at least twenty feet below. Her feet dangled wildly as she tried to get a better hold on the branch, but she could feel it sagging, breaking under her weight. The waterskin fell from her hand as she scrabbled through the leaves, trying to find a more solid grip, and she heard it bounce off the broken boards beneath her. Jirah drew in a breath to scream for help, but before she could, the branch snapped and she fell.

Jirah landed among the broken boards with a terrible din. She lay there for a moment, astonished to still be alive. Gingerly, she moved her arms and legs, testing for any broken bones, and found none. "Ugh." Jirah sat up. Her elbow was scuffed, and there was blood across her shirt where a sharp piece of board had come close to impaling her, but she wasn't seriously injured. After a moment, her eyes adjusted to the dim light.

She was in a large underground cellar, a shaped cave that appeared to have been built into the foundation of the house. It was dark and damp down here, and she could hear the sound of water trickling along the stone walls. Jirah picked herself free of the rubble and noticed passages leading out of the room into darkness. Jirah looked up at the wide hole above her. No matter how loudly she yelled, nobody was going to hear her. She would just have to find her own way out.

Feeling along the wall at the edge of the room, Jirah made her way toward one of the openings. "Maybe there's a torch on the wall, or a lantern or . . . ugh." Her hand slipped into an alcove. It was dark, and there seemed to be spiderwebs between her fingers along with a smooth round stone. Jirah grasped at the stone curiously and pulled it out, turning it to see it better in the light.

It was a skull.

Jirah squeaked, jumping back into the circle of light. The skull fell from her hand, rolling across the floor before her as she skittered out of the way. Now that her eyes were getting used to the darkness, she could pick out details that had been hidden before. There were many long slots in the wall, each one containing a withered and desiccated corpse. Jirah could swear that the shadows in the eyes of the skeletons followed her, staring at her in the little circle of light.

"This is definitely not a house. Not unless the owners routinely buried each other in the cellar." She shivered.

Gulping, she looked up again, but the ceiling was far above her, wholly out of her grasp. There was nowhere to go but forward—into the darkness. Jirah built up her courage and cleaned off one of the desk legs, breaking it away from the rest of the rubble. The wood was dry and brittle. Jirah gathered a few more scraps of dry leaves and twigs, putting some crackly mold into a hole in the desk leg. With another piece of wood and a string, she twisted a thin stick as fast as she could in the hole. After a moment, the moss smoked, and sparks flew. Jirah blew on it carefully until it caught fire.

Armed at last with a torch, Jirah moved slowly down one of the passages in the direction that she guessed was closest to the front of the house. She paused only to pick up her mother's waterskin. "She'd be so mad at me if I forgot that. What is this place?"

Her voice echoed through unexplored passageways. "It's a graveyard," she answered herself, leaning in to stare at one of the withered corpses in an alcove. Some corpses were nothing but bone, others still had skin and muscle attached beneath rotting robes. Jirah reached out tentatively and felt the material of one. It was a faded red, stained with water damage. Something skittered away from the feet of the skeleton, and Jirah took a step back.

"Only a mouse," she chided herself.

The passage ended in a small, circular room that Jirah guessed must be right beneath the main room upstairs. The walls here had once been painted, but were now faded, with chunks of the rock lying in broken piles at the base of the wall. She saw the image of a great bird with red feathers still covering the floor. It was faded in patches beneath pools of stagnant water. The room smelled funny, like moss and years-old dead things, a smell Jirah remembered from the wizard Tudyk's tomb. She could make out a few other paintings—men and women dancing in a fire, roses entwined together, marching dwarves with massive hammers, robed figures that looked like wizards casting great spells. The rest of it was blurred from water damage or chipped away so deeply that none of the original paint remained.

On the far side of the room was a passageway that was not like the one she'd entered. Instead of being flat, the floor there sloped upward, and she could see faint touches of light far up

PILLAR OF FLAME

159

the hallway as if it ended somewhere near the sun. Relieved, Jirah stepped out to cross the circular room, torch in hand, her footsteps plunking softly against wet stone. She could hear soft voices above. She could pick out a few of Lanni's words, and the reassuring tone. It was meant for Koi, Jirah was sure, but it made her feel better too.

Jirah walked cautiously, even though the floor was packed earth under cobblestone, as secure as possible. Her muscles ached from the fall, and she could still feel the burning area in her side where the wood panel had torn her clothes and cut her side. She hurried across the little chamber, keeping the waterskin close to her chest and holding the torch high.

When she reached the center of the room, her torch sputtered. Jirah paused to look at it, afraid that the fire was going out—but instead it grew rapidly. It swelled enough to swallow the entire torch in a rapidly growing ball of flame. Jirah shook the torch, trying to put out the fire, but it only grew larger. Before her eyes, it completely enveloped the torch as well as her hand.

Shocked, she screamed softly, opening her hand to drop the torch. Even as the wood fell away, the fire wrapped itself around her fingers. It felt warm and soft, not terrible at all. Like a cat, the fire warmed and purred against her fingers, snapping and flickering as it grew larger. Jirah shook her hand frantically, trying to shake off the flame. It clung to her skin, not burning her, but surrounding her. It grew half as large as she was. The flames lit the room in weird shadows and spurts of arcing fire. Shadows raged against the walls like warriors in battle. Jirah caught a glimpse of dark images of herself leaping back and forth in darkness, fueled by her wild swatting at the fire.

The flame flared once more and grew as tall as she was. Her hand was trapped in the center of it, white-hot flame springing between her fingers, arcing over the larger form from the tips of her fingers. She found herself facing a humanoid-shaped flame that was exactly her own size and shape. Jirah tried to pull back, to jerk her hand away, but it held her fast with titanic strength. The fire danced with her, imitating every movement, battling with her over control of her hand. Just as Jirah feared the blaze would wrap around her and burn her to death, the fire turned from red to black, sucking inward with the sound of feathers brushing against a strong wind.

Her hair blew forward, and leaves and debris from throughout the cellar rushed toward her, drawn into the fire by the strong wind. Jirah's second scream was encompassed by the rushing sound, lost in the flicker of wild, dancing fire and summer-hot wind. And, in the midst of all this, Jirah felt it again—the tingle. It spread from the hand engulfed in the fire, swelling throughout her body with such a rush that Jirah felt her body tense and arch in its wake. Wild magic coursed in her veins, burning, searing in her blood. Visions swam before her eyes, and languages she did not know whispered into her ears.

Then, in an instant, the fire went out. Each flame was sucked down into a single point, and the radiant light coalesced once more on the palm of her hand. It was brilliant, too bright to look at and so hot that it seared the skin of her palm until she felt her entire hand might turn to ash—then, abruptly, it went out.

Jirah was plunged into darkness.

Heart racing, Jirah fell backward, striking her head and shoulder against a stone wall. She lay stunned and limp and just tried to breathe. Whatever had just happened, it was over. The stone was reassuringly stable, slightly damp, and cold. The incredible light was gone except for white spots swimming in front of her eyes. She blinked them away and tried to see the room again as the feeling in her body returned. Panting in fear, Jirah reached to brush the hair out of her eyes, but stopped her hand when she noticed an odd weight already there. Something cold and flat pressed against her palm.

She clutched it, not understanding what she was holding, and pushed herself to stand against the wall. Her legs felt like jelly and her head throbbed. Everything seemed distant, as though she were moving through a dark fog. She could see the passageway leading up into the light and followed it a few hesitant steps. It ended in something that looked like the back of a painting, with light leaking through along the edges.

By the light at the edge of the doorway, Jirah looked down at her palm. The hand wasn't burned, as she had feared, but whole and pink. In the center lay a medallion made entirely of gold on a long chain of the same material. It was smooth and perfectly round with markings along the edge in a language Jirah didn't understand. Radiating from the center of the medallion was a carefully inscribed spiral, twisting in loop after loop until the final span of it met the edge of the medallion. Jirah turned it over and found the spiral repeated on the other side, twisting this time inward until it vanished into itself at the very center of the circle.

Jirah reached out with her other hand and pushed open the doorway. It swung easily, making a slight scraping noise as the hinges cleared themselves of years of dirt. The room was the one she remembered, with Lanni kneeling over Koi just a few feet away and Eric standing by the windows on the far side. She could hear her father's voice saying, "Why won't they come inside?" But his words made no sense.

"Mama?" she said softly. She felt strange, everything fuzzy, and all she could do was hold out her hand toward Lanni with the unspoken question on her lips.

Lanni screamed as her daughter fell forward through the opening in the wall.

REE SOESBEE

162

CHAPTER

16 EBONHOLDE

I don't understand why you can't just go in. There's nothing wrong in there. It's a bit dangerous, but the floor of the first room seems sturdy," Nearra tried to convince the village leader, Martin. Seven of the villagers stood with her, whether cowed by Loreddion or persuaded by Nearra's story of Koi's injury, Nearra wasn't sure.

Just down the road a ways, they'd found a village called Ebonholde, a small town half the size of Ravenscar, made up mostly of trappers and woodsmen. Martin was in charge—or so everyone they'd been able to find had told them. The big man's muscles were thick and ropy from hard work, his jaw square and stern. Nearra guessed that he was older than Eric, or at least more careworn, for his face was deeply lined. He crossed his arms before his chest and stared levelly at the ruins of the little building. "We don't go inside," Martin said brusquely. "Nobody ever has. Not from this village."

"That's ridiculous." Nearra shook her head firmly. "Someone built that house. Someone used to live in it."

Martin chewed his cheek thoughtfully. Around him, the other villagers whispered to themselves in short bursts. "Nobody ever lived there. It's haunted," he finally replied.

"Haunted?" Loreddion sounded as if he wanted to believe them.

Nearra pressed her lips together, facing Martin. "My friend is in that house, and she's hurt. You said you could help her."

"Yup," Martin said. He was taking a defensive tone, glaring at them both as if they'd tricked him. "But you didn't say where."

"Then help her!" Nearra blurted out.

Martin pointed at the building, jabbing one thick finger in the air like a banner. "I ain't goin' in there!"

Loreddion spun on his heel, marching relentlessly toward the building. "Then I'll bring her out."

He was too slow. Eric stepped cautiously over the broken door of the building, Koi's cloak-wrapped figure in his arms. Behind him came Lanni, holding Jirah tightly against her. Nearra stared, blinking, at her sister. Jirah looked horrible—skin pink as a lobster, as though she'd gotten a sudden sunburn, her black hair jutting out above her shoulders as though she'd been through a windstorm. Nearra had no opportunity to ask if her sister was all right, for the villagers began muttering again at the string of people emerging from their haunted house. Eric lay Koi down on the ground near the headman.

"There, she's out of the house. For the last time, help her," Nearra told Martin.

He did not answer, but knelt down to open the cloak and study Koi's wound. An elderly woman sat down beside him, unrolling a small parcel of bandages and herbs. The others clustered close, though they kept a respectful distance from the Black Robe.

"What happened to you?" Nearra hissed softly to Jirah. Her sister shivered in her mother's arms, eyes wide and fixed on Koi. "Mama, what happened?"

Lanni answered quietly, "She went exploring in the house and came out some kind of hidden passage we hadn't noticed before. She hasn't said a word since she came out of there, but she doesn't seem hurt in any way." Lanni squeezed her younger daughter worriedly.

"It's not a house," Martin replied. He looked up at them while the woman unwound Koi's bandages. "It's a church. That whole area there is a graveyard." His sweeping gesture took in the building and a huge swath of the path and forest beyond. "You go poking about in those trees, you'll find the headstones. I'm told there's a hidden crypt out there too. The kids found it when I was just a wee babe. It got sealed up by the villagers, and they were right to do it too."

Shifting uneasily, Martin frowned down at the old medicine woman tending to Koi. One of the villagers supplied more details without being asked. "That chapel's haunted by the ghost of the god it once tended! The Cataclysm killed the priest! Now there's no god there, no god for us at all. We don't go near it now, or we'll be cursed too." There was a general murmur of assent, and one of the villagers spat on the ground in superstitious fervor.

"Who . . . who was the god it served?" These were the first words out of Jirah's mouth, and they were said so hesitantly that Nearra almost missed them.

Martin shrugged. "Dunno. God's name was forgotten long ago, along with all his symbols and claptrap. They tore it down when the priests were killed. Abandoned. And now it's haunted, they say, by the people buried there and by the god himself—because we forgot him."

"Martin," the old woman called, and the headman knelt down again. "I don't think I can help her. This wound is too deep. Her lung's punctured, and there's been a lot of bleeding. I can give her herbs for the pain, maybe try to sew the wound together, but it won't help her." Suddenly feeling all eyes on her, the medicine woman stammered, "She's dying."

Loreddion flared up, his hands punching forward as though he might strike someone. "She's not dying! If you don't help her, I swear I'll teach you the true meaning of pain. This building will be the last one standing in your village. I'll raze the ground for miles. Ebonholde will be a stain on the ground and nothing more."

Nagato grabbed Loreddion before he could work himself into a real frenzy, but the dark elf tore himself away and raised his fist to the old woman. "I'll see you all dead before Koi breathes her last."

"You leave her alone." Though Martin didn't act intimidated by the Black Robe's threats, Nearra saw the knuckles of his fists whitening. "She's the best healer in our village. If Mathelda can't help you, then you can't be helped."

Lanni reached to help Nagato restrain Loreddion, who looked like he was about to attack the headman. One of the villagers stepped up beside Martin with a sharp hoe in his hand and a severe look to his weathered features.

Nearra didn't notice when Jirah slipped out of Lanni's grasp. While the others were arguing, Jirah bent down by the unconscious kender. Her eyes stared straight ahead as if they saw nothing, and her hand reached toward Koi's wound. Nearra caught a glimpse of something golden in her sister's palm, sparkling in the late afternoon sunlight. "Jirah, what are you doing?"

Eric reached for his younger daughter. "She's making a fool of herself. Lanni, get the girl away." As the rest of the group turned to look, Jirah touched Koi.

Nearra felt a sudden rush of air blowing her long blonde hair out toward her sister. The others felt it too—cloaks billowed and robes fluttered in the newly birthed wind. For an instant, Nearra thought she saw a spark of light around Jirah's hand, a redness shaped vaguely like an axe blade or a bird's wings. Thinking that her sister had set the kender on fire for some insane reason, Nearra cried out and lifted her staff, preparing a spell to dampen any flame.

But no fire appeared, and the light around Jirah's palm flickered only for a few moments, and was gone. Eric, Loreddion, Lanni, and Nagato stood around the kender, frozen. The villagers gasped, some jumped back, and one screamed and clutched the man beside her. The old healer, still kneeling by Koi's side, widened her eyes in surprise. Jirah's hand fell away, and she slumped backward. Eric caught her roughly, pulling her to the side.

"What did you do? What are you holding?" Eric wrenched Jirah's arm up and pulled open her fingers. Inside her palm was a strange medallion that Nearra had never seen before. It was gold and shining, and the symbol of a strange spiral traced its way from one side to the other of the flat disk in Jirah's hand. "Where did you get that? What is it? Jirah, from all your years in my house, you should know better than to use strange magic items without finding out what they are first!"

Jirah tore herself away from her father, clutching the disk tightly to her chest. "I found it in there." She pointed back at the temple. "And I was going to show it to you, but you were all out here, and I thought . . . I thought . . . Koi needed help and I just . . ." Her words trailed away.

"She's healed." The soft voice of the old woman at Koi's side drew all eyes downward again. The cloak was open, and the kender's tunic was lifted to show her ribs where the dagger had been thrust into her side. The bandages—stained red and stiff—were pulled away, but there was no wound underneath. Koi's skin was marked only with a light scar, edged with the clear whitish pink of new flesh. "It's a miracle."

Koi's eyes snapped open, and she took a deep, shuddering breath. "Oi," she said softly. "It's morning already." She tried to focus on

167

the people around her, rolling her eyes back and forth until they fixed on Loreddion. "What's going on?"

Martin was staring at Jirah as though she'd just grown a second head. One of the female villagers rushed forward and touched the kender's side. A man cried out once in alarm, and a third fell to his knees in fear. Martin stepped forward and grabbed Jirah's wrist. He didn't twist it, as Eric had, but only held it questioningly until she lowered it on her own.

"You received this inside that chapel?" he asked.

"Yes."

"And you healed this girl?" Martin indicated the kender with a jerk of his hand. "You used some magic, some strange power?"

Nearra shivered. "My sister isn't a wizard. Paladine himself took magic away from her."

"Paladine?" A gasp went up from the villagers. Martin raised a hand to quiet them, releasing Jirah gently. Loreddion pushed his way past Lanni and Eric, kneeling down beside Koi. The kender would have none of it, untangling herself from the cloak and grabbing Loreddion's shoulder to pull herself to her feet. The Black Robe snorted, a faint smile marking his hair-shrouded features, and shoved her hand away to stand himself.

"I'm not a wizard." Jirah stared at Martin. "I don't have any magic items or strange tricks."

"Then why did you touch her?"

Jirah hesitated. With a small shrug, she answered, "It just seemed like the right thing to do."

"She was called," whispered the medicine woman kneeling where Koi had lain. "The god of that chapel drew them here. He touched her. He's given her a gift."

"That can't be true, Mathelda!" one of the farmers frantically called out to the old woman, clutching his hoe close to his chest as if to hide behind it. "There ain't no gods left on Krynn! They've left us, you know that. All the true healers are gone."

"Then you explain it, Berst," she snapped back at him. The old healer stood, wiping her hands on her apron. "That wound should've killed, but it closed right up when that girl touched it. I've never seen the like. In all my years, I'd have never believed it if I hadn't seen it myself." She placed her hands on her chubby hips, taking a matronly stance. "We've seen that girl perform a miracle here, and there ain't no other explanation."

Haltingly, and with many pauses as he attempted to make sense of it, Martin said, "Now hold on, Mathelda. I've heard rumors from the big cities that the gods are back. We've all talked to the tradesmen who come and buy our furs. There are priests in Palanthas now. And maybe elsewhere." His eyes fell on Jirah.

"She's a prophet," Nearra heard someone in the crowd whisper. Another voice hissed, "She's a holy messenger, sent to bring the gods back to Ebonholde!"

"The gods have returned!" an eager young man cried out. He started waving his hands in excitement, face reddening. "Praise be!"

"We've seen false prophets before," snarled an older fellow who reminded Nearra a bit of her father. The man shook his head, tapping a skinning knife at his belt with a nervous hand. "They try to steal our wealth, and they lie to us to get it." Some of the people nodded slowly, but others seemed unconvinced.

"Please." The young man stepped forward, catching Jirah's arm. "My mother is ill, back in the village. Can you heal her?"

After a moment, another woman pushed through the crowd, kneeling down and grabbing at the hem of Jirah's tunic. "I have a daughter who is pregnant. Will you come and bless the birth?"

"You must help us," called out other voices as people began to crowd around Jirah. "My father . . . my sister . . . I was injured last spring . . . can you heal me . . . heal us . . . help us . . ." others rumbled, clustering around the man with the skinning knife, whispering together strongly in rising anger.

Martin cut between them all, slapping away their hands with a loud shout. He said sharply, "You leave the girl alone, you hear me!"

The villagers' voices fell to a reverent murmur, but did not fall silent. Hands reached for Jirah greedily and tugged at her clothing. Nearra pulled her sister closer, holding the staff out before them in hopes of keeping the people back.

"Chosen or not, she's going to come to my home and speak to me about what's happened," Martin declared. "Tomorrow morning, we'll have a town meeting about this, and we'll get to the bottom of everything." When the villagers seemed reluctant to go, Martin flexed his muscles and crossed his arms belligerently. "Well?"

Martin turned to Eric. Curtly, he said, "Get everyone in your group, all your things, and come with me. I have enough room for you all." Without waiting for a reply, Martin looked down at Jirah. "If that's all right with you, young miss?" he asked respectfully, half inclining his head in a little bow. Eric gaped.

"My name is . . . Jirah," she squeaked shyly. Nearra saw a blush rise in her sister's cheeks.

"Lady Jirah." Martin bowed with great respect, his face sober.

Eric snorted violently, and Jirah corrected the headman. "No . . . just Jirah."

"Come along with me. I won't let them harm you. They're just overeager, filled with rumors from the big city and the superstitions of small-town life." Martin tried to force a smile, but his eyes flicked down to Jirah's clenched hand with a touch of fear. "It's not far."

Nearra and the others followed Martin into the woods beyond

by a small path that did not follow the road. He shooed away the other villagers who tried to follow them, stating again that he would meet with them in the morning. Some still followed at a distance for a while, and Nearra could tell they were watching Jirah's every move.

Koi slipped up next to Jirah, whispering loudly enough that Nearra could overhear, "Hey, so you're a cleric after all!"

"I don't know." Jirah glanced at her parents walking ahead of them. Eric's back was turned and he strode stiffly after Martin, Lanni at his side. Contrary to Eric's stone-faced expression, Lanni's features were screwed into a concerned frown. "I don't know what's going on."

"Well, you healed me—that means you have to be a cleric. Only clerical magic can heal. Thank you for that, by the way. I'd decided to give the whole fear thing another shot after all, so it's good that I didn't die."

"You're welcome."

"Let me see." Koi tugged at the golden chain that hung between Jirah's fingers. Reluctantly, Jirah showed the kender her medallion. "Nope. I've never seen that spiral mark before. What is it? God of dizziness, maybe?" Jirah only sighed.

The path wound upward, slightly following the crest of a hill. Martin's house, a thickly built log cottage whose walls were matted with sod, sat on a hillside. Nearra looked down over the rest of the village as the headman unlocked the gate that led to his front door. Ebonholde was a tiny village, no more than fifteen buildings in all with perhaps as many small houses tucked along the mountain ridge as far as her eye could see. Nearra picked out a hand-painted sign reading "General Store" on one of the sod buildings below, and another sign noted "Inn" that marked the only building in town with two stories and an attached three-horse stable.

She recognized some of the villagers from the group that had been with them outside the ruined church. They scurried about like ants, running from building to building as the warm afternoon sun lit the streets of the little village. Probably spreading the news, Nearra guessed ruefully. By tomorrow morning, even the people in the distant farms would know, the wandering trappers and the people who came in to town only to trade, and Ebonholde would be full of every type of rumor you could imagine. But at least Jirah had found her divine calling. That was cause for celebration, right?

Jirah looked about as far from celebration as Nearra could imagine. Her steps were slow, her head hanging. She still clutched the golden medallion, rubbing her thumb across the markings thoughtfully. Martin opened the door for her, stepping out of the way to let Jirah walk in first. Eric seethed, but Martin pushed him back until Jirah stepped over the threshold. Then he let the others pass.

Martin's house was furnished in dark wood and soft reds, a fireplace as tall as a man taking up most of the west side of the building. Above the fireplace was a stuffed moose's head, the wide antlers jutting out over everyone's heads and sticking between the rafters of the low-hanging roof. Pillows lined small areas near the walls, forming makeshift couches, and two low tables of rough wood made up the rest of the furniture in the main room.

Nagato flopped onto a pile of pillows with a soft sigh. "At last. Civilization." He rubbed his face gratefully against them.

Eric stood near the door, leaning against the wall, and refused food when Lanni offered it to him. Loreddion shoved Nagato aside and sat down on the cushions, taking the plate from Lanni after Eric pushed it away.

"Martin." Nearra sighed, but continued. "What can you tell me about that chapel we were in? We didn't even know it was a temple.

It didn't have any symbols at all, or any sign of religious use."

"Well, no, it wouldn't," the headman replied. "The place was stripped centuries ago. My family has lived in Ebonholde for generations, and the stories have been passed down at least that long. Whatever god was worshiped there, his name was lost long ago."

"You don't even know who the god was?" Jirah asked inquisitively. "Or what this symbol means?"

"I've seen the symbol on a couple of the gravestones out beyond the temple, where the forest's overgrown the path. Other than that, well, like I told you, nobody's been in that building in a dog's age other than kids trying to show off for one another. And I doubt they've been in as far as you have." Martin sat by the fire, pouring hot water into a mug. He added some spices and stirred it with a stick then tossed the twig into the fire, where it blazed brightly. "Maybe you should tell me what happened, La . . . um, Jirah."

Slowly, Jirah began speaking. She told the story hesitantly, never looking up at Eric while she talked. When she got to the part about the graveyard under the building, Loreddion and Martin both sat up curiously. "That must be where they buried the priests," Martin said softly. Loreddion did not add anything to the conversation, rubbing his chin thoughtfully beneath the snarl of his long, pewter hair. Jirah held up the medallion slowly, turning it between her fingers as she described the strange flash of light, and the figure of fire that confronted her in the darkness below the temple.

"That could be any of a number of gods," Lanni said. "Fire is a common theme, from what I remember in the research you've done, Eric. There are several individual deities who—"

"Or it could be the Pillar of Flame!" Koi tossed a pillow across the room. "Ever think of that?"

"I doubt it," said Nagato. "There's no evidence to prove that the Pillar of Flame is related in any way to divine energies. It was created with wizard magic, remember? It certainly couldn't give the ability to heal. That's entirely within the realm of the gods." There was a mutter of assent from Eric.

"Martin, have there been any visitors to town recently? Anyone unusual, possibly a traveling group headed deeper into the mountains?" Nearra asked hopefully. She hadn't forgotten her sister's conundrum, but maybe if they talked about the Pillar of Flame, Eric would be distracted from Jirah.

"No, it's been quiet. We only have visitors when it's trading season. I'd have noticed anyone in town who wasn't a familiar face," said Martin calmly. "Are you looking for someone?"

"Following them, more like, but we lost them," Loreddion grumbled.

"They have to be in the area. When we broke up their camp, they didn't have much in the way of rations. They couldn't have traveled more than another day," Nagato chimed in. "Is there anything unusual in this area, any places where outsiders are regularly seen? A road, perhaps, or an inn?"

"The only inn's here in town, and it doesn't get much use." Martin bit into a ham hock, chewing thoughtfully. "Perhaps the Lady Jirah could use her magic to seek the god's assistance . . ."

"She's not a 'lady,'" Eric snapped. "And she's not a holy woman. She's just a little girl—a foolish one at that, to call on a god she doesn't even know. This could be an evil god, or a dangerous one. Who knows what it wants from her?"

Martin stared, shocked at Eric's rudeness, while Nearra's father crossed the room to face Jirah. "This area wasn't always populated by humans, you know. There have been other races here—goblins, minotaurs. That area below the temple could have been dedicated to any sort of power, and the church built over it to hide the real patron. You're not using this magic medallion anymore, not ever again," Eric said angrily, and Nearra winced. "In fact, give it to me now, girl. We'll melt it down in the fireplace, and no one need ever know what you've done."

"No." The voice startled Nearra—it was her own. Everyone twisted around to look at her, and she said it again, more firmly. "No, Da. She's not doing any such thing."

Martin, too, stood from his pillows and said, "You're overreacting, Eric. And you're out of line. Your daughter's been chosen by a god, and that can't be undone."

While Nagato and Loreddion stared in surprise, Nearra reached out and pushed her father back a step. It was the first thing she'd ever done to disobey him, and her hand trembled in the act. Even as she did it, though, she was deeply sure it was the correct path. "Stop treating her like that. Jirah saved my life while we were out breaking Anselm's curse. She's grown up, and she's done things you've never been able to achieve. She even gave up her magic— her whole life's dream—for our family, and yet you act as if she's disappointed you."

Koi whispered a little too loudly in the corner. "Now he's getting his comeuppance."

Eric looked shocked, but it quickly gave way to anger.

"No, Eric, she's right," Lanni said, not bothering to stand or even to look up. She continued cleaning her arrows and adjusting the fletchings, as though nothing of any importance was happening. In the shadows where she sat, Nearra swore she could see a faint smile on her mother's quiet lips. "Let her speak."

"Jirah said in Palanthas that she felt called to be a cleric. Well, maybe she was right! And if a god's chosen her, then . . . then . . . who are we to say differently?"

"You can't be serious? You're all mad," Eric shouted. "What if this isn't a god, but is some other power? What if it is a god, and it's evil? I won't have my daughter following an evil god!" Eric looked flustered. Jirah glared, as stubborn as her father.

"Martin, you said that the graveyard in the forest had more symbols like this on some of the old mausoleums and headstones?" Nearra asked.

He nodded slowly. "Yes, yes that's true."

"We might be able to discover more about this symbol there," Nearra said. She was firm now, planting her white staff solidly on the ground. "Tomorrow before dawn, before the villagers come to swarm Jirah, we'll go there and look around." Jirah exhaled gratefully at Nearra's words, and hope lit up her face.

"But the Pillar of Flame!" Eric protested. He looked at Nagato for assistance, but the Red Robe nervously picked at his sleeve. "We have a mission, Nearra. One chosen for us by the wizards of Palanthas," her father reminded her.

"No, Da. I have a mission. Me, Nagato, and Loreddion—and Koi and Jirah," she replied. Nearra felt the staff in her hands, and tried to emulate its rigid stance. "Not you."

Eric paused, taken aback. Nearra watched him flounder, trying to think of something to say, his eyes scanning the group. Not a single one of them stepped up to help him. Not a voice was raised on his behalf. Finally, Eric's shoulders fell. Before he could turn and leave the room, Nearra stopped him.

"We need you, Da. We need your knowledge," she said. "You've spent your whole life studying magic items, researching esoteric spells, and living in the very area we have to search. We can't do it without you, but we'll try if you make us. If you choose to leave, that's your choice. Still . . . I'm asking you not to go."

Nearra shifted, looking at Loreddion. "Jirah needs us, and I want to help her. You're a Black Robe, Loreddion. Do you know anything about graveyards?" she asked.

A long, thin smile broke out slowly on the dark elf's face. His voice low and eager, rough like gravel but certain of himself as he replied, "It's my specialty." A shiver zipped down Nearra's spine at the apparent glee on Loreddion's features. He cracked his hands, the tattoos on his wrists shifting in the firelight like living creatures. Nearra remembered Jirah's concern about the dark wizard betraying them in Palanthas, his anger when the conclave demanded he help find the Pillar. Something just felt wrong about the fervency in his eyes, and she was almost sorry she'd asked.

"Then we leave before dawn," Nearra said, trying to regain her surety. "All of us." It was as much a question as a statement, and she looked at her father to see what he would say.

Eric spread his hands in defeat, smiled a sad but earnest smile, and nodded in agreement.

CHAPTER

17   The First Step on the Spiral Path

Wake up, Jirah." Someone was shaking her shoulder roughly. Her body ached from sleeping on an uneven floor, and she buried her head in the pillow.

"Five more minutes."

"No, now. We need to leave soon, and breakfast is already cooked."

Jirah opened her eyes and found Koi's eye disturbingly close to her own. "Gah!" Jirah yelled in surprise. She blinked, and Koi withdrew.

"There's something for you on the table," Koi said in parting, bounding away.

Jirah sat up, rubbing her eyes. The others moved about the cabin in the early morning darkness, packing their things and eating a quick breakfast of juice and leftover pork. Then her eyes fell on the table. Piled high were bouquets of late-summer flowers, loaves of bread, small packages of wooden jewelry and other trinkets, and a set of cutlery made out of a dark stone. "Mathelda's daughter left you a lamb, but I didn't bring it inside. It's in the barn, if'n you want to take it with you," Martin said.

"No, thank you," Jirah said as she pushed off her blanket and stood, her eyes picking out more odd things amid the pile. "What is all this stuff? Some of these things look really valuable. They can't all be for me!"

"Oh, they're for you, all right. The villagers got wind of your magic power to heal, and they're all agog. Left you gifts, they did, hoping to persuade you to heal all their ills," Martin sighed. "Half of them can't afford the things they've given. We're a poor village, so far away from the big city. You'd be a real boon to them if you stayed." Although Martin said it matter-of-factly, Jirah felt guilty. She'd been given this gift in the village temple—even if it wasn't used anymore. And now she was leaving them.

"You don't think I should go," Jirah sighed.

"No, just the opposite. I think they oughtn't rely on one person, 'specially someone they don't know," Martin said. He shook his head. "One wants you to cure her aching joints. This one over here wants you to heal her cow of pleurisy. Another is asking that you come make her nose straight so the boys in the village won't tease her. Fix my door from creaking . . . thinks you're a carpenter, not a cleric . . . speak to my dead aunt about where she's hidden the silver . . ." Martin said with a sad chuckle.

"People are eager to believe in anything they think will change their lives," he continued. "Some of 'em don't even have it bad, but the moment they hear of something they think will make things easier, suddenly they're taken with the thought that their lives are a mess." He smiled at her. "I'm not saying we couldn't use someone with your new talents, milady, just that they oughtn't be relying on you for things they could do themselves."

He patted her shoulder kindly and said, "I'm glad they saw you, and that they know the gods have returned. They haven't had hope like this in a while. It's a good thing, hope, but it shouldn't replace honest work."

"Martin," Jirah said thoughtfully. "When I get back to Palanthas, I'll talk to the clerics there about Ebonholde. I'm sure I can convince them to send someone out here, even if just to visit from time to time."

Martin's eyebrows raised in surprise. "We'd appreciate that. It'd do Ebonholde some good to have a cleric come and talk. Might open the people's eyes a bit. Thank you," the man said.

Jirah shook his hand, sealing her promise. "Will you give these things back for me?" she asked.

"Aw . . . Why would you do that?" Koi asked, pulling her hand out of her pocket without noticing. "Wouldn't that be insulting?" Jirah spared the kender a disapproving grimace, then wrapped up her blankets and readied her traveling pack. The others did the same, quickly readying themselves for their journey. Eric seemed no more excited to be going than he had been last night, but he kept quiet and fitted his pack with deft fingers.

Among her other belongings, Jirah found the golden medallion. She held it between her fingers, feeling its heft, the fine weave of the chain. It wasn't worn or old, nor dirty from being below ground for hundreds of years. On the contrary, the metal sparkled and glistened as if new, though the medallion itself showed faint signs of wear. Perhaps some cleric long ago had worn it close to her heart. Jirah touched the rough pattern of the spiral, felt the weight of the necklace, then slowly spread out the chain. She placed it over her head cautiously. The medallion fell against her chest, and Jirah breathed deeply to see it rise and fall. She looked up with a faint smile, and it faded instantly when she realized her father was watching.

"If you go out the way you came, you won't have to go into the village at all," Martin said, peering out the window past the thin linen shades. "I don't see anyone outside. I'll head down to the inn and cut off any early risers bringing their colicky children to see the new cleric."

Jirah and the others filed out into the misty morning, traveling down the side of the ridge. She saw her father pause just before they entered the treeline, staring longingly down at the village, where, Jirah suspected, he thought to find more information about the Pillar of Flame. Martin waved from the doorway, watching them go before he started to pick his way down the steep slope toward the village. After he had gone, Jirah tugged on Nearra's sleeve. "Nearra, are you certain about this? The wizards in Palanthas are waiting to hear that you've found the cabal," she said.

"They can wait another day."

"But the whole city—the fires that won't light—they need you," Jirah protested.

Nearra winked at her, a smile meant just for her. Jirah remembered that smile from her childhood. Nearra never did it for anyone else. "You're my sister. You need me too," Nearra reminded her. The smile was infectious and Jirah couldn't help but return it, despite worrying about the medallion and Eric. "And I need you. I can't find the Pillar of Flame without my sister. If this helps my sister, it helps me," Nearra finished.

"I wish I'd had a sister," Nagato said as he hiked his bag up farther on his shoulder. "Or a brother. It was lonely, growing up in Palanthas by myself."

Nearra chuckled and teased, "But that's what made you such a good researcher, Nagato. If you'd had a little sister, she'd have poured your ink out the window or written limericks all over your workbooks." Jirah giggled, but Nearra pretended to ignore it. "That's if you were lucky. If you're unlucky, your sister might dump the whole lot in the well one day, just because you beat her in solving a math problem."

Jirah laughed out loud. "I'd forgotten. I was terrible when I was younger, wasn't I?" she asked.

Nearra put an arm around Jirah and said, "Even when you were terrible, you've always been the best sister in the world."

The group went down through the forest and back around to the ruined chapel, all before the sun rose in the sky. They stopped twice along the way to avoid travelers. The chapel lay as it had before, crumbling ruins and broken stone fences, but now Jirah knew its purpose. She could see the temple still shaped in the ruined structure where she hadn't noticed it before—the tall bell tower she'd climbed into, the wide front hall that had been a gathering area for prayer, and the offices and living quarters in the rear for the priests. It must have held as many as ten clerics at one time, long ago.

Jirah noticed the faint markings on the shattered door, faded carvings that decorated the simple wood. The bushes in the front were wild and overgrown, and might once have been shaped by faithful gardeners. In the back, where a forest edged closer year by year, Jirah could see a thin marble roof among the trees. "A mausoleum," she said in an undertone to Nearra. "That must be where they buried the rest of the dead."

Past the temple, the forest grew thick and lush. Trees entwined their branches and roots, and thick grass grew up between them like a wall of vegetation. It took Jirah a while to find any way through into the woods. Only the texture of cobblestones on the ground told her that there was a way in. "Here!" she called, waving. "I've found a path!" She tugged aside thick grass, ripping it out of the earth to see more clearly. A stone lying by the side of the ancient trail proved that she was right. It was carved in the manner of a gravestone, wide and arched at the top, and Jirah could see writing under the moss that grew on its surface.

Nagato's shadow fell over her shoulder. She brushed aside the dirt and showed it to him. "Can you read this?" she asked.

"No," he said, his fingers brushing the letters. "It's neither

Elvish nor human, unless it's some mountain language. That's always possible, of course."

His words were greeted with a jeer from Eric. "As is the fact that it could be goblin, or a hundred other bestial languages." Eric turned to face them both.

"It's neither." Loreddion glanced down at the little tablet as he strolled past into the woods. "Those are stygian symbols." When Nagato stared at him blankly, Loreddion stopped. "I know something that the amazing walking book doesn't know?" Nagato reddened, and Loreddion laughed aloud.

"What does it say?" Jirah asked eagerly.

"Wait a second. Let me enjoy this for a moment. I know more than Nagato." Loreddion spread his hands, taking in a long breath and exhaling luxuriously. "I . . . know more . . . than you. Ahh. That's nice."

"Would you cut that out?" Nagato crossed his arms and fumed.

"All right, all right." At last the Black Robe grinned broadly and resumed what he was saying. "Stygian symbols are a language of sorts. You can't write a book in it or express anything too complex, but it's perfectly serviceable for marking things. Dwarves invented it, they say, but the priests of Chemosh made it popular. They used it to mark graveyards, mostly. Other priesthoods picked it up to carve signs and village markers. This one says, 'Walk not on the dreams of the dead, for they sleep lightly.' It's an old warning—they put it on a lot of graveyards."

"How do you know that? Stygian symbols?" Jirah blurted out. "You aren't exactly the most learned wizard in the world. How do we know you're not lying?"

Loreddion glared at her. "While other little boys were clipping clothespins to cats' tails, I was digging a grave for the squirrel that they knocked out of the tree with their slingshots," he said, looking animated. "Kids like Nagato hid in libraries. I hid in mausoleums. I told you about Cyan Bloodbane and what that dragon did to my country and to my people. And you still have to ask?"

A light lit Nagato's coppery brown eyes. Jirah could tell that Loreddion's words touched something in the Kagonesti wizard. Nagato's tone was casual but his eyes took in the dark elf as if he'd never really seen Loreddion before. "You must have been very lonely," the Red Robe concluded.

"So you'd think," Loreddion said as he stepped over the graveyard marker and pushed through into the woods. "But I wasn't alone."

The walk into the forest was not enjoyable. Brambles clutched at Jirah's clothing and trees clumped so tightly overhead that only the faintest peep of morning sunlight could slip through—and soon enough, nothing at all. Moss and vines crawled over the branches, making the ground slick over knotty roots. Jirah pushed past, occasionally stepping over another marker that bore dates and names that were nearly unrecognizable.

When they finally reached a dark area of the forest where the grass could no longer grow to reach their knees, the graveyard became more recognizable. Here, undisturbed for centuries, the graveyard had become a lush haven of moss and thick earth. It was much larger than Jirah'd thought, with several mausoleums, tall above-ground crypts, rising at odd angles from the broken cobblestone path. It wound through the center of the graveyard around mossy oak trees with trunks as wide as a fat ogre.

"This is creepy," Nearra said, staying close to Lanni and gripping her white staff. It made no sound when she walked, sinking into the thick mossy covering of the graveyard's earth. A tree frog croaked somewhere above her, and Nearra jumped, knocking against her mother. Loreddion snorted judgmentally, Koi sighed enviously, and Lanni almost laughed.

Picking her way through the graves, Jirah spun her arms to keep her balance without stepping on anything that looked like a bump in the ground. "What do these say?" Jirah asked, pointing up at the odd carvings on a mausoleum.

Loreddion walked casually to her side and squinted up at them. "It says, 'Let those who disturb these bones remember they, too, will one day be little more than dust.' It's another one used by the servants of Chemosh."

"Chemosh?" Eric asked. He kept his hand on his axe, staring around at every soft noise in the woods. "He's a god of evil, isn't he?"

Loreddion shrugged and replied, "He's a god of death, and undeath. Is that evil?"

"Undeath," Lanni repeated. She raised an undisturbed eyebrow. "I'd say that's evil magic."

"Death is a natural thing. We all are born; we all die. I knew a healer once who told me that birth is the only medical treatment that is unfailingly fatal. So why be afraid of death?" Loreddion said. "Magic shapes the world using what it finds—trees, air, fire. What are our bodies, if not made of the same stuff?"

Loreddion rapped on the iron grating of the marble mausoleum, making it creak terribly. Jirah half ducked, expecting a ghost to fly out of nowhere.

"Chemosh knows that life is short and death is long," Loreddion continued. "Our bones will grace Krynn a thousand years after our souls have gone into the beyond. There's a dark sleep in death that waits for every living thing on this world, king or beggar. We all dream the same dream when our lives end." Leaning forward, Loreddion spread his fingers on the cold marble mausoleum, pressing them into the dust and mold.

Even Koi shivered. Lanni asked softly, "So this was a temple of Chemosh?"

"Not necessarily," Loreddion said. His hand fell, leaving behind its print. "All graveyards are holy places to Chemosh, no matter what temple guards them. Even Mishakal, the goddess of life—Chemosh's greatest opponent—respects his power here. The temple could belong to anyone. This site belongs to him."

"Here's the mark on the medallion," Nearra said as she stood beside another mausoleum farther along. She stretched up and brushed her fingers hesitantly over a large spiral. "But this . . . I recognize this. That's a bison."

"The bison of Kiri-Jolith, actually," Eric told them. "God of soldiers and warriors."

"Yes, this looks like a warrior's tomb," the Black Robe concurred. "See the shield carved inside?" He pointed through the iron grating, at the four coffin-shaped pedestals against the walls. "One, or maybe all, of those probably contained someone who died in battle."

Lanni knelt beside another marker. "Here it is again. But this looks like a tree, and here's a strange mug-looking thing. Maybe a beer mug?" she pondered aloud, wrinkling her nose. "God of drinking?"

Loreddion crouched beside her and rubbed some of the moss away. "It does look like a mug. I don't know. Maybe a god of dwarves? Sometimes the same god will have different symbols in different areas. Chemosh is called the black goat in some lands, the dark daughter in others, and in some ogre lands, he's represented by a giant mouth that can never fully be fed."

"So two people could worship the same god who has different sigils?" Jirah asked.

"It happens." The dark wizard shrugged.

"I know this one," Nearra said. She touched the headstone of another grave. "Hiddukel. The god of Kirilin, the god that made Anselm betray the other wizards." She eyed the medallion Jirah wore around her neck with apprehension. "You don't think . . ."

"No, I don't," Jirah said firmly, her hand clutching the golden disk.

"But how can you know?" Lanni sat down on the stairs of a mausoleum while the others continued to wander through the graveyard. She thrust the tip of her bow into the ground and raked at the dead leaves there. "How can you serve a god when you don't even know its name? That's not possible."

There was an uncomfortable silence, and the wind shook the trees forlornly, making the tree frog croak eerily once more. "Goldmoon did," Nagato piped up unexpectedly. All eyes turned to him, and he flushed, tugging at one pointed ear.

Jirah frowned at him. "Who?"

"Goldmoon?" Nagato looked from face to face. "You've never heard of her?"

"I have. She was a hero of the War of the Lance, wasn't she? Some sort of barbarian?" Koi straddled one of the larger gravestones, kicking her feet as if she were riding a pony.

To Jirah's surprise, Nagato nodded. "Exactly. She was a barbarian from the wildlands, and she was the first one to know that the gods had returned. She and her friends went on a quest to find a blue crystal staff—the staff of the goddess Mishakal, but Goldmoon didn't know that at first. All she knew was that a goddess had appeared to her and given her a mission. The symbol had long been forgotten, you see, so it didn't mean anything anymore." Nagato drew a twisting figure eight on the ground and tapped it with his finger. "Mishakal's symbol."

Koi kicked the sides of the gravestone. "What happened to her?"

"Mishakal made her a priestess and gave her the power to heal. She was the first cleric on Krynn when the gods returned, the first person after the Cataclysm to bear healing magic. I read about it in tales of the war. Without Goldmoon and her faith, the gods might not have returned. It takes the faithful to ignite the fires of belief." Nagato steepled his fingers. "That's what faith is—belief in the unknown, even without proof."

"But Goldmoon found out—about Mishakal," Nearra prompted.

Nagato's head bobbed up and down. "Eventually. But then again, Mishakal is a goddess of good, someone who speaks to her followers often. Other gods are more reclusive. Some might even still be away from Krynn—might not have returned yet. I wouldn't even know where to start on identifying a god like that. And what happened to Jirah might have been some magic that was set there when the gods vanished. The god involved might not even be paying attention."

Jirah stared at him. With a sinking feeling, she remembered the feeling when the medallion first appeared, the strange fire and the bird painted in red on the floor. It had been there a long time, that was certain, and Martin said nobody had ever gone into the building. "You mean I might never know?"

"We'll see," Nagato said gently. "There are a lot of books in Palanthas, and the clerics of other gods might have the ability to recognize that symbol, even though we don't."

Koi added, "And the god might come to you in a dream, or send an avatar, or show himself in a ball of flame or something. Or kill you in your sleep." She sighed. "Lucky."

"Look at this," Loreddion interrupted. He hadn't been paying much attention to the conversation. He'd wandered much farther into the graveyard and now reached up to pull a tangled mass of vines from a marble mausoleum near the center of the graveyard.

Jirah stepped forward and pushed her way past an ancient oak tree toward Loreddion, trying to see the symbol he was outlining with his hand. "That's not a god," she said, looking at it curiously. "Wait a minute. I know that mark!"

Three crescents, intertwined, all on fire.

"It's the symbol of the cabal!" cried Jirah.

At that moment, there was a shout from the woods, and twenty men with copper rods stepped out of the brush, surrounding them.

CHAPTER

18   Digging up Bones

One of the cabal agents hefted his copper rod to his shoulder, hurling it like a javelin. It sailed through the air, red gem flashing, and struck Nearra in the side. Most of the men standing in the woods were dressed in the familiar black outfits that the companions had seen before, but some—no more than five or six —wore strange golden robes decorated with crescents in black, red, and silver.

"Hey! They brought wizards!" Koi cried, tugging her boom-stick from her belt.

"Where did they come from?" Jirah yelled. Eric grabbed Nearra as she sagged from the power of the copper rod, her eyes wide and glazed.

"Does it matter?" Loreddion growled, crossing his arms and leaning back against the mausoleum.

Eric lay Nearra gently on the ground and reached for his axe, raising it swiftly to block another rod that flew through the air toward them. The metal rang against the blade of his axe and turned away to bounce and slide among the tombstones. Moving to stand over her daughter, Lanni nocked an arrow and loosed. The arrow sank deep into the man's chest.

Nagato swept his golden wand out of his sleeve and pointed it at one of the men in golden robes. Bubbles swirled from the wand's tip, rushing on a gust of wind toward his opponent. The man raised his hand and spoke a word, and a bluish shield sprang up in front of his palm. The bubbles burst upon reaching it, spraying greenish foam everywhere. Behind his shield, the man smiled. Nagato fell back.

"You're not going to help?" Koi paused and stared at Loreddion.

"Nope."

"You're kidding."

Lanni shot two more arrows at their fast-moving attackers. One bit into a man's arm, but the other flew wide and stuck, wavering, in a tree. Koi met one attacker running, clearing his knees out from under him with a single harsh blow. The man flew against the side of the mausoleum, struck his head, and fell only inches from the Black Robe's feet. Koi looked up at Loreddion, who poked idly at the man with his toe. "Nope," the dark elf said. "Not kidding."

Eric had three men with daggers fighting him at close range, their blades weaving in and out as he swung his massive axe to keep them at bay. Jirah scrambled over to Nearra, lifting the copper rod that had struck her.

"Good idea, Jirah!" Koi yelled, gesturing wildly at one of the mages. "Get 'em!"

Jirah nodded and rushed forward through her father's attackers, dodging a thin bolt of blue light. The mage who had cast the spell cursed and began to chant again as ice formed on one of the tombstones. There were four mages, Koi saw clearly now, one at each cardinal point of the graveyard, standing just outside of the twisting paths and marble markers. The graveyard proper where the markers stood was the only clear area in the woods, surrounded on all sides by thick undergrowth and tall, widely branched trees. The cabal had hidden among these trees, but now slowly moved out into the clear area of the graveyard.

To the west side of the graveyard clearing, where a massive oak tree spread huge limbs to block out the sun, Jirah cornered the mage who had cast at her. She gripped the rod, readying herself to fight, and then charged. Jirah swung the rod in both hands, the red gem flashing like a ball at the end of a street bat—and struck the mage full in the chest.

The red gem did not flash. The mage did not fall. He lifted one hand, and a blue stone inset into a golden ring twinkled. He grinned down at her, and Koi suddenly realized how much taller than Jirah the man was. He backhanded Jirah, sending her sprawling, the copper rod falling uselessly from her hand. He spoke another word, pointing down at her, and the cold ray sprang up from his palm again. It struck the girl, and Jirah's scream was frozen into a block of solid ice. Koi stared at the ice statue that had been Jirah, and thought she saw the girl inside the frozen pillar blink.

"Holy flying fish!" Koi looked at Loreddion. "Are you going to help us now?"

"Nope."

Koi growled, blocking two daggers even as they spun through the air toward her. She didn't look at the black-garbed cabal member, but she knocked him expertly in the groin, and when he hunched over, in the back of the neck. He sprawled next to the other at Loreddion's feet. "Loreddion! We're in trouble."

"You're not in trouble—yet." His dark eyes flashed beneath the veil of his hair, and Koi suddenly felt cold and alone. Jirah's protests and accusations in Palanthas after the first thieves struck returned to her mind.

Koi couldn't continue the conversation immediately. She saw another mage lowering his hands, fingers waving through the air as though he were combing invisible strands of hair. As he made the movement, small bolts of lightning began to rain down all over the graveyard. Lanni lowered her bow, quiver nearly empty, and lifted Nearra's limp body in her arms. She dragged Nearra under the eave of one of the larger mausoleums. Koi saw Nearra starting to move, fingers clenching around the white staff she still held near her chest.

Eric swung his axe in wide swaths, hurling back his attackers. "They followed us!" he roared. One of the lightning bolts struck the ground near him, hurling Eric to his knees. He struggled to stand up again as more of the black-clothed cabal agents threw themselves on him.

Nagato started in surprise, pointing at the mage who had summoned the lightning bolts. "That wasn't a real spell! They aren't wizards!"

Koi turned to Nagato. "What?"

"They're using magic items. That bracelet is magical. I saw him twist it just before the lightning started. And the one who got Jirah, he has a ring!" Nagato shot again with his wand, fluffy pink bubbles soaring through the graveyard. "Break the items, and they can't cast spells any more!"

"Did you hear him?" Koi kicked Loreddion. "Break the magic items! You can do that, can't you? Throw some kind of spell to rip the ring off his hand?"

"Not my kind of magic," he replied implacably.

Koi was ready to tear out her hair. She struck another of the cabal agents with her boomstick, calling on its power to hit him with an earthquake. The man howled and fell over, flopping on the ground between two graves. He kicked like a hooked fish, bouncing up and down from the power of Koi's weapon, but even that didn't keep the kender's attention. She turned on Loreddion, eyes shining with hurt. "Are you working for them?"

He chuckled wickedly, and behind the curtain of his angled pewter hair, Koi saw a sharp smile. "I hate people who don't do their research." Loreddion pushed off from the marble wall, his hands curling like claws. "I hate people who sit in libraries and don't learn anything. And I hate arrogant jerks who think that magic is just something you shoot out of your fingers or draw on the floor in chalk." He stepped toward her, feral grin glittering in the darkness.

The kender fell back, heedless of the cabal agents who flooded into the wide graveyard. She dodged one instinctively, allowing the man's dagger to slide against one of the tombstones. Confident, the four "mages" moved forward. They wound through the paths that led among the graves, creeping ever closer to the small group of resistance near the center mausoleum square. Lanni and Nearra still crouched under a mausoleum's sheltering roof while Eric—nearly overwhelmed, with six men surrounding him—defended them. More closed in on Koi and Loreddion warily, daggers and copper rods in hands.

Nearly the last of the group left standing before the barrage, Nagato's crazy bubble wand was wreaking havoc, turquoise and violet bubbles billowing through the air with every sweep of his arm. Two of the cabal agents wandered about, clearly confused. They stared at the tree branches above them and staggered back and forth with odd smiles. Another sat on the ground, digging into the earth with his fingers and making snorting sounds like a pig. Koi was impressed with the reedy diviner's fortitude, but all the book learning and library research in the world hadn't prepared Nagato for a fight against so many opponents. He was outnumbered and had only a wand against four other spellcasters. Koi knew he'd be overcome in a matter of minutes. "Loreddion! We're going to lose our lives!" she howled desperately.

Loreddion shoved Koi against the mausoleum, exchanging

places with her. "Magic is alive. And it is the only life I need."

"You betrayed us to the cabal?" Koi couldn't believe it. Her hand fell limply to her side, the boomstick loose between her fingers. "I thought you said you'd show me fear. I thought you were our friend."

"I *am* your friend." Loreddion turned his back on her. "These people didn't do their research, Koi. You want to know the first thing my master taught me when I started to learn magic?" Koi shook her head sullenly, and Loreddion raised his arms without looking back. His voice was smooth, the words stretched out with dark pleasure.

"Never fight a necromancer in a graveyard."

Loreddion called out to his magic, a long command that sounded like poetry. Magic flowed from him in waves and settled deeply into the ground. Tombstones shook, the mausoleums creaked with ghosts of the past suddenly released from the depths of sleep. Loreddion's chanting rang out across the graveyard, and suddenly Koi realized why the Black Robe had been waiting.

All of the cabal spellcasters were within reach of the graves.

Withered, rotting hands split the ground, throwing up ancient dirt and scattering worms. Grinning skulls ripped through the earth, and yellowed arms scrabbled at the ground, climbing out into the light of day. One of the yellow-robed mages shrieked as creaking fingers locked around his knees and ankles.

Ruined, leathery faces gaped from the mausoleums, thrusting mummified arms through the iron bars of their gates. The metal rattled, shaking with the force of the undead behind it, and burst open. Shrieking hinges accompanied pallid moans. Maggot-ridden mouths with lolling tongues widened in glee at their newfound freedom. From below, the graves broke open and sod fell back over shredded blankets of moss.

"Throw fireballs," Loreddion snarled, the words arrogant and critical. "Divine the future." He raised his hands, the fingers clenched like talons. "Fools. I know the future of every creature that draws breath on this world. That future is *death*." Revelling in pure power, Loreddion lowered his hand to point at each of the four cabal mages in their yellow robes. The vicious undead horde plowed toward them in a great mass of bone and stinking, mottled flesh. Green hands reached out to grasp golden robes, and one of the mages screamed. Loreddion roared at him, "Magic trinkets and fairy lights won't help you against the cold, hard reality that comes at the end of your last breath." The cabal mage faltered, dragged down by the dead hands that grabbed at his limbs.

The reanimated corpses swarmed in shuffling clumps toward the agents with daggers. Many of them fought back, but the blades of their daggers sank into putrid flesh with a squelching sound. Punches landed ineffectually, and only the copper rods had any use; striking a zombie with one seemed to end the enchantment, causing the corpse to fall back to the ground, a withered heap of bones once more.

But there were far too many undead and far too few copper rods.

Koi saw the walking corpses rip items from the yellow-garbed men, shattering bracelets and crushing rings. Loreddion directed them with a sweeping hand, a composer in a deadly symphony. The cabal fell back. Eric's axe swung down on one of his three attackers, felling the man—who then rose again to become part of Loreddion's spell. Glassy, newly dead eyes turned on the other agents in black, and he raised his dagger against his former allies.

Yelling in fear, the cabal agents fell apart. Faced with horror on every side, stripped of their magic and forced to fight the dead bodies of their own friends, they scattered, screaming. Loreddion's hollow laugh boomed out. He clenched his fists. "Run," he growled, stepping forcefully after them. Skeletons and zombies roamed everywhere, a great cacophony of death, chasing the agents of the cabal down twisted, mossy paths and among overturned marble markers. "Run all you like. They'll catch you eventually." Loreddion watched the zombies and skeletons shuffle after their prey, following them in to the woods with relentless, ambling strides.

Koi lowered her boomstick, staring after him. For once, Loreddion was animated, shaking the long hair out of his face and striding after them as though he would chase them to the ends of the earth. "Run, cowards! One day, death will find you too!" He laughed merrily, striding powerfully across the newly turned grave soil.

One of the gold-robed mages fell before the onslaught of undead. Some cabal members did not follow the black-garbed thieves, but instead ran toward one of the stone mausoleums—the one, Koi noted, engraved with the symbol of the Crescent Cabal. The first one there struck the iron grate with his open palm, speaking a word in the language of magic. The gate flew open, and he stepped back to push the others inside.

"I guess you're not going with them." Koi chuckled, shaking her head as she realized what Loreddion had done. The Black Robe had saved them all. Hearing the sound, Loreddion looked back over his shoulder.

"You really thought I was a member of the cabal?"

She started to shake her head, then sighed and shrugged. "Yeah."

"And that I would betray the whole group, turn you over the cabal to be tortured and killed?"

"Maybe." She stuffed her boomstick in her belt, her eyes furtively following the last of the walking dead. They chased dark figures through the vine-laden trees. A few, too slow to continue the chase, slowly sank back into their graves with a windy sort of sigh.

Loreddion leaned forward, sticking his face into hers. "Scare you?"

Koi stopped short. She arched an eyebrow and glared at him. "No." Koi thought she saw the ghost of a smile creep over Loreddion's features, but then his usual mask of sullen arrogance returned. "Heck of a try, though."

Leaning back with a sigh, Loreddion walked toward the mausoleum bearing the cabal symbol, stepping over a few zombies too rotted to give chase. "The cabal went in here," Loreddion said quietly. "But my question is, why didn't any undead come out?" He stepped just inside the mausoleum's clean marble floors. "No dust." Loreddion squatted and ran his fingers across the marble. "Someone comes through here fairly often."

Inside, Koi could tell that none of the coffins were opened, none of the crypts disturbed.

"Some of the graves didn't open either," Koi noted, pointing back at smooth stretches of earth. "But you don't seem worried about them."

The necromancer wrinkled his nose with a belligerent huff. "The bodies in those graves were cremated, most likely. You can't raise ash into zombies. There's nothing to hold them together."

"Remind me to put cremation in my will," Koi said.

Loreddion stood up, glancing back at the others. Eric helped Nearra to her feet while Nagato worked a counterspell to free Jirah from her icy prison. Most of them gave wide berth to the open graves, and the Red Robe kept glancing into the forest as though trying to catch a glimpse of the zombies that were still shambling among the trees.

"Mausoleums don't usually have cremated remains," Loreddion continued. "There's no use putting ashes inside a marble building—it'd just be overkill. These places are made to protect bodies, and this one's got two perfectly good alcoves in use. Grave tenders slide coffins into those alcoves and then plaster them up and write the name and date."

"Did you see where they went? The gold-robed cabal guys?" Nearra asked worriedly, hanging on the iron grate of the mausoleum. Koi thought she looked a little green, probably from the cabal's copper rods—or the zombies. Koi cocked her head, getting a better look at Nearra's face. Definitely the zombies.

"Through here." Loreddion pointed at the mausoleum's back wall. "I think there's some kind of a door in here, one they didn't want us to find. There's something in here, some way to escape. But I don't know how they opened it. "

From the doorway, Nagato volunteered, "There's probably a lever somewhere, a way that they open the door without leaving a trace. Can you find any sort of switch or button? Perhaps a torch holder that spins to the right or left?" He gestured largely, sleeves flapping about. "Maybe there's an illusionary wall. Try to poke your head through the stone!"

Everyone in the party turned to stare at Nagato, and the Red Robe slowly dropped his arms. "Sorry. I got a bit overexcited. Carry on." He smiled, blushing.

Loreddion tapped along the plaster wall. When he got to the farthest alcove, Koi heard an empty, thunking echo behind it. "That's not a normal coffin marker," Loreddion said with a frown.

"We don't have the time to figure out how they use the secret door. We just have to get inside." Eric pushed past Nearra, Jirah, and Lanni.

Koi walked farther into the crypt. "Whatever's down there, it must be a big place to have so many people living in it. Here were twenty-four folks, all ready to attack us with just a day's notice." Koi tried to add it all up, but it just didn't make sense. "The graveyard isn't that big, and it's old, so they couldn't have just dug a place to live under the ground. Everything would have collapsed." Her words trailed off as Eric used his axe to smash open the plaster covering on the crypt. It broke in chunks, pieces scattering across the marble floor.

"There was a big area under the temple, where they kept the bodies of the priests," Jirah recalled. "That's where I got the necklace. But the room wasn't big enough to go under the graveyard." Her hand fluttered to the medallion on her chest. She nudged aside the larger pieces of plaster with her toe, stepping closer to Loreddion and her father.

Behind the wall, instead of an alcove for a coffin, there was a small stairway leading down. Eric started to place his foot on the first step, but Nagato grabbed him. "What if there's a trap behind this false wall? Or what if there are more cabal members down there?" Nagato whispered. He squeaked and shoved forward as the group crowded into the mausoleum. "We should take some time before we go down there—cast divinatory spells, do some research on the area. Who knows what's under this graveyard?"

"The cabal knows." Nearra stepped down the stairs, her white staff giving off a faint glow in the darkness. "And that means we have to know too." Koi noted the stern look on Nearra's face, the way her hand tightened on the ancient white staff. She was right. They had no other choice.

Nearra led the way down the stairs with only the glow of Anselm's staff lighting her steps. Koi shrugged and trotted after her. One by one, the others followed into the dark.

At the bottom of the staircase there was a single room. Koi had to admit, it wasn't at all what she had been expecting. The room was square, the floor covered in intricate tilework. It wasn't a large room, more like a very wide hallway. Nearra stepped out onto the floor. Koi saw three figures running ahead of her, golden robes flapping with each broad step. "There they go!" she yelled, pointing.

Eric pushed past her into the room, clenching his fist about the hilt of his axe. He ran down the hallway, Loreddion and Jirah only a half step behind him. Lanni nocked an arrow swiftly into her bow.

"E'li," Nagato whispered. "Look!"

Koi saw what had been lighting the hallway, and she blinked. There was a large round portal glowing in a soft reddish swirl. Sculptured birds' wings swept along the edges as though it were a doorway forged in feathers of bronze. The metal birds were alight with magic, fire leaping to form a hoop larger than a man between their swirling wings. Through the wavering heat of the blaze, Koi could see a great chamber of lava and fire. Like the inside of a volcano, lava poured down high obsidian walls, cascading in rivulets into a pool at the bottom. An arched bridge of stone rose from the other side of the portal, stretching across the pool of lava to a larger ledge on the other side where Koi could see movement.

From the center of the lava pool rose a massive column of living flame. Faces writhed, smiling or screaming, speaking in a whisper that was just out of hearing. Like a giant pillar, it turned slowly over the lava pool, radiating heat and magic in a wide aura. The air around it shifted, arching with flares of fire that spun outward as it rotated, and the kender was certain, without knowing how, that she was looking at the Pillar of Flame.

The first of the three mages leaped into the portal, scorching his robes in the flame. The waves of rippling heat wavered and swallowed him whole. Suddenly, he was standing on the arched stone bridge on the other side. Flat and distant, he looked back, and Koi caught a glimpse of fear on his features. She stifled her jealousy and turned to look at her friends.

"They're getting away!" Nearra's yell was muffled by the sound of the flames.

It felt almost close enough to touch, the heat of the portal blazing against Koi's face and hands. The second cabal agent leaped through, turning to reach to help the third across. The last man stumbled, almost in Eric's grasp, and hurled himself through the portal to get away. "We have to jump through!" Jirah yelled, continuing on, but Loreddion grabbed her by the shoulder and pulled her back.

"We don't know where it goes!" he yelled over the sound of the boiling lava and roaring flames. "We might not be able to make it back." The Black Robe took in the portal in all its glory, his eyes flashing from side to side, measuring its power.

Lanni lowered her bow and Koi her boomstick, stepping out of Nearra's way as she descended the last of the stairs. Nagato followed quickly. "It's closing!" he yelled, and he was right. The flames around the edges of the brass portal were flickering out, smoke rising from them to obscure the portal. It flickered, wavered, and began to fade. The image of the Pillar beyond it shimmered and slipped from view.

Suddenly, just before it was entirely closed, Eric lunged toward Jirah. His hand wrapped around the medallion that she wore and snapped the chain around her neck. Spinning on his heel, he hurled the medallion into the portal. It flew, chain dangling behind it like the tail of a kite, and sank into the last vestiges of fire and smoke. Nearra swore she heard a faint clattering sound as the medallion landed on the stone bridge on the far side of the portal—and then, it was gone.

The portal flickered into darkness, and all was silent.

CHAPTER

19   THROUGH THE GLASS

W hat have you done?" Jirah screamed, fists pounding on the stone wall where the portal had been. The circle of brass stood silently, the birds no longer afire. The portal was now nothing more than a large ring of intricately carved brass without even the faintest hint of enchantment sparkling across its surface. Jirah spun and yelled at her father. "What did you do?"

"Eric!" Even Lanni was shocked. She held her bow in limp hands, the arrow falling loosely between her fingers.

Nearra and Nagato approached him, walking past a stunned Koi and a mildly amused Loreddion. This time Jirah wasn't crying. She wasn't hiding behind her sister nor was she weakly protesting Eric's action. Instead she stood, feet wide apart and eyes burning, facing him. "That was mine!" she yelled again, her voice echoing in the dim hallway.

Nearra spoke a soft word, and the light of her staff increased to brighten the room. She could see faint patterns on the floor, etchings of crescents along the walls of the mausoleum's basement, all leading to the bronze ring embedded in the floor at the other end—the ring where Jirah was standing, refusing to back down. **203**

"I did what was necessary!" he retorted. "I won't have my daughter serving an evil god!" But something in his voice rang false, and his eyes shifted from face to face.

"Da," Nearra said, raising a hand and pushing past Nagato. "Tell us the truth."

"What do you mean?" he protested. "I *am* telling you the truth. That holy symbol is evil. I could feel it. We could all feel it."

"I couldn't feel anything of the sort," Nagato snorted haughtily. "And I'll thank you not to tell me what I think about something that has yet to be researched. We can't draw conclusions so swiftly, not without more proof."

"It's a ruined temple in a graveyard! The god probably picked her because she was young and naive! How much more proof do you need?" Eric's eyes darted between them as he searched for words. "I was trying to protect my daughter."

"No, you weren't," Jirah's voice cut through, reducing Eric's action to ultimate simplicity. "You were just getting in the way."

Loreddion nodded. "Girl's got a point, old man. Ever since she got that thing, you've been on and on at her, but I haven't seen her do anything but help other people. She healed Koi. Fought in that graveyard like a tiger. Evil god or not, she's done good by you."

Nearra reached for Eric's shoulder, turning him to look at her. "You're lying, Da. Tell us the truth."

Eric crumbled in his daughter's grasp. He sank to the floor, sitting on his heels and hanging his head. "I had to do it. Believe me." He reached for Nearra's golden hand and stared forlornly out at Jirah. "I had to protect my family."

"Eric, what are you talking about?" Lanni asked.

"The cabal," he answered softly. "They said they'd hurt the girls. They burned our house down. They nearly killed Nearra, and Jirah's too small to understand what they could do to someone without magic like her. Like me."

"I'm not that small, Da." Jirah sounded stung, but her eyes softened.

Lanni knelt beside her husband. "Eric, tell us what you've done."

Slowly, the story came out. "I met these men a few years ago in Palanthas. They were researchers, like myself. We exchanged ideas, and I told them about the curse on our family. They helped me place Nearra in Cairngorn Keep. They traded me texts to study." Eric sighed, looking up at the ceiling to avoid his wife's eyes. "In exchange, I let them use our house as a way station from Palanthas to the stone table and on to the Pillar of Flame."

Nearra tapped her fingers on her staff, obviously irritated. "You knew about the Pillar of Flame? Where it was, what it did, how to get to it? And you never told us?"

"No," Eric said grimly. "I never knew its location. Only that it existed, and that the Crescent Cabal was researching it. When the pillars were created, each was given a key. That key allows the holder to command the magic of the pillar. But the key to the Pillar of Flame was stolen many years ago by a young spy within the Crescent Cabal. They never caught the one responsible. They've been searching for him—and the key—ever since."

"Why didn't you tell us this?" Jirah spat, still angry.

Eric sighed. "Tell you that I'd been working for the cabal? Out of the question. Worse, just a few days before you arrived, cabal agents brought me a sealed message—it was left for me to find in the barn. It told me that you had been sent by the conclave of Palanthas to find the Pillar of Flame. I was to deliver the key to them—or else my family would be killed."

"Oh, Eric." Lanni embraced him. "That's how you knew the girls were coming. No wonder you weren't working down by the river. But this is terrible. I wish you had told me. I could have—"

"Could have what? Lanni, the lower ranks of the cabal may be thugs and item wielders, but the real power behind the Crescent Cabal are the mages. I can't cast spells. How was I to protect you?" He looked first at Nearra, then Jirah. "Any of you."

"Have any of you seen a portal like this before?" Nagato asked, crawling over the bottom of the feathered portal. He studied it closely, his face an inch from the metal. "Koi? Loreddion?" Perhaps grateful to edge away from the family argument, the kender and the Black Robe went to help him, examining parts of the metal ring. "It's astounding. So complex, and yet so simple. Look at the work on this feather! If I didn't know better, I'd say it was made by dwarves."

"Gnomes would be my guess," Loreddion huffed. "Although it hasn't exploded yet."

Nearra softened. "That's why you wanted Jirah and me to come with you and not return to Palanthas."

"Yes," he answered. "When I discovered you didn't have the key, that you knew even less about the Pillar than I did, I was so afraid. The cabal wouldn't believe me if I told them you didn't have the key. They knew you were researching them, ferreting out their trail, and they wouldn't stop until they found us."

"Why would they attack us? We don't have the key." Koi frowned. She crawled up the side of the brass ring and swung from the top, annoying both wizards who were nearly knocked over by the kender's swinging feet.

Nodding, Nearra turned back to Eric. "Koi is right. Your story makes sense, Da, as far as it goes. But why did you throw Jirah's medallion into the portal? What does that have to do with the key?"

"Don't you see?" Eric's face lit up. He spread his hands, pointing at Jirah and up in the direction of the ruined temple. "This portal was put here by the Crescent Cabal generations ago, after the temple fell. The spy escaped through here with the key. He must have hidden it nearby, slipping back into society and maybe back into the cabal itself, when they couldn't figure out who it was. It's a good guess that the key is nearby—that it was here. Don't you see? It had to be the medallion." Eric desperately rushed on, "Giving it to them was the only way to make sure they'd never try to find us again."

Nagato, who had been scanning the wall and eying the bronze ring of the portal, turned back to the conversation again. "If the cabal didn't have the key, how were they putting out the fires?

"They're doing research on the Pillar to create another key," said Eric. "That's probably why the magic is going crazy and turning off fires all over the world."

"Yzor," Nearra guessed. "That's what Yzor is doing."

Eric nodded. "I'd only heard the name once before you came. The note was signed with that name."

Jirah stomped across the hallway to bristle at her father. "Da, I understand that you were trying to save us, both from the cabal and from whatever power watches over that medallion, but how can you be sure?"

"The cabal has been looking for the key for a very long time. They were very careful not to tell me anything too specific. I did research on things living underground, divination spells, protection from fire—all of it sounds just like the kind of thing Jirah saw in that room under the temple!"

Loreddion rolled his eyes. "It also sounds like a dragon hoard, lost city, or gully dwarf village."

"Dragon hoards are rough places," Koi chimed in. "I know. I was in one, just before the fires went out in Kenderhome." Her face fell at the tragic memory. She reached into her hair and withdrew one of the trinkets tied there. "Got this there, in fact."

A single bronze feather.

As she held it up, a reddish sparkle fluttered down the spine of the little token. An echo of that spark flashed in the center of the portal, and one by one, the birds' eyes opened. Nearra and the others stared in shock as the bronze birds moved, began to spark, and then to burn, and the red center of the portal slowly returned.

"It's opening," breathed Nagato.

It seemed unbelievable that one of Koi's hair bobs would be having such an effect on the metal ring, but there was no denying it. Curiously, Koi waved the feather, watching as the fire in the portal followed every movement, swaying to the right and to the left.

"Where did you get that?" Eric asked the kender. He stared at her as though he'd never seen her before, as if she'd just fallen out of the sky and into the room.

"In a cave, where a fire-breathing dragon was making a brand-new dragon hoard," Koi explained. "He was a young red dragon and had just moved into the cave when I saw him. He came from somewhere down south, maybe near Palanthas, and he didn't have much of a . . . why are you all staring at me like that?"

"Underground, fire breathing, very dangerous. Lived near Palanthas," Loreddion repeated, ticking each off with his fingers. "So he could have found it when he was here, in a cave where the spy thought it well hidden. Sounds like the Crescent Cabal was closer to getting the key than you thought. But I don't think they knew Koi had it."

In the background, the portal continued to glow, swelling open like a flower blooming against the wall. Nagato stepped back, shielding his eyes from the hot blaze of the fire.

"They knew when it came into Palanthas, though. That's what they've been doing by turning off the fires!" Jirah's eyes lit up as an idea struck her. "They were trying to track the key."

"That's why the fires in Kenderhome went out?" Koi lowered

the feather, and the portal's fires dimmed. "And in Palanthas? The magic was following me?"

Nagato chimed in, "That's why they attacked my house. They knew one of us already had the key—but they didn't know who. The cabal's so centered on wizards, I bet they'd never have thought a nonwizard would have the key. The key must work without needing a wizard's magic to fuel it, but they didn't know that. But we should hurry; it's getting brighter. I don't think we have much time."

Ignoring him, Nearra rushed on. "That's why they kidnapped you and Loreddion, and were coming after me—but not Koi or Jirah."

Face creased with worry, Eric rose and put his arms around his wife. "They'll figure it out soon enough. They'll be able to track us wherever we go, just by putting out the fires around the key. The Crescent Cabal won't stop until they have it in their possession."

"Then we have to face them," Nearra said stubbornly. All eyes turned to her, but for once, the attention didn't make her nervous. She faced the fire on the bronze portal, taking a moment to gather her thoughts. Was this the right thing to do? And more, could she do it? The words weren't difficult, but making herself say them was a huge effort of will. "Loreddion, Nagato, Koi, Jirah, and I. We're going through the portal, and we're going to face Yzor." By now the portal was blazing as hot as the inside of a bonfire, lighting the room and sweeping waves of warmth as the wings of the birds moved. Through the center they could once again see the far room, and shadowy figures moved in the distance through waves of steaming heat.

"Nearra!" Eric protested. "You can't go in there alone. Lanni and I—"

"Da," she cut him off firmly. "You did all this to protect Jirah and me, so you know how I feel. You and Mama aren't part of this. We've been asked to help Palanthas, and I'm going to uphold that promise." Nearra saw Jirah nod. "I need to know that you and Mama are safe."

Eric's shoulders sagged. "You don't want me to come because I'm not a wizard."

"No!" Exasperated, Nearra ran a hand through her long blonde hair. "You just don't get it, do you? Being a wizard doesn't mean you're all-powerful. It doesn't make one person better than another. Thousands of people live without magic every day, and they're happy. Some of them are powerful, or rich, or famous, and all without casting a single spell." Hot waves of superheated wind pressed Nearra's silvery dress to her skin. They could hear a faint roar now from the far side of the portal, as if something there noticed the opening they had created. Time was short. "Da, trust me. *Magic won't help you.*"

"We have to go," Lanni said gently. Eric nodded and stepped away from Jirah.

"Where will you go?" Jirah asked. "So we can find you when this is all over?"

Eric frowned, rubbing the small beard on his chin thoughtfully. "We'll have to hide pretty well; the Crescent Cabal is thorough. I don't think they'll put too much effort into looking for us once this is over, though. And anyway, I hear Kenderhome is nice this time of year. There will certainly be lots of work for a woodsman once the fires have returned." Koi laughed out loud in agreement.

Eric put his arm around his wife and smiled at his daughters. "It sounds like I have a lot of thinking to do. We'll talk about this after you're done . . . in there. Take care of each other."

"We will, Da." Nearra hugged him and embraced her mother tightly.

Turning to the kender, Nearra lifted her staff resolutely and stamped it on the ground. "All right. Everyone ready? We're going through."

CHAPTER

20 THE DEVIL INSIDE

The portal shimmered and blazed, rippling heat rising from the flames to fill the ring in the center of the bronze wings. The fire roared as wide and strong as it had when the cabal mages ran through, and on the other side, Jirah could see dark shapes running to and fro on the ledge across the arched stone bridge.

Koi had wanted to be the first one through, but Nagato stopped her. "If you go through and it closes, then we're stuck here without the ability to open the portal again," he said. She nodded, holding the blazing feather high.

Nearra was the first to go. She sank into the rippling air and appeared within the picture on the other side, standing on the stone. Jirah didn't wait to be told. She held her breath, put her arms out in front of her, and jumped through the ring. The air felt too hot and sticky, pressing against her skin like a giant soap bubble. There was a stretching feeling, as if her body were taffy pulled in a long, thin string. Then the bubble broke, and Jirah stumbled forward, falling sharply, and found herself face-to-face with an obsidian floor.

Jirah raised her head. The heat was incredible, and sweat already poured down her body from the sudden rise in temperature. Lava bubbled all around her in great pools, and far above, she could see through the thick smoke to a strangely starry sky framed in a circular ring of stone. "It's a volcano," she said, awed.

The Pillar of Flame rose from the center of the largest pool of lava, fire flowing upward in a giant column. Lava washed in great waves against the bottom of the pillar. Jirah pushed herself to her feet as Nagato and Loreddion materialized through a shimmering hole in the stone wall behind her. She could see Koi still on the other side, tucking the feather into her pocket as she stepped into the portal. A fraction of a second later, the kender tumbled out on their side, regaining her footing with the quickness of a cat. She looked back at the wall, realizing as Jirah did that there was no mark, no ring nor other delineation of the portal save the heat shimmering against the stone.

"Don't close it," whispered Nagato.

"I wasn't planning to," Koi said, leaning in with a wink.

"Do you think they noticed us?" Jirah scrambled to her feet.

"Yeah," Nearra replied grimly. Jirah turned to look across the obsidian span. She could see three figures crossing the bridge toward them from the far side, their dark shapes outlined sharply against the Pillar of Flame. "I think they did."

The column of flame wavered, shifting from side to side. Images of faces rose in the smoke and fire, twisting as though fighting to be free. The pillar crackled and arches of fire erupted from it, shooting wildly to either side of the mountain. Rocks exploded from the walls, raining down into the lava. Huge splashes of thick, red magma shot up against the walls, searing the stone. "What are they doing?" Koi yelled.

"They're trying to use the Pillar of Flame!" answered Nagato. "But they can't control it."

"They must be afraid that we know how to use the key. Da said they were trying to make a new one—they must be using it, and it's not working." Nearra widened her stance as the three figures on the bridge got closer with every passing breath. "But we don't have time to worry about that."

She was right.

The two men crossing the bridge wore golden robes such as they had seen before, glittering and shimmering in waves of heat. Baubles shone from their fingers and hands. Each clenched one of the copper rods of the cabal, red gems winking in the brilliant light of the Pillar of Flame. But these two men didn't grab Jirah's attention the way the third figure did. She stood taller than they, nearly six feet in height, and her slender body was wrapped in gold and bronze scale armor. A light, black tabard hung out at the edges of her armor, fanning like a skirt at the top of her legs. Her hair was black too, spiked in a short, violent bob above ruthless features. She held a sword in each hand, no burden to her muscular arms, and spun the weapons about her body with the precision of a circus performer. A thick, black cape whipped behind her with each step she took across the bridge.

Even at this distance, Jirah could see her eyes. Sharp and gold, slanted like an elf's but with no hint of smile to them, they shone with an unnatural light that made her skin look even paler. She strode across the bridge, uttering commands with a strange, bitter lilt to her voice. The two cabal mages—item-users, really—were quick to obey. A third man in black leathers ran from behind her, reaching to grasp the woman's forearm, and Jirah could just make out what he was saying: "The shard is ready, Yzor. We don't need the key anymore." He pointed behind her, fluttering his hand to the other side of the bridge. "We can still escape."

"Escape?" She paused, spinning on one heel to face him. "Coward. You would flee from children?" Her sword slipped into his stomach with a stunningly quick strike. The man gaped, staring down at the weapon that pierced him, and Yzor backhanded him with the hilt of her second weapon, sending the man spinning. Screaming, he fell backward, arms whirling like windmills, and pitched off the arc of the stone bridge. Jirah turned her face away from the gruesome sight, but the sound of his body splashing into the lava told her his end.

Yzor continued crossing the bridge, her eyes fixed on them. Nagato fell back, pressing his back against the wall next to the portal and whipping out the slender golden wand. Koi and Loreddion stepped forward.

Koi sniffed the air, smelling the thick burn of sulfur and the hot wave of ash that marked each breath. "Not much like Kenderhome," she said wryly. "But I never really liked it there to begin with." The kender slapped her metal baton against her palm, sizing up their opponents. Beside her, the Black Robe grinned sharkishly, teeth glinting behind the thick wave of his steel-colored hair.

"No undead here to help you out," Koi chuckled. "I'll take two. You get the one on the left. He's kind of stringy looking anyway."

"Chemosh's grinning skull you will, shorty. You can have the scraps when I'm done with all three!" He spoke a quick, rhythmic phrase, and his hands glowed purple. A strange, ectoplasmic substance swelled in the hollow of his palms then shot out like a cannon toward Yzor and her two followers. Instead of stepping aside, Yzor leaped to meet it with a terrible grin, striking the ball of energy with her sword and cutting it cleanly in two.

Koi ran forward, engaging with the golden-robed man on the left. Her boomstick flashed out, striking once, twice, three times, but never met flesh. Each blow was blocked by the man's copper rod. The red gem flashed when it hit Koi's silver rod, but the kender only laughed. "You can stop it from making a boom, but you can't stop it from being a heavy piece of metal!" She cracked it through the man's guard at last, connecting with the man's shin. There was a sharp snapping sound, and he fell to his knees, his expression pained.

The second golden-robed cabal member raised his hands swiftly, crossing his forearms with a snapping gesture. Jirah saw something around the man's wrists flash. A bolt of lightning careened from his flashing metal bracelets, snapping through the air toward them. Jirah threw herself out of the way, clutching her head in her hands. Nagato squeaked, a shrill sound of fear, but Nearra threw herself in the path of the lightning bolt without hesitation. She held up her white staff and the lightning struck it with a roaring crack, shaking the foundation of the obsidian bridge.

Jirah stifled a scream, lying on the floor of the bridge. "Nearra!" she yelped, looking up through her hands. She expected to see her sister blown to bits by the impact, but Nearra stood like a marble statue in her silver dress, white staff still shining with the heat of the blow.

"*Daya burun!*" Nearra yelled, the language of magic hanging thick in the air. The staff shivered, and the shadow of a bird passed over the ground on which she stood. Jirah heard the sound of wings pressing against the air, feathers sliding on the hot wind of the volcano. Like a ghost, the transparent image of a white owl rose from Nearra's staff. It beat its great wings over her head, silvery eyes flashing in the firelight, and shot forth toward their opponents.

Yzor's chiseled features shaped themselves into a terrifying scowl. She struck at the bird with her swords, moving faster than anything Jirah had ever seen in her life. Even the lightning bolt had been easier to track than the trail of Yzor's weapons as they cut through the air.

Jirah crawled forward, trying to push herself up despite shaky legs, and saw something bright sparkle down by the lava. She squinted, trying to see through the rolling waves of heat—it was her holy symbol.

Magnetized, Jirah scrambled forward on all fours, getting as close to the edge of the lava as she could. On an outcropping just a few feet past the rippling edge of magma, the spiral sigil dangled from its broken chain. The heat didn't seem to affect it, but it glistened and swung on the wind raised by the Pillar's arching flames. Jirah tried to reach out for it, but it was too far. The heat of the magma forced her to snatch her hand back.

The man kneeling beside Koi raised his hands to his head and shouted a command word in a language the kender didn't recognize. A blue-green gem on a small coronet beneath his hair flashed, and the coronet shimmered. The magic overwhelmed the man, swallowing him in a sudden burst of greenish light. Koi jumped back, readying her baton for another strike.

The man's arms stretched, his featured blurred, and within a second a giant bear with claws like long daggers stood where he had been. Koi blinked, surprised, but quickly rejoined the attack. With four legs, the man's ruined knee was far less notable. He attacked with short, clawed strokes, raking Koi's armor and leaving half-inch marks in the thick hide.

Loreddion readied another spell, but Yzor's second minion was swifter. The man in the golden robes jerked a steel ball from the pocket of his robe, hurling it at Loreddion. The ball exploded outward in midair, steel bands spinning out from the center of the sphere in long, twisting ribbons. Before Loreddion could finish his spell, the whipping strands of the ball surrounded him, twisting about his limbs and shrinking back together like a collapsible prison. In a heartbeat, Loreddion was trapped inside the steel, arms and legs akimbo, sealed in a maze of steel ribbon and iron bands that kept him from moving. He fell to the ground, writhing in the small space left to him, unable to do more than twist slightly between the metal bands.

"What are you doing?" Koi yelled to him. "This is no time to play around!"

The Black Robe fixed her with a dark stare from behind the bars. "Very funny, Koi. Ha ha," he said without mirth.

The bear launched another attack, ripping the bridge with each swing of its claws. Koi blocked the first paw, but the second came at her from the other side, slapping against the kender's face and hurling her to the ground. The claws drew long, bloody marks on the kender's cheek and throat. Jirah saw Koi flinch once, and then she lay dazed with her boomstick clenched in one fragile hand. The bear turned toward Nagato with a low, eager growl.

On the bridge, the man who'd thrown the steel prison readied his copper rod and came down the hill of the bridge toward them. Loreddion struggled in the magical cage while Nagato and Nearra continued to concentrate on their spells—they were easy prey. The bear roared, its claws slashing red arches above Koi's body.

"*Avatio!*" Nagato yelled. From his wand, a lazy stream of purple and orange bubbles rose into the air, spewing from the mouth of the little golden serpent. They fluttered low against the the bridge, moving toward Yzor. Although the bubbles were beaten back and forth by the pounding wings of Nearra's spectral bird, they continued on their path unerringly toward the woman with the two swords.

Yzor fought Nearra's ghostly bird, her weapons flicking back and forth beneath the bird's talons. The bird drove Yzor forward and back, tilting dangerously over the lava that stretched like a river under the bridge. Bubbles rolled up the hill against all logic, sweeping under Yzor's feet.

The Red Robe still concentrated on keeping magic flowing steadily toward Yzor, making the bubbles from his wand roll against all gravity up the arched bridge.

The bubbles reached Yzor and her companion before they could strike, and Jirah saw what Nagato had done. Some of the bubbles stuck to their shoes, and others hardened like marbles beneath their feet, causing both Yzor and the golden-robed mage to totter uncertainly. Yzor had been so concerned with the spectral bird that she hadn't seen the bubbles coming, and the suddenly uneven footing was a surprise.

The bird swept down on them, a great breeze springing up from its flapping wings. Swoops of ghostly feathers struck Yzor's shoulder and the man's chest, throwing them off balance. In the moment when the bird struck, Yzor launched her own attack, double swords cleaving through the bird's magical body. The owl screeched, vanishing, but it was too late. Entangled in sticky threads, marbles rolling beneath their feet, Yzor and the man in the golden robes pitched, careened, and fell from the arch of the dark bridge.

Jirah clenched her fingers in her teeth, but this time, she watched. It seemed that it took them forever to fall, the man's golden robes fanning out all around him. However long it was, it wasn't time enough to scream, and he vanished into the magma with hardly a sound. The red muck encased him, sucking him down as he thrashed about in the lava for only moments before he disappeared beneath thick ripples of molten stone.

Yzor, on the other hand, did not fall in.

Still holding her swords in each hand, Yzor fell from the bridge feet first, plunging like an arrow toward the magma. But just before she struck, something amazing happened.

Two great black wings opened from Yzor's back. What Jirah had mistaken for a cloak was in fact thick furls of leather, now lifting and widening to hold her aloft. Like a bat's wings, they beat the air and sent great drafts of searing wind sweeping across the lava. Jirah stared openly. "Is she part dragon?"

Nagato was the first to answer, his wand hanging loosely from his hand. "Part demon, actually, I think. That must be how she withstands the heat here day in and day out." His voice shook in fear and looked up to meet Yzor's golden, hate-filled eyes.

The bear didn't fall—another advantage of four legs, even if one was broken—but skittered away from Koi to regain its footing. Koi pushed herself up, dazed and blinking, shaking her head. She stared at the dark figure of Yzor, stunned, and grinned from ear to ear. "Well, I'll be a monkey's uncle. I've never seen a demon before. It may not be scary, but it's a start!"

Yzor's wings snapped downward, hurling her up through the volcano's fire. She thrust her swords deeply into their scabbards, then spun on one wing and dived to brush just above the lava. Plunging her hands into the lava, Yzor scooped up thick handfuls of lava that oozed between her fingers. Her wings beat furiously, and she spun upward once more. A dark speck against the blazing light of the Pillar of Flame, she soared in an arc over the dark bridge.

Koi fell back beside Nagato, grabbing the bars that held Loreddion and shaking them. The bars were yellow and orange, sucking up the temperature of the volcano and conducting it so well that some parts of the cage seemed almost to be glowing with heat. She jerked her seared hands back, crying, "Ow! Hot!" and stared in at the elf.

"Let me help you," Nearra offered as she bent to tug at the bars, wrapping her fingers in the skirt of her dress against the heat. Even so, her dress began to smoke, and she was forced to let go.

"Don't worry about me," Loreddion growled, so low that Jirah could barely catch the words. His robes were smoking, and he had wrapped one long, dark sleeve about his hands where he held on to the bars. "I'm tougher than a little heat. Get out there and show her that you're a wizard of Palanthas."

Koi swallowed hard, turning to face the bridge again. "Nearra, what do we do?"

Loreddion's hand shot out and caught Nearra's golden one through the bars, holding her still a moment longer. "Don't let them beat you. You're better than that."

Nearra stared at him and nodded slowly, her face breaking into a tight-lipped smile.

Above them, Yzor soared for a moment longer on the hot winds, then stooped like a falcon to attack.

CHAPTER

21   AT LAST

Nearra dodged to the left, and a ball of molten flame splattered on the stone where she'd stood only a moment before. Nagato squawked, slapping at his robe where a spot of the stuff had caught on fire as Yzor swept down from above. She carried handfuls of the sticky stuff, hurling lava the way a child might throw mud at a playmate. And all the while, that horrible smile lit her features, half savage and half amused. Nearra shuddered at how close the thick magma had come to her skin.

"*Petatani!*" Nagato chanted, his voice quavering but earnest. Suddenly a shield sprang up around them, golden and shimmering with light. "It won't hold long," he said, wiping sweat from his brow. "You'd better think of something—fast!"

Nearra's eyes widened. "Me?"

"I trust you, Nearra." Nagato faced her, a weary little smile playing on his lips. Though he was dusty with travel, his red robes torn and scorched, his little smile reminded her of how he had rescued them outside Shoikan Grove. "We all do."

"But I can't . . ."

Nagato's hand closed over hers. "I believe in you."

Nearra's dream swept back to her: *Bodies in the water, the dark red of their blood matching the scarlet magma that surrounded her now. The old man holding a scrimshaw of Palanthas, telling her . . . telling her . . .*

"Stand between Palanthas," Nearra breathed, remembering. "And the flame."

Yzor landed, her wings sweeping through the magma on either side of the bridge. She drew her swords once more, the blades glowing with heat. Her armor shone, golden and fiery, and her short black hair was like the night sky after a bright sunset. She marched toward Nagato and Nearra, pausing only a moment at the edge of the Red Robe's shield. With a muscular shrug of her shoulders, she plunged one of her swords through the shield. Nagato's protections stretched and tore open from the force of the blade.

Nearra squeezed Nagato's hand and turned to face Yzor. She caught a glimpse of Jirah to the side, crouched at the edge of the lava. "Jirah!" Nearra yelled. "I need your help!" But her sister didn't listen. She was staring out over the lava fixedly. Nearra had no time to find out what had captured her attention, for Yzor was only a few steps away, and the shield around them had collapsed into sparks that fluttered down onto the barren stone.

Yzor's sword came down like the flickering tongue of a serpent, and Nearra barely had time to raise her staff to defend herself. Although she expected her staff to shatter into pieces from the magic and strength of Yzor's weapon, the sword careened away as though it had struck an iron wall. The second strike came up beneath Nearra's guard, but she felt the staff righting itself, lending her the fraction of time she needed to place it before the swinging blade. Yzor snarled, blocked again, and stepped back to reconsider her assault.

Standing a bit back from Nearra and with his hand still on his wand, Nagato whispered, and the little golden serpent came to life. Orangey bubbles began to trickle from its jeweled head.

"Not this time," Yzor snarled, quickly stepping beyond Nearra's guard and lashing out toward Nagato. Her blade sank into his arm before he could move.

Nagato cried out, and the wand fell from his fist, but he snatched it up again with the other hand. He clutched his injured arm close to his body, his blood matching the scarlet of his robes.

Loreddion wrestled like a captive animal in the bars of his tight-fitting cage, ignoring the smoke that rose from his skin where he touched the ever-increasing heat of the metal. Yzor had stepped too close to the cage, and Loreddion's arm shot out to grasp her wing. He tugged on it with all of his strength, and Nearra heard a horrible tearing sound as bone parted from its socket. The flesh of Loreddion's arm sizzled and turned a severe, blistery red, but he did not let go. Yzor spun, screaming, and the motion only served to further wrench the wing. Her sword struck toward Loreddion, but before it could land, he threw himself back in the cage, tearing the wing off completely. Her weapon crashed with a ringing sound on the bars, knocking the cage to the side and leaving a massive cut in the metal.

Loreddion's fingers slowly opened, one by one releasing their burden. He let the wing fall to the ground with a dark and murderous grin.

"You are a fool." Yzor's voice was ages old, rough and without compassion. "My wing will grow back."

"Maybe so," Loreddion said. He faded against the burning hot metal of his cage, strength at last falling from his arms and legs. His grin, however, was still sharp. "But not today."

Yzor roared in rage and reached through the bars for him. Before she could grasp the dark elf's smoldering robe, Nearra opened her hand, palm facing the demon, and shouted in the tongue of magic, "*Es!*" Ice sprang from the center of her strangely golden hand, striking Yzor in the back. Yzor fell to her knees with the force of it, her ruddy skin paling.

"You've hurt her!" Nagato said gleefully.

"Ice!" Nearra cried. "Yzor's a creature of fire! She can't stand the touch of ice." Yzor's flesh was cracked and blackened, as the cold sheen of ice stretched across her ruddy flesh. But she was quickly back on her feet again.

Yzor shuddered, regaining her balance. The wound to her wing and the touch of Nearra's spell had shaken the half-demon. Nearra squared her feet and spoke the spell again. "*Es!*" The second spray of ice coated Yzor's shoulder where her wing had been. Her sword arm froze, locked in ice and frost, white creeping down her arm, freezing her elbow, seizing her wrist. Dropping her sword, Yzor raised the hand to her face, forcing her fingers to close against the ice. She scowled, furious, and the thin coating shattered.

"*Es!*" Nearra yelled again, and another bolt of ice rocketed from her hand, but this time Yzor was ready. The half-demon leaped aside and the ice shattered against the stone. More magma leaped from the widening cracks, melting the smooth ice in an instant. One wing flapping, the half-demon wobbled, off balance, teetering on the edge of a newly formed precipice. The ice slowed her movements, and the loss of one wing made her unwieldy. For a moment, Nearra dared to hope that they might win.

Shaking off the crust of ice, Yzor smiled. She reached back to grasp the wing still attached to her torso. With a vicious tear, she ripped it from her body without flinching. She tossed the leather sail close by the wing that Loreddion had dropped. Nearra took an involuntary step backward, her heart pounding against her ribs.

Farther up the bridge, Koi crawled forward, dragging her baton before her. The bear noticed the movement and growled, arching up to wave both massive paws in the air. When the paws came down, the force of the blow split the stone, causing cracks to run like spiderwebs across the smooth surface of the bridge's base. He stomped toward Koi, and the kender was forced to scrabble sideways to avoid the hot lava that sprayed up between the cracked stone of the bridge.

The bear pounded Koi again, knocking the kender dangerously close to the edge. Bashing the bear over and over with the baton in her hand, Koi was giving as well as receiving. The blood that smeared her face didn't taste like her own and she could tell the bear was moving more slowly than when the fight started.

"You like that?" she asked, dancing forward heavily. "Want some more?"

The bear limped, one eye blackened and swollen shut, its fur matted with blood. The kender could feel her armored shirt hanging in tatters from the constantly tearing claws, but she didn't care. The fight made her blood rush and her head sing, and that was as close to fear as she'd ever come, even when she charged the dragon. Then suddenly, with a powerful blow, the bear's paw caught her. Though the claws missed tearing off her face, it spun her around completely and nearly knocked her off the bridge. She grabbed hold of the stone as she fell, struggling to keep herself steady.

As she scrabbled to keep hold of the bridge, Koi's opponent shifted back to human form. He stood over her, drawing out a black ceramic disk from his robes. He raised it to break it open and unleash unknown magic, but a swift kick from Koi into his wounded knee forced the golden-robed wizard to fall on the ground at her side.

"You want to use magic?" Koi growled. She stared viciously through the metal eyes of her cat's-head helm. "Try this."

"No, Koi!" she heard Nearra yell. That girl was always yelling in combat, like some kind of squawking bird. Koi smiled. She kind of liked that about Nearra.

Koi didn't reach for her earthquake stick, instead holding aloft the bronze feather. Yzor spun in an instant, her eyes fixed on Koi's prize. Over the lake of magma, arching with fire and twisting, screaming faces within flames, the Pillar shifted and moved. As if drawn to Koi's presence, great gouts of fire roared down toward her, striking the bridge with huge plumes of flame. The golden-robed cabal member screamed, forgetting his enemy, leaping to get behind Koi before the wave of flame reached them. "Wow," murmured the kender, staring into the flame. "That's really neat."

The fire swept across the bridge in a great wave, swallowing them both whole.

"Koi!" screamed Loreddion, and Nearra felt her heart leap into her throat. Nothing could possibly survive that heat, the focus of the entire Pillar lashing out onto one small point. The magma all around the center of the bridge splashed up in great fountains. Nearra heard agonized screams inside the fire, the sizzling of flesh and the snapping of bone plunged into a violent furnace. Within the roar of the flame, the screaming slowly and horribly died.

The wave receded, the Pillar of Flame swelling above them with awesome, untapped power. It seemed to Nearra that the faces and vision within the flickering fire were more animated, catching her attention in fevered dreams that centered on visions of destruction and woe. "It's cruel," she murmured. "Cruel and uncontrollable."

Perhaps not. A single, smoky figure remained on the bridge. Small, sturdy, with a helmet shaped like the maned head of a cat, Koi clambered to her feet, the feather still in her hand. The bronze glinted, drawing Nearra's attention uncontrollably to it—even as she knew Yzor's would be.

"It didn't hurt me. Completely surrounded by fire, and not a burn. The key must have protected me. You know what?" Koi cocked her head and shot Nearra an impish wink. "For all that I fuss about kender and things they find 'interesting,' that *was* actually kind of neat."

Whether Koi didn't notice Yzor or didn't think the half-demon was a threat, Nearra didn't know. "Koi!" Nearra yelled, lunging forward. "Watch out!"

Yzor was already moving—had been moving from the moment she'd seen the key. Nearra was close behind her, but Yzor's strength and speed were such that she outdistanced the girl quickly. The sword in Yzor's right hand flashed, left hand still stiff and slow from Nearra's ice spell. Koi blocked the sword with her metal baton, able to keep up with Yzor's strikes only because of the ice. But Yzor was far stronger than the kender, and her attacks pounded Koi ever backward toward the edge of the bridge.

"No!" Nearra struck out with her staff, trying to trip Yzor. Her opponent was sure footed and leaped over the slim, white wood. Her icy hand reached easily to grip Nearra by the throat. The pressure was intense, choking Nearra and silencing her magic. Yzor snarled and pulled Nearra close. Inches from her, eye to eye, Nearra could see faint, sharp fangs among her teeth.

Staring at Nearra but talking to Koi, Yzor growled, "Give me the key."

Nearra tried to tell Koi not to do it, forbid her from dealing with the half-demon, but any sound was crushed beneath Yzor's iron grip. The kender moved forward, boomstick in hand, and Yzor swung her arm out over the magma. Nearra's feet kicked into open air, heat swirling up her silvery skirt and against her body. She clung to Yzor's arm, fully aware that if the demon opened her hand, Nearra would go spinning into the magma.

"Give me the key," Yzor demanded, her words clipped and deliberate, "and I will trade your friend's life for it."

Koi held out the key slowly, the bronze feather turning between her fingertips. Yzor reached for it.

At the last moment, Koi dropped it, and Yzor instinctively bent forward to grab the feather before it struck the stone. The motion brought Nearra forward too, her feet brushing the dark arch of the bridge. Yzor's hand lightened on her throat for just an instant, and Koi was ready and waiting in that brief moment to strike.

Nearra pushed against the stone, throwing herself forward as Koi's baton snuck in beneath Yzor's guard. It struck the half-demon in the stomach, doubling her over, allowing Nearra a moment to wrench herself free. Yzor gave no real thought to either of them, nor to the pain of Koi's attack. Her fingers clenched about the bronze feather, clutching it and lifting it high in triumph.

Nearra reached for her staff, which had fallen to the side in the tussle. Although the heat around her was fierce, the staff felt cool and comforting in her hand. Koi helped her to her feet. Nearra spared a glance at the others. Loreddion, limp in the cage, its iron bars glowing white and gold with heat, appeared not to be aware of his surroundings. Koi's hand was clenched tight around Nearra's arm, the other readying the boomstick, waiting for the right moment. Nearra saw her glance down at the cracks in the bridge, gauging the magma that spurted through them, and knew that the kender no longer planned on surviving the battle.

"We can't let the cabal have control over the Pillar," the kender said, lowering the faceplate on her helm.

"I know," Nearra said simply. Nagato was behind them, his wounded arm wrapped in the torn sleeve of his red robe. He, too, seemed to understand, a faint smile trying to bloom on his dark features, coppery gold eyes gentle.

At this moment of utter defeat, Nearra looked for her sister, hoping to have Jirah close one last time. She scanned the platform at the end of the bridge where they stood, but could not find her. Nor was she near Loreddion's burning cage, or at the portal, which still shimmered and waned on the wall behind them. For a moment, Nearra thought perhaps Jirah had gone back through—but no. Jirah was far braver than that, even if Nearra wished she'd gotten to safety. She'd never abandon Nearra, not now, not ever.

Then Nearra saw her. Down by the edge of the magma, Jirah sat back on her heels, an exultant look on her face. She grinned in triumph, waving a long stick made of two cooking spoons lashed together with her belt. Hanging from the end of it was the golden chain, and at the end of that, Jirah's medallion. "I've got it!" she cried out, dropping the holy symbol into her hand. Though it must have been super-heated from the fire and the magma, it did not burn her, and Jirah gazed down on it fondly, like a lover too long parted from their sweetheart.

"At last!" Yzor crowed, feather in one hand and sword raised in the other. "The Pillar of Flame is mine to command!" She spun, pointing the feather at Koi and Nearra. A violent ripple rushed up the towering column of flame, and a snakelike tendril of flame parted from the body of the Pillar. It whipped down to the bridge right where they were standing, forcing Koi and Nearra to hurl themselves down, sliding and rolling awkwardly on the stone, down the arch of the bridge. More tendrils began to shiver and explode from the Pillar above, reaching down to obey Yzor's commands without a word spoken.

"Now," she smiled, pointing the feather toward them once more. "You all die. No one defies the Crescent Cabal."

Gazing adoringly at the spiral in her hand, Jirah breathed softly. "At last . . ."

CHAPTER

22 PROMISES

Jirah could hear the fighting on the bridge. It seemed far away right now. The disk in her hand held her attention and left little room for other thoughts. Still, bits filtered through.

"Koi!" Nearra spun the kender toward her. "Can you get Loreddion out of that cage before the heat kills him?"

"I'm not a thief," Koi protested. "I'm a fighter."

"You're a kender," Nearra said firmly. Koi shrugged, grinned, and darted back toward the cage. Slowly awakening from her daze, Jirah scrambled from the edge of the magma and made her way toward the others. She could see Yzor exulting in her prize, the bronze feather catching the glow of the firelight. Another great arc of flame burst from the Pillar at just that moment. It swept the ground, whooshing toward them the way a man washes leaves from his porch with a bucket of water.

Nagato was quicker despite his wound. He called out in the language of magic, raising another golden shield. The fire slammed against it, pouring over it like a tide. Jirah, just at the edge of the shield, jerked her toes behind the barrier as the wave threatened to light her boots on fire. Nagato's shield held, but wavered under the onslaught. Nearra joined her voice to the chant, redoubling the strength of the magical wall.

Jirah could hear Yzor laughing maniacally, hurling bolt after bolt of fire from the Pillar. The half-demon gestured again, and the magma all around them began to rise, filling the cracks and spilling over the edges of the bridge. The portal behind them snapped shut in a wink as Yzor closed her fist.

Yzor took three long strides from the center of the bridge, twirling the bronze feather. Fire leaped up all around her, boiling up the Pillar from the magma below. Great plumes of smoke obscured the top of the volcano. Jirah could have sworn that the Pillar doubled in size, unleashing power exploding from its sides, showering torrents of sparks down over the bridge.

"You have given me the key, so I will grant you a quick death—on one condition." When Yzor stopped, fire spun down to ring her, swirling and crackling like a living thing. Her dark eyes narrowed. "Tell me who the traitor is."

Fire roared again, charring the magical shield to black ash. Flakes tore from the edges, and the wall faded from gold to an ash gray. Jirah crawled over to the cage, watching as Koi sprang several of the bars out of place. "Easy enough," the kender grumped. "Don't fight the demon, Koi, oh no. Go pick locks that a kender child could open between biscuits." She looked calmly over at Jirah. "Help me get him out of there."

Jirah grabbed Loreddion's shoulders, and Koi his arms, and together they drew the unconscious elf out of his burning-hot prison. Jirah reached to check his pulse, but Koi knocked her out of the way, delivering a ringing slap to Loreddion's pale cheek. "Get up, pansy," she said with a grin. "You're missing everything."

Loreddion's eyes fluttered in confusion. Her smile faded as he sank back into unconsciousness. Koi lifted his hand, studying the raw burns. Loreddion's robe hardly moved at all, his breath growing too shallow to lift his chest. When she spoke again, her tone was softer. "Lor?"

Remembering what had happened at the ruined chapel, Jirah clutched the golden medallion close to her heart and reached out to place her hand on Loreddion's forehead. He was burned badly, the skin on both arms charred as black as his robes, his face marred by the long red scar of one of the metal bars. Jirah squeezed the disk, whispering softly, "Please don't let my friend die."

Obligingly, the metal in her hand grew warm, and Jirah felt a tingle through her arm. She felt it spread throughout her body, washing over her hand and into Loreddion's form. It was as though she could see it somehow, feel the warm blue of it, a silky motion inside her bones. Like a sheet floating through the air, the magic settled over Loreddion. His eyes opened once more, and the burns faded from his arms. New skin crept across his hands, leaving undamaged flesh behind.

Loreddion raised his hands to look at them. A thin trace of scars now coated his forearms, thin spiderwebs over his tattoos. It marked his face with a single silver line up one cheek and over his left eye. But save those small reminders, no other sign of the burning remained. In amazement, he raised his eyes to Jirah. "Thanks."

Stunned, Jirah nodded.

Fire lifted Nearra's dress in a whirling ball of light, rocking her from side to side and setting her silver dress alight. "Tell me who helped you, who betrayed the Crescent Cabal, or I will destroy you!"

Nearra pounded her staff on the ground. The fire went out, but more was quick to follow, brushing against the hem of her skirt. "We don't know!" she cried out.

"Liar! Someone is helping you. We already know there is a traitor who stole this key. Now you will lead us to him." Tremendous columns of magma bulged from the lake, billowing in waves and cascading over the bridge. "And if you won't tell me, then you are of no further use to me."

The magma flowed over the bridge freely, overrunning the span of the bridge between them. Now the five stood on an island in the lava, blocked on all sides by the thick, molten stone. "I will find the traitor, with or without your assistance, but you can help yourselves by giving me the information now," Yzor snarled. "This is the only time I will ask. Speak . . . or die."

Jirah looked down at the spiral disk in her hand as the sea of lava overflowed. Even if they could survive a few moments longer, what good would it do? The cabal had the key. They had the shard—whatever that was—and they had a plan.

All Jirah had was a small, circular piece of gold.

"Help us," Jirah begged. "Save my sister. And I promise"—she paused, then finished her statement, sure of every word—"I'll be your cleric, whoever you are." There. She'd said it. The medallion didn't flinch, glow, or get warm. Nothing changed inside her. She felt no sense of communion, heard no angels singing, no avatar sprang into being to defend her. Jirah gulped, unsure if whatever power watched over the spiral sign had even heard. Stupid to believe, she thought. The cleric in Palanthas was right after all. The gods themselves didn't want her.

Fine. She'd do it herself. Sparks flew past, white hot, blurring her vision, and the magma rose even farther up the path. She had to think of something—had to find a way. The spiral medallion hung in her hand, chain drooping down. Then, suddenly, when all hope was lost, Jirah had an idea.

"Nearra!" she called over the sound of flowing lava and hissing stone. She spun on one heel, yelling at the top of her lungs. Thick smoke choked her, and the smell of sulfur and ash was cloying. "Nearra! The feather!"

"What?" Confused, Nearra spared her a blank glance. On the archway, Yzor stood beneath the swollen Pillar of Flame, exulting in her victory.

"Loreddion!" Jirah grabbed him, pointing toward Yzor. "The spell you used on the vegetable monsters, the one that made them stand still. Can you cast it on Yzor?"

"The paralyze spell?" He cracked his knuckles. "Won't hold her for more than a couple of seconds."

"It'll be enough for Nearra to get one good shot." Jirah pointed at the feather and gestured to Nearra. "Hit the feather with your ice bolt when Loreddion holds her still!"

Nearra lowered her staff and gauged the distance quickly.

Before she could cast anything, Nagato screamed, "NO!" His eyes were wide with panic. "Jirah! That's a terrible idea! Nearra, you can't!"

"No time to explain!" Jirah answered, pointing at the advancing figure of Yzor. Nearra looked back and forth between them. Jirah couldn't afford Yzor overhearing the plan as she marched down the arch of stone toward them. "Nearra, please. Trust me."

Spinning on her heel, Nearra beckoned to Loreddion. "Do it."

The Black Robe laughed, pleased by such wicked sport, and clenched his hands around an invisible ball of energy. Pointing it at Yzor, he commanded, "*Capik!*"

Yzor stiffened. Clearly fighting against the spell's effect, her steps ground to a halt midstride. Loreddion's spell caught her in an invisible web that froze bone and muscle. She stood at the edge of the magma around their island, feather in one hand, sword in the other—a momentary statue of herself.

Nearra's finger stabbed out sharply. "*Es!*"

In the same breath, Nagato screamed, "No!" once more, leaping toward the others. His robes swirled out behind him. Nearra's ice bolt streaked toward the frozen Yzor even as Nagato collided with her. The weight of his body knocked Nearra into Loreddion, and the elf into Jirah, sending the lot of them sprawling onto the stone. Only Koi still stood, baton limp by her side, staring at Yzor, the ice-bolt, and the feather with a perpetually quizzical stare.

The ice bolt hit the feather.

With a roar, they were caught up in a terrible explosion as the feather shattered into dust. In the instant that the feather broke, Yzor broke free. She screamed as the key was destroyed.

Above her, the Pillar of Flame rippled again, and the fire turned black and gold like Yzor's armor. The twin columns of magma exploded, raining down through the volcano and searing into the stone on both sides of the lake. The Pillar itself began to whirl and spin, fire streaking out at all angles in a wild puzzle of whiplashes. It scarred and shattered the stone walls of the crater and devastated the arch on which Yzor stood. As the bridge collapsed into the magma, Yzor screamed.

"That won't stop her!" Koi exclaimed with a frown.

"No." Nearra pointed up above them, her view clear as she lay on her back against the stone. "But that will!" Above them, the lip of the volcano was collapsing, sides crumbling beneath the frenzied implosion of the Pillar of Flame. "Run!"

Down the last bit of the bridge they raced, throwing themselves against the wall at the edge of the room. They clustered back against the rock near where the portal had been first opened and sought shelter beneath the lip of an overhang. Rocks pounded into the center of the lava pool, but they were protected from the collapse—for now.

Wild lashes of fire and the rain of magma cracked great ledges from the stone and they hurtled down into the magma pool. Cracks appeared in the walls, breaking open the stone. "The mountain is falling!" Nagato gasped. "This overhang will fall too, and we'll be crushed. Or worse, the ground here will crumble and we'll be pitched into the lava."

"Hey, look." Koi pointed casually to the side. "The portal's open again." And indeed it was. Through it, Jirah could see the cold and reassuring stone of the old mausoleum, fluttering in and out of view as the portal's magic warbled with the Pillar.

"Go!" Nearra shoved Nagato off her. "Through the portal!"

Stumbling and white-faced, the wizard was quick to do as she said, nearly falling through the magical door. He fell onto the stone on the other side, a heap of shaking limbs, but safe.

Loreddion rushed past Jirah, but Nearra stayed to help her sister up. As the Black Robe jumped through, the lip of rock on which they stood trembled and shook. Koi followed Loreddion through the flickering portal, looking back for the sisters. The edges broke apart and fragmented under the heat of the rising magma and the pressure of the collapsing walls. They could no longer see Yzor, buried as the half-demon was in a massive pile of rock and lava, and the entire top of the mountain seemed about to collapse inward and crush them all. Nearra pitched forward and nearly fell into the lava. As she stumbled, her white staff rolled from her hands. It fell into the bright red liquid and floated for an instant on top of the magma before it slowly began to sink beneath the red waves.

Jirah moved without thinking. She plunged her hand into the molten stone to grab the staff. It wasn't as though she thought it wouldn't hurt her, but more like she did it on instinct. All she could think of was that the staff was Anselm's. It was all that remained of their family heritage. Jirah jerked her hand back, lava dripping from her fingertips. In her hand, the staff blazed with heat from the Pillar's core. A shimmer passed down it, then faded, leaving the staff unblemished by the fire into which it had sunk. Jirah stared. She turned to her sister and held it out.

"How did you . . . ?" Nearra began, staring. "The key's broken. It couldn't have protected you."

There was no answer to give to her sister. Jirah shoved the staff into Nearra's hands, and the two stared at each other. A ripple passed through the stone at their feet, and a great hunk of mountain wall began to crumble away above them, pitching down past the ruined and fading Pillar of Flame into the sea of liquid stone.

Jirah and Nearra clasped hands, white palm warm against golden fingers, and together they jumped through.

CHAPTER

EPILOGUE

Palanthas spread before them, a river of fire-light in the evening dusk. Torches burned along thin, curving streets, and at the center of the city's hub, a great tower flared with illumination. People carried lanterns that glimmered, and children's laughter could be heard through windows lit with the warm glow of candlelight.

"We did it." Nagato still held his right arm close to his chest, though the wound was no longer there. Jirah's magic had healed him.

Nearra looked over at the Black Robe, noting the scar through his left eye and down his cheek. Jirah was getting better. Nearra sighed, her horse stamping idly against the ground as the others passed her by. They had taken extra horses from Eric's barn in the woods as they passed by. Nothing else of their family's remained. The home they grew up in was a burned husk. It didn't even feel like home anymore. Maybe nothing ever would again.

Jirah spoke unexpectedly. "Something bothering you?" Jirah quirked an eyebrow and paused in the twilight. As she spoke, her hand reached to brush against the medallion that hung around

her neck. Since the volcano cavern, they'd spoken little about what happened there. They kept their comments to the journey, or family matters such as wondering where their parents were now or hoping for the future. They never talked about the past.

Nearra paused to let the others go by, waiting for a moment alone with her sister. When the other horses were several steps ahead down the path to the city, Nearra confided, "There are so many questions left to answer. Destroying the Pillar of Flame saved Palanthas and restored fire to the city—probably to Kenderhome as well."

"But you don't think that was the end of the Crescent Cabal's plan." Matter-of-factly, Jirah summed up all of Nearra's fears.

"Yzor spoke of a 'shard.' She talked about a traitor whom she claimed helped us, but we don't know who. There are pieces moving here. There's a great game that we don't see, Jirah," Nearra said to her sister. "I don't think the cabal is finished with whatever they're trying to do."

"One of the things we know about the cabal is that they were planning to seize control over all wizards. They want to take magic into their own hands and control its use," Jirah answered. "I don't see why that would change."

Nearra faced her sister, a light evening breeze blowing golden locks into her eyes. "You think that's still their plan?"

Jirah sighed and tugged at her horse's reins lightly. "When Nagato was looking through his dusty tomes, he mentioned that there were four Pillars—Fire, Earth, Water, Air."

"You think there are three more?"

Holding her medallion pensively, Jirah sighed. "I'd bet on it."

Nearra turned back to the city. "How do we find them, Jirah, if you're right? Does . . . does your god tell you anything about that?"

"The god of the medallion—whoever it is—doesn't talk to me." Jirah flushed.

"But the magic of the medallion saved us. You saved us all in the volcano." Before Jirah could cut her off, Nearra rushed on, blue eyes flashing. "You guided my shot, didn't you? I couldn't have hit that small a target from so far away. I'm not a very good shot. You're much better with a bow, and it's nearly the same thing. Did you use a prayer? Perhaps some divine force guided you, told you what to do?"

Jirah paused and shifted in her saddle. "There was nothing, Nearra. I called on the medallion, but it didn't listen. You made that shot yourself." She looked uncomfortable, twisting the golden chain between her fingers. "I don't think I helped you at all."

"But you did." Nearra wanted to hug her sister, comfort her as she had done when they were children, but something in Jirah's manner stopped her. That little girl, so scared and unsure, was gone. Nearra didn't entirely recognize the young woman who stood in her place. Nearra sized up her sister with a long, sharp gaze. "You've changed."

"Have I?" Jirah's voice was completely unconvinced. She looked toward the city and shrugged.

Nearra didn't answer. Whatever was going on in Jirah's mind was beyond her. She saw her sister's finger trace the spiral on the medallion thoughtfully. Whatever path Jirah was on, Nearra couldn't walk it for her. She could only stand beside her, as Jirah had done when Nearra needed her. Aware that Jirah was uncomfortable, she changed the subject back to the Crescent Cabal. "Do you really think we'll find them again?" Nearra looked out over the Palanthas, the twinkling firelights, the quiet peace that lay over the city below.

"I don't think we'll have to."

Something in Jirah's voice chilled her. She glanced over at her sister, but Jirah started her horse walking away, down the path toward Palanthas, the holy symbol still clenched in one hand.

Nearra suddenly remembered her dream—the one that had started it all, brought her to Palanthas, showed her the way to go, and guided her to the salvation of the city. She thought about Jirah's words. Somehow she knew that her sister was right.

The Crescent Cabal would find them.

The story continues in . . .

QUEEN OF THE SEA

ELEMENTS, VOLUME TWO
by Ree Soesbee

Four Elements
Three Dreams
Two Sisters
One Final Test

A tempest off the coast of Krynn threatens to overwhelm Palanthas, and once again the Wizards' Conclave sends Nearra on a treacherous journey. As Nearra works to uncover the Crescent Cabal's machinations, her sister, Jirah, struggles in the service of her newfound anonymous god. With the storm raging around them, Nearra must locate the Queen of the Sea and the Pillar of Water. But will the evil Crescent Cabal find them first?

Available July 2007

Find out how it all began in . . .

TEMPLE OF THE DRAGONSLAYER

by Tim Waggoner

THE NEW ADVENTURES

A Practical Guide to Dragons
By Sindri Suncatcher

Sindri Suncatcher—wizard's apprentice—opens up
his personal notebooks to share his knowledge of these
awe-inspiring creatures, from the life cycle of a kind copper
dragon to the best way to counteract a red dragon's fiery
breath. This lavishly illustrated guide showcases the wide
array of fantastic dragons encountered on the world of Krynn.

The perfect companion to the Dragonlance: The New
Adventures series, for both loyal fans and new readers alike.

Sindri Suncatcher is a three-and-a-half foot tall kender,
who enjoys storytelling, collecting magical tokens, and
fighting dragons. He lives in Solamnia and is currently
studying magic under the auspices of the black-robed
wizard Maddoc. You can catch Sindri in the midst of
his latest adventure in *The Wayward Wizard*.

For more information visit www.mirrorstonebooks.com

For ages ten and up.

THE NEW
ADVENTURES

Want to know more about the Dragonlance world?

Want to know how it all began?

A RUMOR OF DRAGONS
Volume 1

NIGHT OF THE DRAGONS
Volume 2

THE NIGHTMARE LANDS
Volume 3

TO THE GATES OF PALANTHAS
Volume 4

HOPE'S FLAME
Volume 5

A DAWN OF DRAGONS
Volume 6

By Margaret Weis & Tracy Hickman

For more information visit <u>www.mirrorstonebooks.com</u>

For ages ten and up.
Gift Sets Available

KNIGHTS
OF THE
SILVER
DRAGON

Written by series creator Matt Forbeck, this special two-part KNIGHTS
OF THE SILVER DRAGON adventure will rock Curston to the core!

REVELATIONS

Five years ago, treasure hunters destroyed a seal deep in the Dungeons
of Doom, releasing hordes of monsters upon the people of Curston.
An ancient prophecy predicted the city would face the fiends
from the Abyss again.

PROPHECY OF THE DRAGONS
REVELATIONS, PART 1

It's up to Moyra, Driskoll and Kellach to make sure the prophecy doesn't
come true. It won't be easy with the return of Lexos, who seeks a key that
has kept the seal locked for the last five years. Lexos has a few surprises up
his sleeve, but what the Knights find behind the seal might be
the biggest surprise of them all.

THE DRAGONS REVEALED
REVELATIONS, PART 2

As fiends soar the skies and monsters prowl the streets, the Knights have
but one hope left: the dragons that long ago pledged to protect their order.
Zendric readies the ritual for recalling their winged allies, while the
Knights race back to the Dungeons to restore the seal. There is just one
thing they aren't prepared for: a traitor in their midst.

**Ask for KNIGHTS OF THE SILVER DRAGON books
at your favorite bookstore!**

For more inf [   ] verdragon.com

KNIGHTS OF THE SILV [   ] Vizards of the Coast, Inc.
in the U [   ] f the Coast